ACCLAIM FOR COLLEEN COBLE

"Filled with the suspense for which Coble is known, the novel is rich in detail with a healthy dose of romance, allowing readers to bask in the beauty of Washington state's lavender fields, lush forests and jagged coastline."

—*BookPage* on *The View from Rainshadow Bay*

"Prepare to stay up all night with Colleen Coble. Coble's beautiful, emotional prose coupled with her keen sense of pacing, escalating danger, and very real characters place her firmly at the top of the suspense genre. I could not put this book down."

—Allison Brennan, *New York Times* bestselling author of *Shattered* on *The View from Rainshadow Bay*

"I loved returning to Rock Harbor and you will too. *Beneath Copper Falls* is Colleen at her best!"

—Dani Pettrey, bestselling author of the Alaskan Courage and Chesapeake Valor series

"Return to Rock Harbor for Colleen Coble's best story to date. *Beneath Copper Falls* is a twisting, turning thrill ride from page one that drops you headfirst into danger that will leave you breathless, sleep deprived, and eager for more! I couldn't turn the pages fast enough!"

—Lynette Eason, award-winning, bestselling author of the Elite Guardians series

"The tension, both suspenseful and romantic, is gripping, reflecting Coble's prowess with the genre."

—*Publishers Weekly*, starred review for *Twilight at Blueberry Barrens*

"Incredible storytelling and intricately drawn characters. You won't want to miss *Twilight at Blueberry Barrens!*"

—Brenda Novak, *New York Times* and *USA TODAY* bestselling author

"Coble has a gift for making a setting come to life. After reading *Twilight at Blueberry Barrens*, I feel like I've lived in Maine all my life. This plot kept me guessing until the end, and her characters seem like my friends. I don't want to let them go!"

—TERRI BLACKSTOCK, *USA TODAY* BESTSELLING AUTHOR OF *IF I RUN*

"I'm a long-time fan of Colleen Coble, and *Twilight at Blueberry Barrens* is the perfect example of why. Coble delivers riveting suspense, delicious romance, and carefully crafted characters, all with the deft hand of a veteran writer. If you love romantic suspense, pick this one up. You won't be disappointed!"

—DENISE HUNTER, AUTHOR OF *THE GOODBYE BRIDE*

"Colleen Coble, the queen of Christian romantic mysteries, is back with her best book yet. Filled with familiar characters, plot twists, and a confusion of antagonists, I couldn't keep the pages of this novel set in Maine turning fast enough. I reconnected with characters I love while taking a journey filled with murder, suspense, and the prospect of love. This truly is her best book to date, and perfect for readers who adore a page-turner laced with romance."

—CARA PUTMAN, AWARD-WINNING AUTHOR OF *SHADOWED BY GRACE* AND *WHERE TREETOPS GLISTEN*, ON *TWILIGHT AT BLUEBERRY BARRENS*

"Gripping! Colleen Coble has again written a page-turning romantic suspense with *Twilight at Blueberry Barrens*! Not only did she keep me up nights racing through the pages to see what would happen next, I genuinely cared for her characters. Colleen sets the bar high for romantic suspense!"

—CARRIE STUART PARKS, AUTHOR OF *A CRY FROM THE DUST* AND *WHEN DEATH DRAWS NEAR*

"Colleen Coble thrills readers again with her newest novel, an addictive suspense trenched in family, betrayal, and . . . murder."

—DIANN MILLS, AUTHOR OF *DEADLY ENCOUNTER*, ON *TWILIGHT AT BLUEBERRY BARRENS*

"Coble's latest, *Twilight at Blueberry Barrens*, is one of her best yet! With characters you want to know in person, a perfect setting, and a plot that had me holding my breath, laughing, and crying, this story will stay with the reader long after the book is closed. My highest recommendation."

—ROBIN CAROLL, BESTSELLING NOVELIST

"Colleen's *Twilight at Blueberry Barrens* is filled with a bevy of twists and surprises, a wonderful romance, and the warmth of family love. I couldn't have asked for more. This author has always been a five-star novelist, but I think it's time to up the ante with this book. It's on my keeping shelf!"

—HANNAH ALEXANDER, AUTHOR OF THE
HALLOWED HALLS SERIES

"Second chances, old flames, and startling new revelations combine to form a story filled with faith, trial, forgiveness, and redemption. Crack the cover and step in, but beware—*Mermaid Moon* is harboring secrets that will keep you guessing."

—LISA WINGATE, *NEW YORK TIMES* BESTSELLING AUTHOR
OF *BEFORE WE WERE YOURS*, ON *MERMAID MOON*

"I burned through *The Inn at Ocean's Edge* in one sitting. An intricate plot by a master storyteller. Colleen Coble has done it again with this gripping opening to a new series. I can't wait to spend more time at Sunset Cove."

—HEATHER BURCH, BESTSELLING AUTHOR OF *ONE LAVENDER RIBBON*

"Coble doesn't disappoint with her custom blend of suspense and romance."

—*PUBLISHERS WEEKLY* ON *THE INN AT OCEAN'S EDGE*

"Veteran author Coble has penned another winner. Filled with mystery and romance that are unpredictable until the last page, this novel will grip readers long past when they should put their books down. Recommended to readers of contemporary mysteries."

—*CBA RETAILERS + RESOURCES* REVIEW OF *THE INN AT OCEAN'S EDGE*

"Coble truly shines when she's penning a mystery, and this tale will really keep the reader guessing . . . Mystery lovers will definitely want to put this book on their purchase list."

—RT BOOK REVIEWS ON THE INN AT OCEAN'S EDGE

"Master storyteller Colleen Coble has done it again. The Inn at Ocean's Edge is an intricately woven, well-crafted story of romance, suspense, family secrets, and a decades-old mystery. Needless to say, it had me hooked from page one. I simply couldn't stop turning the pages. This one's going on my keeper shelf."

—LYNETTE EASON, AWARD-WINNING, BESTSELLING AUTHOR OF THE HIDDEN IDENTITY SERIES

"Evocative and gripping, The Inn at Ocean's Edge will keep you flipping pages long into the night."

—DANI PETTREY, BESTSELLING AUTHOR OF THE ALASKAN COURAGE SERIES

"Coble's atmospheric and suspenseful series launch should appeal to fans of Tracie Peterson and other authors of Christian romantic suspense."

—LIBRARY JOURNAL REVIEW OF TIDEWATER INN

"Romantically tense, but with just the right touch of danger, this cowboy love story is surprisingly clever—and pleasingly sweet."

—USATODAY.COM REVIEW OF BLUE MOON PROMISE

"[An] outstanding, completely engaging tale that will have you on the edge of your seat . . . A must-have for all fans of romantic suspense!"

—THEROMANCEREADERSCONNECTION.COM REVIEW OF ANATHEMA

"Colleen Coble lays an intricate trail in Without a Trace and draws the reader on like a hound with a scent."

—ROMANTIC TIMES, 4½ STARS

"Coble's historical series just keeps getting better with each entry."

—LIBRARY JOURNAL STARRED REVIEW OF THE LIGHTKEEPER'S BALL

THE HOUSE AT
SALTWATER POINT

Also by Colleen Coble

The

HOUSE *at* SALTWATER POINT

COLLEEN COBLE

The House at Saltwater Point

© 2018 by Colleen Coble

Published in Nashville, Tennessee, by Thomas Nelson. Thomas Nelson is a registered trademark of HarperCollins Christian Publishing, Inc.

Thomas Nelson titles may be purchased in bulk for educational, business, fund-raising, or sales promotional use. For information, please email SpecialMarkets@ThomasNelson.com.

ISBN: 978-0-7180-8582-7 (library edition)
ISBN: 978-0-7180-8580-3 (trade paper)

Library of Congress Cataloging-in-Publication Data

CIP data available upon request.

Printed in the United States of America

18 19 20 21 LSC 5 4 3 2 1

For my darling Elijah,
cutest baby in the world!

Chapter 1

Neutral paint colors allow the prospective buyer
to imagine their own furnishings in the space.
—EXCERPT FROM ELLIE BLACKMORE'S
HAMMER GIRL BLOG

Two construction workers carried in the orange ladder splatted with dried paint blotches and old drywall mud. The top of it nearly crashed into the new chandelier dangling twelve feet overhead in the foyer.

Ellie Blackmore darted forward to prevent disaster. "Careful!"

She moved under the glittering crystal light fixture so the workers couldn't come closer. Paint fumes stung her nose and mixed with the salty sea breeze blowing through the open door. This home was nearly complete. She'd start staging it as soon as it was cleaned and the ladders, scaffolding, scraps of hardwood, and cans of paint were gone. If luck was with them, she and Jason would make over fifty thousand dollars' profit on this project. They already had three interested buyers, so she hoped a bidding war would drive the price even higher.

The dark hardwood floors complemented the soothing gray walls in the open floor plan. She walked through the kitchen and touched the marble countertops, then snapped several pictures for her blog, *Hammer Girl.* Their clients tended to like genuine marble, high-end cabinets, and solid wood floors—and she was happy to deliver. She went to the first of the boxes the workers had hauled in and lifted out decor items. Though she'd have to wait for the cleaning crew, she could put the boxes in the rooms where she wanted them.

Mackenzie, Ellie's younger sister, came down the hall into the kitchen. She looked like she was still in high school, but she'd graduated college with a degree in Asian languages at twenty-one, plowing through the rigorous studies in three years. She'd been offered prestigious positions at several major universities across the country, but she'd chosen to teach at a local college, mostly because she didn't want to leave Ellie.

A dark stain marred her white shorts, and her royal-blue tee held a smear of gray paint. "The master bedroom is ready for staging." She ran her fingers through her curly brown hair.

"Thanks so much, Mac. You didn't need to work like this on your day off, but I really appreciate it."

Mac's blue eyes softened when they lit on Ellie. "The two of us have always been a team."

Jason Yarwood strode into the kitchen and lifted his thatch of sun-streaked brown hair to wipe his damp forehead with the tail of his T-shirt. He and Ellie had co-owned Lavender Farm Homes for five years, and last year they'd turned a good profit for the first time. They'd become known for the highest-quality flips in the entire Olympic Peninsula area, and they had more business than they could handle with kitchen and bath remodels making up the bulk of their jobs.

Jason was twenty-eight and handsome, though his mouth often held a sardonic twist that had appeared after his divorce from Mackenzie. "I wouldn't mind testing the air-conditioning. This is crazy hot for Washington. It has to be ninety out there." He didn't look at Mac, whose smile had vanished when he entered.

Ellie stepped to the thermostat and kicked on the air. "This heat wave could break anytime." She shut the door behind the workers carrying out the last of the construction debris.

Lavender Tides rested in the rain shadow of the Olympic Mountains. While the area was no stranger to high humidity, the hot temperatures they'd had this week were out of the normal seventies they usually enjoyed for October.

Mac went to the door. "I'm so excited about the tall ship regatta. They get here in two weeks. I want to have *Lavender Lady* ready to join in."

Ellie took off her glasses and polished away the condensation. "That's wonderful!"

Mac had been fascinated with tall ships since she and Ellie had seen their first one in California during a Disneyland vacation when they were five and seven. Mac had bought an old tall ship five years ago and had worked hard to restore it. Ellie suspected her obsession with the boat had contributed to the failure of her marriage.

Mac still hadn't looked at Jason. "I'm ecstatic! I just need to find more crew. Want to be part of it?"

The strain between Mac and Jason set Ellie's nerves on edge.

"I don't think you want me vomiting on your new paint." She'd tried to like sailing, but her stomach never cooperated, and she wasn't the strongest swimmer in the world.

"I know, but I had to ask. Want to grab lunch at the Crabby Pot? I can show you what I've gotten done on the ship."

Ellie slid her glasses up on her nose, then glanced at her watch. Nearly eleven already. "I wish I could, but I'm going to that moving sale at the Robb house in half an hour. I just have time to get there. How about I come out to the ship and see it before your birthday dinner tonight?"

"Okay, that will work."

Jason began to pick up pieces of scrap wood. "I really want that Robb house when it goes to auction. I don't think it will go higher than we can afford."

She hadn't told him, but Ellie was tempted to keep the house for herself. She'd fallen in love with the floor plan and the view of the bay from the backyard. "It's a huge project, but it's going to be beautiful when we're done."

"We can handle the size of the reno." Jason glowered at Mac, who still hadn't looked at him. "Am I invisible, Mac? Maybe I'd like lunch. You didn't even say hello."

Mac's eyes narrowed. "You can get your own lunch."

Jason glared back, then walked out and slammed the door without another word.

Ellie sighed. "Why do you have to antagonize him all the time? He still loves you, you know."

"I don't understand why you're still partners with him. You're the genius behind Lavender Farms. You can hire anyone to do the brute labor. You don't need him. It infuriates me to constantly run into him."

"And I can't understand why you can't muster a little courtesy! You were married to the man for two years. There has to be some kind of feeling left."

"There is—it's called hatred." Mac brushed at the stain on her shorts. "If you loved me, you'd cut him loose. He's gone so much anyway, kayaking in that inflatable he keeps in his truck. You do most of the work."

"That's not true. Jason works hard." Ellie took a step back. "Our partnership goes back to before you knew him. Jason is like a brother to me. He brings a lot of business savvy to Lavender Farms. Don't pull me into your feud."

"You don't understand anything about relationships, Ellie. You've never even had a serious boyfriend. You're so afraid of letting someone down like you did Alicia, you never take a chance on loving anyone. You don't know what it's like when someone breaks your heart."

Ellie gasped and pressed her hand against her chest. They never spoke of their little sister's death, and to have it thrown in her face now was like a knife to the heart. "You blame me for her death too? You always said it wasn't my fault."

Tears flooded Mac's blue eyes and she rushed for the door. Ellie thought for half a second about going after her, but her pain was too raw. They both needed to cool down.

Even as she wandered the rooms in the estate sale, Ellie mentally ticked off all she wanted to do in this house. In her mind she already owned it, and the more she saw of the room sizes and high ceilings, the more she liked it. The superb view from the big windows at the back of the house looked out on Rainshadow Bay, and she caught sight of Mac's ship docked there.

The Robbs had owned this house for fifteen years, and Ellie used to babysit for their son. Terrance Robb had grown up in town and had gone on to work for the CIA. He'd recently been transferred to an upper-level position at Langley, and Ellie suspected half the people perusing the contents were hoping to see him or his wife, Candace. Everyone in town had been curious about what he'd be doing in Virginia and hoped to ferret out some spy details. The truth was much more mundane since he worked in the accounting department. Spies worked in other countries, and Terrance's job was simply one of support.

She paused at a large cabinet with various items inside. She spied a vintage mah-jongg set in a blue vinyl case and grabbed it. Mac would love this. Ellie had already gotten her a bracelet for her birthday, but this would be a nice bonus gift. She tucked it under her arm and tried to sidle past a petite, dark-haired woman who was frowning at her.

"I was about to buy that." The woman looked to be in her twenties and of Asian descent. She held out her hand. "May I have it, please?" She had a slight Asian accent. Her high heels and slim-fitting dress had to have cost a fortune.

"Sorry, it's a gift for my sister." Ellie started past her, but the woman made a grab for the box. "Hey!" Ellie clamped her other hand on the game before the woman could snatch it out of her arms. "What's wrong with you?"

The woman's face contorted, and she stepped closer to Ellie. "Give me the box!"

"Is something wrong?" Jermaine Diskin got between her and the woman. Jermaine was an African American flight paramedic who worked for Zach Bannister. He and his wife, Michelle, owned a lavender farm on the outskirts of town.

The woman glared at him. "She has my mah-jongg box."

Jermaine's pale-green eyes narrowed. "I saw her pick it up first. Get lost, lady, or I'll call the cops. I saw Deputy Rosa Seymour in the other room."

The woman clenched her fists, then spun on her three-inch heels and brushed past Ellie.

Jermaine stared after her. "That was weird. I hope you don't mind that I interfered."

"I was thankful you did. I've never had to fight for an estate-sale purchase before." She looked down at the box. "I've heard some vintage games are worth a lot of money. Maybe this one is, but I wasn't going to resell it. It's for Mac's birthday."

"Glad it all worked out then. You'd better buy it and get out of here before she comes back."

Ellie thanked him again, then paid five dollars for the game. When she neared her old blue pickup, she frowned. Both tires on the passenger side were flat. Who would slash her tires? Would the woman have been so angry about losing out on the mah-jongg tiles that she would have done something like this? It seemed extreme.

A black Taurus with tinted windows drove by slowly as she called for roadside service. Roy's Service Station had a truck there in fifteen minutes. She kept her eye out for the vandal as she waited for new tires to be put on her truck, but she saw no one suspicious. She stuck the mah-jongg tiles in her toolbox for safekeeping.

She paid Roy's employee, then climbed behind the wheel to go pick up Mac for their dinner out. The marina parking lot was nearly empty, and she pulled into the spot beside Mac's BMW. Mac's clipper, *Lavender Lady*, was gorgeous in the sunlight. Her sails were down, and her masts soared toward the clouds. Ellie often wished she could share her sister's passion for sailing. She loved the water and the scent of the sea, but all the sailing terms confused her.

She parked her truck, then walked out onto the dock. Seagulls landed near her feet, and their black eyes looked up for a snack. "Sorry, guys, I didn't bring any bread." Where was Mac? Ellie thought she'd be on the dock or near her car waiting. Maybe she'd lost track of time.

She cupped her hands around her mouth. "Mac!"

No one answered her but the squawk of the closest seagull and a toot from a ferry out in the bay.

Mac's skiff bobbed in the water next to the ship, but there was an inflatable raft bumping against the dock Ellie could take out. She stepped into it and steadied herself as it rocked in the waves. She sat down and rowed out to board the boat. She tied off next to the skiff, then climbed the ladder to the deck.

She looked down and bile rose in her throat.

A pool of red congealed on the tile floor about four feet from the railing on the starboard side. A lot of blood.

She tried to swallow, but all the moisture evaporated from her tongue. "Mac?" Her voice came out as a whisper. She rushed along the deck and followed the blood to the railing. There was no sign of Mac in the blue waves lapping at the hull.

She fumbled her phone out of her purse and dialed 911. Mac couldn't be dead, not on her birthday.

Chapter 2

You've heard to trust your instincts.
That piece of advice never fails.
—HAMMER GIRL BLOG

S hauna Bannister stood on the bow of the ferry and watched the island of Hope Beach draw nearer. The sea air had curled her black hair into something that resembled Frankenstein's monster's bride, but she made a vain attempt to smooth it back into place. The scent of salt and sea wrapped around her in a caress. They were finally here after an eventful honeymoon, and she couldn't quite believe she was about to see her brother again after all these years.

Zach dropped his arm around her, and she welcomed his warmth. "Traipsing all over North Carolina in search of my brother isn't much of a honeymoon for you, Zach."

"We had a great honeymoon. This is just an extension." His

lips brushed her temple. "I'm with my beautiful bride, and that's all I want." He pointed out two dolphins jumping beside the boat. "This is going to be an exciting week."

While they couldn't really label their honeymoon "great" after barely escaping with their lives, it had only made them stronger. And more in love.

She tipped her head back to stare into his deep-blue eyes. "You're sure it's him?"

"As positive as we can be without a DNA test. From what I can tell, he doesn't know he's adopted, honey. You have to be prepared for some initial disbelief that you're really his sister and he's who you say he is."

Disbelief. Would he reject her? He'd been old enough when he disappeared that he should still have some memory of her, shouldn't he? She'd looked it up, and some people remembered bits of their childhood from age two. They'd spent a lot of time together, and she clearly remembered his adorable freckles and the cowlick in his blond hair. He'd been a cute toddler and was probably a handsome man now.

She pressed her hand against her stomach. "The butterflies are trying to escape."

He tucked a long strand of her dark hair behind her ear. "We'll weigh them down with something sweet once we hit the island. I hear there's a great place for lunch and ice cream in town."

Taking time to eat would give her a chance to calm down. They'd landed in Norfolk last night and stayed at a hotel, then flown on a charter flight to the Dare County Airport this morning where they'd caught the ferry.

"Sounds good." She leaned her head against his shoulder.

"I'm so nervous. In my daydreams he recognizes me immediately and we hug until we're breathless."

A troubled frown wrinkled his forehead. "It's not going to be like that, babe. I think deep down you know that. A lot of time has passed. He spent most of his life in Japan. There's no guarantee he even remembers Washington."

"I remember lots of things from when I was two and three."

His embrace tightened. "And he went through a lot of trauma when he was ripped from his family after watching his mother die. He might have blocked out most of it."

She knew Zach was trying to make sure her expectations were realistic, but the thought of a negative reaction from her brother was disconcerting to her. She pulled away and watched a seagull regard her with inquisitive eyes from a nearby railing. "Maybe this was a bad idea. I probably should have called first and talked to his parents."

"No, we're doing it right. I could be wrong, you know. He might recognize that black hair." He twirled a lock of hair around his finger.

She smiled and leaned against his chest. Being married to Zach was wonderful. He'd found her brother, Connor, all by himself as a surprise. How many men would do that? "We should probably call and check on our boy."

"I talked to Alex while you were in the bathroom, and he was heading to the beach with Marilyn to go tide pooling. I'm sure she has her phone with her if you want to call."

"Of course you called. You're a good dad."

His eyes crinkled in a smile. "I try. He's easy to love. And so is his mother." As the wind ruffled his dark hair, he wrapped his arm around her waist and they turned to watch the ferry dock at

Hope Beach. "I hear we can rent bicycles in town. That would be a fun way to tour the island."

"We're booked at Tidewater Inn, right?"

"Yes, they have a van picking us up. Looks like a nice place. It's a few miles out of town, and the van runs back and forth every two hours."

Zach had planned all this down to the last detail. "Let's drop off our stuff, then head into town. I'd like to at least get a glimpse of Grayson before we approach him." It would be hard to remember her brother's new name, Grayson Bradshaw.

"We could ask about him at the hotel too. Maybe the manager knows him or his family. It might be good to have a little more information before we attack."

She sputtered a laugh. "I sure hope he doesn't feel like it's an attack."

He steered her toward the gangway. "It's going to be fine. Don't worry so much. We'll get through this. Even if he needs some time to absorb it all, I think he'll want to get to know his amazing sister and nephew. You'll see."

She could only pray he was right.

Ellie's eyes felt raw and scratchy from crying. The sheriff and his men had been all over the ship and found no sign of Mac's body. It was clear she'd gone into the water. With that much blood Ellie didn't see how Mac could have survived. One of the deputies had even spotted a few fins in the strait, and she shuddered at the thought that they might never find her sister's body.

The cold wind laden with the smell of kelp cut through her as they headed back to the parking lot. She reached her truck and opened the door. "I need to tell Jason. I tried to call our dad, but he's out of the country on a safari. He won't be back to civilization for another two weeks."

"Sorry to hear that. You could use the support." Sheriff Everett Burchell, a burly man in his forties with a slight resemblance to Elvis, pulled a pad of paper from his shirt pocket. "Mackenzie and her ex don't get along great, do they?" His tone was too casual.

Ellie caught her breath. "You can't suspect Jason."

"I have to look at everyone, Ellie. Even you. This wasn't an accident."

"Maybe she fell and hit her head. Head wounds bleed a lot. She could have been disoriented and fallen overboard. Aren't you going to call in some divers?"

"I already did. They'll be here any minute. Now, about your sister. When did you see her last? And do you know where I can find Jason?"

Ellie pressed her lips together. She'd seen enough movies to know law enforcement always thought a relative was to blame.

Tires squealed behind them, and she turned to see Jason's new Chevy pickup pull up behind her. The door flew open, and Jason bolted from the vehicle with the engine still running. He rushed to Ellie's truck.

His brown eyes were vivid in his pale face. "I heard Mac was attacked. She's all right, isn't she?"

"She's missing," the sheriff said. "I'm glad you're here though, Jason. I have a few questions. When did you see her last?"

"Just before lunch. She was painting at a flip we're doing. She left the house to get some lunch. I didn't see her after that."

He ran his hand through his sun-streaked brown hair. "Wait, am I a suspect?"

The sheriff's smile didn't reach his dark-blue eyes. "It's just routine to talk to everyone close to her. Did you argue?"

Jason looked away and sighed. "It's impossible to talk to Mac without arguing. She's been even more quarrelsome in the past couple of weeks. I mostly try to stay out of her way, but it's hard to do when I'm partners with her sister." He glanced at Ellie. "Tell the sheriff how bad she's been."

"I don't know what you mean, Jason. She hasn't been quarrelsome."

"Then you've never seen her bad side," he shot back. He stalked away from Ellie's truck a few feet, then wheeled back around. "What happened out there? I heard there was blood."

Ellie nodded. "A lot of blood. And the trail leads to the railing and over the edge."

"You mean she went overboard?"

"Ellie, please let me handle this," the sheriff said. "Back to my questions, Jason. You said Mac was quarrelsome lately. Can you give me some examples of what you mean?"

Ellie was interested in hearing his answer herself. Mac had been a little quiet lately and hadn't always answered her phone, but the closest they'd come to an actual quarrel was today when Mac had practically drawn a line in the sand between her and Jason.

Jason stared off toward the boat. "That crazy tall ship flotilla idea, for one. She got into an argument with the city council about it. They didn't think it was worth the cost to bring it here for the seafood and Dungeness crab festival. They wanted to postpone it to next year's lavender festival, but she wouldn't hear of it. She seemed to think it would draw in the crowds and didn't believe the cooler weather would affect that at all."

Ellie shook her head. "Sailing has been her passion for years. This is nothing new, Jason."

"You never seem to notice how unpleasant she can be."

Sheriff Burchell raised a thick brow. "Sounds like you don't like your ex-wife much, Jason."

"Sometimes she makes me crazy, but I'd never lift a hand to her."

Ellie put her hand on the sheriff's forearm. "He wouldn't, Sheriff. I've known Jason a long time. He's a good man."

The sheriff grimaced. "Anything else out of the ordinary with her that you can think of?"

"She was dating some Coastie guy," Jason said. "You might check him out. Dylan Trafford. I heard she dumped him recently."

Ellie winced. He wasn't helping his case by revealing how obsessed he was with Mac's relationships and behavior.

"That so?" The sheriff jotted down the name on the pad. "Anything else?"

"Not that I can think of." Ellie hoped to derail Jason from giving the sheriff more reason to suspect him. She looked over the sheriff's shoulder. "Looks like we've got some help coming. The town has heard she's missing."

She recognized the Diskins, the Baers, and attorney Kristy Gillings at the forefront of townspeople heading for the beach and the forest with flashlights. She spotted some of Mac's co-workers as well as the sheriff's wife. Stuart Ransom, the fire chief, waved at her as he began splitting the searchers up into quadrants.

One person broke away from the group and rushed toward Ellie. Michelle Diskin had been Mac's best friend since they were children, and the two of them were close. Her parents had moved from Korea to Washington when she was three, and Mac had quickly picked up Korean as a child from playing with Michelle.

Ellie opened her arms, and Michelle fell into them. "She can't be dead." Michelle's shoulders shook with sobs.

"They're looking for her." Ellie gave up the struggle to maintain her composure and wept with her.

Michelle pulled away and swiped her eyes. "We have to find her. I'll text you if we see anything." She turned and ran back to the searchers fanning out across the shoreline.

For the first time since finding the blood, Ellie had a small sliver of hope. Their friends would try their hardest to find Mac. If she was out there, they'd find her.

But when dawn grew pink and gold in the eastern sky, Mac was still missing.

Ellie drove home to shower and change clothes. Her eyes were gritty from crying, and her head throbbed. She went up the steps to her front porch and frowned. The door was ajar. While Lavender Tides was generally safe, the town hadn't escaped the country's drug problem, and break-ins happened.

She pushed open the door and peered inside from the safety of the porch. A casserole sat on the floor just inside the door, and her breath came out in a *whoosh*. A neighbor hadn't gotten the door latched. That had to be all it was. But even as she reassured herself, she remembered her slashed tires.

Chapter 3

A building is only as beautiful as its
construction—the parts you can't see.
—HAMMER GIRL BLOG

Hope Beach, North Carolina, was a beautiful place with its thick sand dunes and clear blue waters. Grayson Bradshaw veered around a group of tourists who had blocked the sidewalk in front of the Oyster Café, then hurried away from the Coast Guard station in the harbor as fast as his lame leg would allow.

He worked in the Seattle area and was here to visit his parents, but an urgent phone call had summoned him from vacation. This station was the closest for reporting in. The commander here had relayed the full details of his new assignment.

Coast Guard stations up and down the West Coast had been on high alert ever since a seized shipment of two tons of cocaine worth twenty million dollars had gone missing three days ago.

The stuff had simply vanished from the evidence hangar. He was being called back to Washington to investigate the seizure's disappearance, and he'd have to board a plane for Seattle tomorrow.

As a sworn civilian investigator for the Coast Guard Investigative Services, or CGIS, for the past three years he'd been on the trail of Tarek Nasser, but the terrorist was a phantom, and every time Grayson got close to apprehending him, he'd slipped away, only to reappear in another part of the country.

His wounded leg throbbed, and he rubbed it. Thanks to Nasser, he was stuck at a desk, but even worse, his best friend, William Lacy, was in a grave. This time Grayson knew more about Nasser, and he'd get him. The man would pay for what he'd done.

Glancing in front of him, he saw the same couple he'd noticed yesterday. If it didn't sound so paranoid, he would have thought they were following him, but Hope Beach would be filled with tourists for a few more weeks. Their sunburned skin showing below their shorts and short-sleeve shirts was a good indication they weren't natives. He guessed them to be on their honeymoon, though, and the way his neck prickled when he saw them staring had to be just adrenaline from being tapped for a special assignment.

He crossed the parking lot toward his SUV but stopped when Chief Petty Officer Alec Bourne hailed him.

"Heck of a time to be called back to work. You just got here to enjoy yourself. Anything I can do?" Six two with blue eyes and an easy smile, Alec naturally drew people to him. He and Grayson had been friends from school but only saw each other on Grayson's rare trips home.

"I'd appreciate it if you could keep an eye on Mom." Grayson's mother had been recently diagnosed with diabetes, which was why he'd come home now. She looked okay, but he'd seen her sneaking Snickers bars in the night. That wasn't going to stop the disease. Dad was no help either. He'd long ago quit objecting to anything she wanted to do. She ruled the roost with a steely green-eyed gaze and a determined manner.

"Will do." Alec's gaze went over Grayson's shoulder. "That couple seems to be heading straight for us. Know them?"

He turned to see the honeymooners. "Nope."

The woman had her sights fixed on him, and a tentative smile lifted her full lips. Her nearly black hair was twisted atop her head in a messy knot that gave another inch or so to her height of about five two, and her green eyes were startling against her pale skin. The man with her had a protective hand at her waist. He was about six two or so and held his muscular build erect. His dark-blue eyes went from the woman to Grayson and back again.

A jolt of déjà vu shot up Grayson's spine. The woman reminded him of someone, but he couldn't think who.

The man swiped dark-brown hair off his forehead. "Grayson Bradshaw?"

Heat radiated off the pavement, and Grayson squinted in the sun trying to think of a reason they would want to speak to him. "That's right. Have we met?"

The man glanced at the woman, who clasped her hands in front of her and tilted an anxious smile up at him. She took a step closer. "I'm Shauna. Shauna Duval." She bit her lip and glanced at the man. "Well, Shauna Bannister now. That part's still new. This is my husband, Zach Bannister. We live in Lavender Tides, Washington."

Shifting from foot to foot, she was as nervous as a seaman recruit in a room full of admirals. "Is there something I can do for you?" He vaguely knew Lavender Tides was near Sequim, though he'd never been to that area other than to the Coast Guard station at Port Townsend.

"I knew this would be hard." She made a visible effort to drop her hands to her sides and force a smile. "I think you're my brother, Connor Duval, who went into foster care following an earthquake in the Olympic Mountains in 1995."

He started shaking his head as soon as she said the word *brother.* "I've only got one sister, and she lives in Okinawa where we grew up. I'm sorry," he added when he saw the disappointment surge into her eyes.

Zach shoved his hands into his pockets. "I'm pretty sure of the information I tracked down. You were adopted by Granger and Fiona Bradshaw six months after the quake. You were two, so you wouldn't remember. They didn't tell you?"

His chest tight, Grayson took a step back and shook his head. "I'm sure they would have told me about it if it were true. Look, I'm sorry you came all this way, but you're very wrong. Nice to meet you."

Shauna said something, but he couldn't hear it past the blood roaring in his ears. Why was he feeling such panic over a case of mistaken identity? He'd tell his parents about it tonight and they'd all laugh about it.

He practically fled to his SUV to get away from those two. What a weird thing to have happen now. His mother would be appalled at his lack of manners, but those people should have been more sure of their facts before they showed up with such wild assertions.

Grayson waved at Libby Bourne, Alec's wife, as he drove past Tidewater Inn on the narrow road to his parents' cottage. The shingle-style house was across the road from the sand dunes, and the sea salt left the plants and shrubs his mother had planted looking straggly and forlorn. He parked in the oyster-shell driveway and stepped out into the ocean air.

His mother rose from in front of a leggy rosebush as he approached. She brushed the dirt from her hands on her khaki shorts that revealed how much weight she'd gained since he'd seen her last. "I didn't expect you back for a while. When do you have to leave for Washington?"

"Tomorrow." He stared at her short blonde hair, so like his own, and it was further confirmation the Bannister couple had their facts wrong. "Where's Dad?"

"He was walking the beach. Here he comes now."

Grayson waved at his dad strolling across the road. At fifty, Granger Bradshaw still possessed a military bearing even though he'd been out of the navy for ten years. There was little gray in his thick brown hair, still cut short. Since retirement he'd spent his time golfing and fishing.

His dad stopped at the foot of the porch steps and brushed his wife's cheek with a kiss before smiling at Grayson. "There you are, son. Tell us all about your new assignment."

Grayson told them about the cocaine theft. A jet ski revved in the waves behind the dunes, and he raised his voice a bit. "I might be gone a few days, or it might be weeks. I'll keep you posted."

His mother studied his face. "I thought you'd be excited at this opportunity. You seem a little distracted."

Her green eyes were nothing like his, and his bulky height of six five dwarfed his father's six-foot frame. He'd never for a moment entertained the idea that he might be adopted, and it was silly to let it nag at him. The easiest way to resolve it was to talk to them.

"A couple from Lavender Tides, Washington, tracked me down today. I'd seen them hanging around me since yesterday. The woman tried to tell me she was my sister and that I'd disappeared after an earthquake. Crazy, huh?"

His mother went still and her eyes widened. She glanced at his dad and wet her lips. "I-I see. Did she give her name?"

His gut twisted at the way his mother stepped closer to Dad and took his hand. "Shauna Duval was her name before marriage."

"Lavender Tides, you say?" Dad set his other hand on her shoulder. "Fiona, I knew we should have told him."

She batted his hand away. "Granger, how could you!" His mother turned and rushed up the steps to the door, which banged behind her.

"Dad? It's true, then?" His throat was so tight he barely managed to force the words out. He blinked and tried to squelch the sense of being adrift at sea.

His father's brown eyes looked moist and his face resigned. "It's true."

Grayson took a step back and shook his head. "You can't be serious. I'm adopted?"

How could he have forgotten something so important as another family? A sister? Something about the woman had seemed familiar, but that was crazy, wasn't it?

His father settled on the porch step. "Have a seat."

"I don't think I can." Grayson wanted to pace, to shout and yell at the puffy white clouds floating by. This perfect day had taken a drastic and unwanted turn.

So many memories from childhood rose to his mind. Beachcombing in Okinawa, playing with his sister, Isabelle, in the yard, making cookies with his mom. Every part of who he was revolved around those memories. This couldn't be happening.

His father pulled out a roll of mints and popped one in his mouth. "We were foster parents, and you were about two when we got you. You screamed every time I got near you at first. We assumed your dad was either not in the picture or wasn't good to you. You had quite a few injuries from the earthquake. A concussion, a broken arm, and lots of cuts and bruises. We'd been told a rafter fell on you. You had regressed speech and didn't say anything at all the first six months, then you started repeating everything you heard. We'd been told no one claimed you, so it was assumed your parents had died in the quake."

"They never looked for me? You never heard of this Shauna?"

His dad shook his head. "As far as we knew, no one was looking for you, so we started adoption proceedings as soon as we could. I was stationed in Lavender Tides when we first got you. As soon as the adoption was final, we shipped out for Okinawa."

Grayson's earliest memories were in Japan. Nothing sounded familiar about an earthquake or Washington. Even a toddler should have remembered something that traumatic.

"What about Isabelle?" Right now he'd like to get on a plane and visit his sister, hear what she had to say about all this.

"She doesn't know."

Grayson paced the sandy grass as he absorbed the news. It

hurt like the dickens that the sister he adored wasn't adopted too. It would have been easier to accept if she had been as well.

"I need to take a walk. This is too much to take in." He jogged across the road and ignored his dad calling after him.

How was he supposed to find that cocaine with this news hanging over his head?

Chapter 4

The costliest renovations are on things you
can't see like plumbing and electrical.
—Hammer Girl Blog

Sheriff Burchell's office was located in a building built in 1895. Ellie nodded to the receptionist, who motioned her back to his office, a musty-smelling room with greenish-gray paint that would have fit right in with its original color. The old wooden bookshelves were battered as well and held a picture of the sheriff and his deputies receiving some awards along with a picture of his wife, Felicia.

Burchell rose from behind his desk. "You been sleeping at all?" His dark-blue eyes missed nothing, and she knew he had to see the dark circles under her eyes, even behind her glasses. She felt like she'd been tossed against ocean rocks for the past forty-eight hours, but she held her shoulders back as she shook his hand, then settled onto the worn chair across from him.

"Not much. I hope you called me down here to share good news." Mackenzie's body hadn't surfaced, which meant Ellie had managed to hang on to a slight thread of hope on her sister's fate, even though logically she knew the chances of finding Mac weren't good.

He stroked a long, seventies-style Elvis sideburn. "I wish I had better news. We do have preliminary confirmation that the blood is Mackenzie's; at least it's the same blood type. We ran all the fingerprints we found at her house and on the ship but came up with nothing other than hers and known friends or family members." He cleared his throat. "Including Jason's prints."

She ignored his comment about Jason. The sheriff couldn't seriously suspect Jason. "No unaccounted for hair or fibers or anything?" What she knew of forensics came only from TV and movies, but she desperately wanted some hint on how to find out what had happened to Mac.

He shook his head. "We're still looking at those things. We seized her computer, but nothing seems relevant to her disappearance. It's all university business as far as we can tell."

"Could I take a look?"

He pursed his lips. "I don't think that would be helpful, Ellie. I've got my best detectives working on it."

"Maybe a student took her." It was a long shot, and she knew it even before the sheriff raised a brow. "You never know."

"For what reason?"

She pushed her glasses up on her nose. "I don't know."

The sheriff was doing all he could, but maybe Mac's

coworkers would tell her things they were reluctant to tell the sheriff. It was worth a try.

Her muscles ached from lack of sleep as she rose. "I'll let you get back to work. Please let me know if you hear anything."

"Will do."

The university where her sister worked was on the outskirts of town. Ellie found her way to her sister's office and swallowed hard when she saw the yellow police tape across the door. Across the hall was the break room, and she should be able to find some of the other professors there.

Ellie yanked open the door and stepped into the room flooded with sunlight from the big windows overlooking the parking lot.

Two women and a man seated at a break table together looked up. Darcy rose first. About forty, her short, round figure implied softness that was missing in the sharp hazel eyes under red hair that owed most of its color to a bottle.

She embraced Ellie, and the lavender scent she wore enfolded her as well. "Ellie, I don't know what to say. We're all grieving."

Ellie clung to her for a long moment. "I'd hoped to find you all here. I still can't believe it."

"We can't either." Darcy pulled back, and her hands moved to grasp Ellie's shoulders. "What can we do to help?"

"You've been looking for her like the rest of the town has. I think that's all we can do now." People had come by the house with food and hugs, and she'd seen searchlights out every night since Mac disappeared.

Penny Dreamer had been waiting her turn to greet Ellie.

In her fifties, her hair was pure white, and she had chiseled features and clear blue eyes. Mac had always called her the Fairy Godmother because of her calm, helpful manner. She'd been widowed for ten years and had two grown boys. Her students loved her, and she'd always said she never wanted to retire.

Darcy stepped back and let Penny grab Ellie. She closed her eyes as she sank into the comfort of Penny's embrace. The woman could hug like nobody's business, and she always smelled of lemon and frankincense essential oils. Inhaling the aroma could calm a charging bull.

Ellie's eyes burned, and moisture forced its way past her determination not to cry. Crying always made her glasses fog up. She swallowed and pulled back, then dug in her purse for a tissue. It was hard to talk past the lump in her throat. These women loved Mac fiercely.

She glanced at the man, Isaac Cohen, who taught government and politics classes. He wore an impeccable navy suit that enhanced his black wavy hair and dark eyes. Mac had been interested in him when she first started teaching at the university, but he hadn't been interested in her. They had become good friends, though.

He reached out and took her hand. "I haven't been able to sleep from worrying about Mackenzie. She's a special person."

Ellie squeezed his hand. "Thank you."

Penny pulled a chair out from under a long table holding computers and equipment. "Sit down. Want some coffee or anything? Darcy brought in donuts, and they're still warm."

Ellie shook her head. "I haven't been able to choke down more than tea and toast." She waited until the teachers pulled out chairs opposite her and settled. "The sheriff said he talked to you."

They looked at each other. Darcy shrugged but didn't say anything.

Penny bit her lip and shook her head hard enough that her white bob bounced against her cheeks. "They have to find out who did this. The deputy took her computer and everything."

"So she never said anything to you that might explain who could have hurt her?"

The teachers all shook their heads.

"All I knew about was her breakup with Dylan. He said she'd been a little paranoid about him and thought he might be watching her," Penny said.

"I forgot to ask the sheriff if he'd talked to Dylan. Maybe he knows something."

Penny put her arm around her. "I wish we had some sort of clue to share, but there's nothing."

Ellie's throat thickened. "Thanks. I'd better go." She fled the building before she could burst into tears again. No amount of crying would find her sister.

A car drove slowly past. Was that the same black Taurus that had driven by her after her tires were slashed? She stared at it, but the tinted windows prevented her from seeing anyone inside. It probably wasn't even the same one.

She'd hopefully figure that out, but first she'd call the sheriff and ask him about Dylan. Maybe he'd attacked Mac in a rage.

Grayson couldn't count the number of times he'd passed the stately Georgian mansion called Tidewater Inn. Its status as *the* boutique hotel in the area was well deserved from what he'd heard, though he'd never had an opportunity to stay there. When he approached the front door, his stomach roiled as he caught a whiff of the shrimp boil going on at the beach in front of the hotel.

What would he say to her, that woman who claimed to be his sister? He'd waited several hours to come, and even now he couldn't quite process it all. An earthquake. No matter how hard he tried, any memories of something that traumatic refused to surface. Nothing much existed for him before playing on the beach in Okinawa with palm trees and impossibly green mountains looming in the distance. According to his parents, he'd been three when they moved there. He and his sister had spent a lot of time splashing in the warm Pacific Ocean waters.

He at least owed the woman the courtesy of hearing her out. And apologizing for his rudeness earlier.

He opened the door and stepped into the inn's lobby area. No one manned the reservation desk. "Hello?"

A pretty woman in her early thirties stepped through a door. Her light-brown hair was up in a ponytail, and her amber-brown eyes smiled at him. "Hello. I'm Libby Bourne. Checking in?"

He recognized the name as the inn's owner, Alec's wife. "I'm looking for Shauna Bannister. I'm Grayson Bradshaw."

"Alec's friend! It's good to finally meet you." Her smile widened. "Shauna and her husband are taking a walk on the beach. They just left, so you can probably catch them on the way to the pier."

"Thanks."

He exited into the sunshine and headed down the dunes to the water. The scent of saltwater wafted to his nose. If he'd looked toward the water when he got out of his SUV, he probably would have seen them. He kicked off his sandals and dug his toes into the warm sand. The beach always soothed him.

He inhaled and squared his shoulders as he moved toward the pier. His long legs ate up the distance quickly, and he spotted the couple strolling hand in hand toward the sinking sun. Should he call out to them or just hurry to catch up?

He decided on the latter option. The last thing he wanted was for her to fix those expectant eyes on him and watch him approach. The thick dunes made jogging difficult, so he veered toward the water and picked up the pace on the packed, wet sand.

He slowed when he got five feet from them. "Hold up a sec."

Shauna and her husband—was it Zach?—stopped and turned. Her face lit up when she saw him, and her lips curved up in a welcoming smile. Were those tearstains on her cheeks? The husband maintained a warier expression, and Grayson couldn't blame him. He hadn't been exactly welcoming when they'd approached him.

He dropped his sandals to the sand and stopped about three feet from them. "I, uh, talked to my parents. What you said about the earthquake appears to be true."

Her green eyes acquired extra light. "They admitted they got you after the earthquake?"

He nodded. "Dad had always wanted to tell me, but Mom wouldn't let him. I'm still trying to process it all." He looked her over better. "We don't look much alike. Where'd I get all the blond in my hair?"

"Mom used to say a fairy left you under a lily pad. No one else in the family had your hair color, but those recessive genes played out, I guess."

"How old were you?"

Her lips curved in a tender smile. "Eight. I remember you well."

That would make her thirty-three. The sea breeze freshened and brought the squeals of boaters with it. He tried to think of what to say. Did he ask about his birth parents now or what? He had no idea what the proper etiquette was when you found out your whole life was a lie.

Zach's wary expression softened. He shrugged off his backpack and dug out an old quilt. After spreading it on the thick sand, he settled on one corner and patted beside him for Shauna to join him. "Have a seat, Grayson. This could take a while." Shauna sat beside her husband with her knees tucked under her.

Grayson settled as far away from them as he could on the farthest corner. "I need to apologize for before. I was rude."

Shauna shook her head, and a stray lock of black hair swung against her cheek. "I should have called and given you some warning. Or sent a letter explaining it all. It's no wonder you were shocked."

"That's no excuse for how I acted. I'm really sorry. You seem like a nice person, and I hope I didn't hurt your feelings."

She shot a quick look at her husband. "Nothing that isn't easily forgiven."

He studied her face and wished it brought back a memory of some kind. All he could dredge up was an uneasy sense of familiarity. "So, what happened exactly?"

"We were with our pregnant mother at a grocery store in Lavender Tides, Washington."

"I'm heading to that area tomorrow to investigate some missing cocaine. The Coast Guard base where my investigation will center isn't far from your town."

She smiled. "We'll be back in another five days. You're

welcome to stay with us. Or at my house that's sitting empty since my son, Alex, and I moved in with Zach. Alex is five, and he will be over-the-moon excited to have an uncle."

Would it be a terrible idea to get to know her better? And he had a nephew. The blows just kept coming. "Thanks, I'll think about it. Go on."

"There was a play area in the store, and you and I were having fun. Then everything started to shake and rattle. The ceiling caved in, and we were trapped for two days. Our mother went into labor and delivered a baby girl I named Brenna. Mom died. You were having a lot of trouble breathing after we were rescued, and they took you away. I was told you died. Brenna too. Our dad said you'd both died."

Tears glimmered on her lashes, and she sent her husband an appealing glance. He took over the tale. "We recently found out that your dad didn't think he could take care of three kids with your mom dead. He never tried to find you and Brenna. I talked to one of the CPS workers and found out what had happened to you. So here we are."

Pressure built in his chest. His father had just turned his back on him and forgotten his existence? "I see."

Shauna rubbed her forehead. "It was a terrible thing he did, but I hope you can forgive him. He was an alcoholic, and he's dead now. I'm sure you had a better life with your parents than I did with him."

Grayson wasn't ready to examine how he felt about his abandonment. "What about Brenna?"

Zach shook his head. "I haven't been able to find a trace of her yet, but we're not giving up."

The guy really seemed to love Shauna.

Grayson hated hotels, and the thought of digging into the mystery of his beginnings held some appeal. "I think I'd like to take you up on your offer. I'd hate to intrude on newlyweds, so staying at the empty house might be the best idea."

Chapter 5

The right tool always makes the job easier.
—Hammer Girl Blog

The barn looked empty as Grayson, Sig Sauer in hand, crouched behind a line of bushes with other members of the Coast Guard team. His bum leg didn't allow him to go in during the takedown, but he helped man the perimeter. His fatigue had dropped off the moment he landed and found out his team had a lead on Tarek Nasser's whereabouts. His adrenaline was as high as the moon beaming down. In a perfect world, clouds would have obscured any light from the heavens, and he hoped the clear night sky wasn't an omen of failure.

Cuffing Nasser tonight was all he cared about. He saw a hand signal to move and crept forward past the cover and into the moonbeams. Not a glimmer of light showed through the barn's windows. Several dark man-shaped shadows crept forward and opened the barn door. He was on their heels and bit back a sneeze from the scent of old hay and straw.

The team swept what appeared to be an empty building while Grayson walked the perimeter of the yard and the attached fenced area. When he first saw someone clambering over the fence in the back paddock, he thought it was one of the team, but this figure wore a hoodie and jeans. The soles of the guy's sneakers gleamed in the moonlight.

He yelled for backup and took off after the guy. Shoving his gun in the holster, he put on all the speed he could muster with his bum leg and climbed the fence after him. The guy was fast, though, and all Grayson could reach was the side of the backpack the guy had slung over his shoulder.

Grayson's fingers tangled in the back loop of the shoulder strap, and the bag slid off the guy and into Grayson's hands. He started to drop it while he ran after the fleeing terrorist, but common sense told him he'd never catch him, not with his leg.

Which was why he spent most of his time at a desk. He didn't have to like it, but he had to recognize facts.

He'd started to turn back toward the barn when a bullet whistled close to his left ear. He ducked down behind a fallen log and drew his weapon. The muzzle flash showed him the guy's position, and Grayson returned fire. Two Coasties joined him, and he motioned for them to circle around to each side of the shooter.

A bullet splintered the tree by his head, and he shot toward the flash of fire he'd seen. The guy yelled and toppled over. Grayson crawled over the fallen log, and crouching low, he hurried to where he'd seen the man tumble into the tall weeds. The sharp scent of gunpowder stung his nostrils, and he slowed his pace as he neared the fallen figure.

One of the Coasties reached the guy first and touched his neck. "Dead." He rolled him over, and moonlight illuminated the man's face.

Grayson shouldered the bag. "Nasser's second in command, Omar. Our intel was spot-on. We just didn't get here in time to nab Nasser. Losing Omar won't make him happy, though. I'll leave you guys to finish up here. I want to see if we got anything of value in this bag."

He carried the backpack to his SUV and opened the passenger door. Under the glare of the dome light, he pulled out the contents: a half-full bottle of Evian, a tube of ChapStick, several notepads with Arabic scribbles, a MacBook Air with its silver edges battered, an army-green jacket, two pens, a GPS unit, a USB drive, and a satellite phone.

He grabbed the phone and pulled up the last call. He'd let the tech department check it out. They might be able to get a GPS fix on whatever numbers had been dialed on this phone, though it was anyone's guess whether Nasser had moved on. He had probably been here with Omar and not at the number this phone had called, but it was worth a try.

Grayson's phone vibrated in his pocket, and he pulled it out. The number was blocked, but he answered it. "Bradshaw."

Someone clapping on the other end filled his head. "Very good, Bradshaw. Doesn't it tick you off that you can never get me? I'm the phantom you'll never catch."

"Omar's dead, you know."

Nasser went silent for a long moment, and his voice vibrated with anger when he finally spoke. "You're lying."

"Want me to send you a picture?" Grayson straightened and turned to look back at where the team was scouring the grounds.

"I'm going to get you, Nasser. You can't run fast enough or hide well enough to get away from me. Sooner or later it's going to happen."

Nasser didn't answer, and Grayson realized the terrorist had hung up. The tech team would discover what goodies they'd acquired. He'd receive a video and other files while he was in the air. At least Grayson had a lead to follow up on the cocaine theft, and with any luck, it would direct him to Tarek.

The courthouse had been built in the late eighteen hundreds and sat atop a small hillside overlooking the downtown area of Lavender Tides. The food trucks were doing a brisk business, and the aroma of shrimp and crab lingered in the air. Ellie parked on the street and looked at the small group of people waiting on the lawn. She had a few minutes before the Robb house auction was scheduled to start, so she called Sheriff Burchell's number.

He answered on the second ring. "Sheriff Burchell."

"It's Ellie Blackmore, Sheriff. Is there anything new on my sister's disappearance?" It had been several days—surely there was something.

"I was going to call you, Ellie. We had a tip that Mackenzie was spotted in Hamhung, North Korea, yesterday. According to the caller, the ship was staged to look like she'd been killed, but she was actually spying for North Korea."

A stone formed in Ellie's stomach. "That's a lie! Mac would never do that to her family. You don't believe it, do you? It's the most ludicrous thing I've ever heard. A spy! Good grief, she's a college professor."

"The caller sent over a picture. It's being evaluated for authenticity, but it appears to be real."

"I don't believe it." She thought she'd shouted the words, but they came out as a whisper.

Could it be true? She didn't want to consider the possibility. "What about Dylan Trafford? Did you check him out?"

Ellie had never liked the guy, who was full of himself and ordered Mac around. If Mac was afraid of Dylan, at least it was some kind of clue.

The sheriff broke into her thoughts. "Not yet. He's been out at sea, which makes him less of a suspect anyway. Listen, I have another call coming in. I'll let you know what I find out."

Ellie put her phone into her purse, then exited her pickup and headed up the walkway to the courthouse. She saw several other possible buyers milling around. She didn't want this house to slip away, but this was the last place she wanted to be. It didn't seem important with Mac missing and likely dead. She understood now what people went through without closure. Stuck in limbo, she found it impossible to concentrate on much of anything else.

The auctioneer, a portly man Ellie didn't recognize, stepped forward. "We're going to get started, folks. The opening bid is one hundred thousand."

Ellie raised her hand, and the war was on. After fifteen minutes, she had purchased the home for two hundred thousand dollars—a steal for sure, but more than she'd hoped to pay. The place was in serious disrepair and would take several months to restore. She wasn't sure she could afford to keep it after the remodel, but she had to try.

She made payment arrangements and took the house key, then went back to her truck. She texted Jason to let him know she'd bought the house, then started the pickup and headed to their new purchase.

Sunshine sparkled on her window, and she rolled it down to breathe in the scent of pine and sea. As she perched her elbow on the door, she saw a black Taurus approaching at too fast a speed. Was it the same one she'd noticed after her tires were slashed? This stretch of road had a forty-miles-per-hour speed limit, and the guy had to be doing at least seventy.

She frowned and slowed so the car could pass her, but it did the same and stayed on her bumper. The sun glaring on her back window prevented her from making out more than a vague outline of the person driving.

When the first tap came on her bumper, she managed to keep her truck on the road and steered toward the shoulder. The driver probably didn't even know she'd been hit. Then the next blow came, hard enough that it pitched her head back, then forward. The steering wheel lurched under her hands, and her vehicle headed for the deep ditch along the side of the road. She fought the truck and managed to bring it to a stop before it rolled over into the ditch.

Her chest was tight, and she could barely catch her breath. She had to force herself to release her grip on the wheel. The Taurus was nowhere to be seen. She got out and checked for damage—nothing but a small dent in a bumper that had already seen its fair share of accidents over the years.

Still shaken, she got back into her vehicle and carefully drove back onto the road and headed for her destination. That felt like a deliberate attack, and she resolved to call the sheriff as soon as she was safely parked in the driveway.

She reached the Saltwater Point house and parked, then called the sheriff's office. He wasn't in, so she told the deputy handling the call what had happened. He took down all the information, but she didn't have any real details to tell him. That make of car was common, and she had no license plate number.

She exhaled and dropped the phone back into her purse. She got out of the truck and looked over the Saltwater Point house. It was the only house on Saltwater Point, and the land alone was worth what she'd paid. Her practiced eye noted the cracks in the circular driveway. More work.

A fog blew in from the Strait of Juan de Fuca and swirled around the smooth cedar facade of the home she'd purchased. Her taste normally ran to contemporary coastal properties, but this traditional cedar house had been one she'd admired from the first moment she'd seen it when she was a girl. She'd already named it the House at Saltwater Point. If she didn't get to keep it, the name would play well in ads.

An unfamiliar SUV parked in the driveway caught her eye. Who was here? She pushed her glasses up on her nose and got out. Maybe someone else interested in the property? If so, he was out of luck. The black SUV was empty as she passed it, and no one was at the front door. As she neared the entrance, she saw the door standing open, and the back of her neck prickled.

She pushed it open the rest of the way. "Who's there? You're trespassing." The musty odor of an empty house wafted toward her.

Footsteps came her way, and she held the key in her hand like a weapon as a tall man with blondish hair came into view. He had shoulders as broad as a linebacker, but the bulk narrowed at his hips. His slight limp looked out of place with his muscles.

His blue eyes narrowed when he saw her standing on the portico. "Ellie Blackmore?"

She took a tighter grip on her key. Big men always made her feel smaller and more diminished. Her father had been a big guy prone to using his fists when she or Mac misbehaved. "I'm Ellie Blackmore. Who are you and what are you doing in my house?"

He quirked a brow. "Sorry, I didn't mean to upset you. Your partner told me I'd find you here."

The tenseness eased from her shoulders. A new client? "What can I do for you?"

"I'm trying to find the cocaine your sister stole." He slid a large hand into his breast pocket and retrieved a badge. "Grayson Bradshaw with the Coast Guard. CGIS."

Cocaine? Stole? She retreated several steps as she translated what he'd said. The CGIS was the Coast Guard Investigative Service. She glanced at his badge.

"Step aside." She backed up on the portico. "My sister didn't steal any cocaine. That's the most ridiculous thing I've ever heard. Mac would hardly take an aspirin, let alone drugs. She's a professor."

He returned his badge to his pocket. "You talked to her about the cocaine?"

"I can't talk to her. She's missing, probably even dead." Tears burned her eyes at the admission. She'd been clinging to hope as best as she could, but this big bear of a man had flustered her with his wild accusations.

No matter what the sheriff said about Mac being in another country, Ellie was sure her sister's body was floating in the sea somewhere waiting to be found and brought home.

Chapter 6

Saving what's real, true, and solid
is always the best plan.
—HAMMER GIRL BLOG

G rayson welcomed the opportunity to do what he came here for and pushed away the déjà vu that had hit him when he had gotten off the plane an hour ago.

He squinted in the bright sunshine. The feisty brunette had her fists clenched as if she'd like to punch him. Her earnest eyes were more golden than brown. As close to amber as he'd ever seen. His size could be intimidating to women, and she was eyeing him with a dubious glare, so he stepped away a few more inches. She was kind of cute standing there with such a pugnacious stance. The huge black glasses didn't hide enough of her face to keep him from seeing her perfect skin and high cheekbones.

He folded his arms over his chest. "I have an appointment with the sheriff tomorrow afternoon, and I hope to get to the bottom of the theft. All the evidence points to your sister."

Her lips parted, and a harsh breath escaped. "You are all set to railroad her into something she didn't do. She's missing! That stupid picture means nothing." She looked away.

His ears perked. "What picture?"

She caught her full lower lip between perfect white teeth. "The sheriff will tell you anyway. He claims a tip came in that Mac isn't dead, that she is in North Korea. I don't believe it. She'd never run off like that and make us think she'd been murdered. Never!"

He didn't know the woman or her relationships well enough to comment on them, but if he had a dollar for every time he heard that kind of avowal, he could retire at the beach. "You'd be surprised what people will do. And North Korea would make sense. She's an Asian language expert."

"Not Mac! I know her too well to believe something like that." One perfectly shaped brow lifted. "What are you doing *here* anyway? Mac has nothing to do with this place. I just bought it in an auction."

He dug out his phone and said nothing as he held a picture from his phone under her nose. It showed Mackenzie inside this house talking to Terrance Robb and another man. "Recognize either of the men with her?"

The pink washed out of her face, leaving her cheeks colorless. "That's the owner of the house, Terrance Robb. The other guy is a man Mac had been dating. Dylan Trafford."

"So tell me what this looks like. The cocaine is gone, and Trafford is missing along with your sister. Looks to me like they took the drugs and went off to enjoy the high life." He already knew Trafford was out to sea and not really *missing*, but maybe prodding her would produce a nugget of information.

When she swayed, he started to steady her, but she shook her head and stepped away. "Just because she was here with them doesn't mean anything. She broke up with Dylan two weeks ago. And he's not missing—he's been out on a boat."

He shrugged. "Probably to throw suspicion off her. The picture in the sheriff's possession may be found to be authentic, then how will you explain it?"

She blinked, and some color came back to her face. "Nothing you say could make me doubt my sister. Now, if you'll excuse me, I want to check out the house I just bought."

"I'd like to look around if you don't mind." When a frown wrinkled her brow, he shrugged again. "I can get a court order if you'd rather."

"But why?"

He held up the picture on his phone again. "It's probably nothing, but I want to be sure."

"Fine. You can check it out, but the place is empty." She pushed open the door.

"Hey, mister." A little girl with a wagon hauling Girl Scout cookies came up the walk.

Ellie stepped past him to smile at the child. "You've got a heavy load there, honey."

The girl nodded, her black curls bouncing. "Want to buy some?"

"I sure will. I'll take two boxes of the peanut butter ones."

"Thanks, lady!" The girl picked up two boxes and handed them over, then accepted Ellie's money with a huge smile. She peeked up at Grayson with a questioning smile.

"I guess I'd better buy some too." He couldn't let Ellie outdo him. "I'll take three boxes of chocolate mint ones."

The little girl's smile went up in wattage as he handed over the money and took the cookies. "Thanks!" She walked away from the house excited.

"You're good with kids. You have any of your own?" He wanted to kick himself for directing the conversation to something so personal.

She shook her head. "Not married and no kids, but I like to encourage an entrepreneurial spirit." She lifted a brow. "You?"

Touché. "Nope. I've traveled around too much in my duty stations to get serious about a woman."

He followed her inside the house. The sea salt and sand had done damage to the floor over the years, and it was nicked in places. The finish was worn in the walk paths, but the place had good bones. An oak board ceiling's natural color bounced light from the windows to the floors. The plaster walls bowed out from the lath in places, and the kitchen hadn't been updated in twenty years, but he could see beyond that.

He pointed to the bowing plaster. "Looks like you'll have to remove the lath and plaster, then put up drywall."

She shook her head. "They make what are called plaster washers I'll use with a drywall screw to tighten it back to the lath. Authentic plaster adds character to a home, and I like to keep it when I can."

The young woman was cute in a girl-next-door kind of way. He hoped she wasn't about to learn a hard lesson about the secrets people keep. "How'd you learn so much about remodeling? Most women aren't interested in home repair."

"My dad was a carpenter, and he taught me a lot when I

was growing up. We kids often helped him." A ghost of a smile lifted her lips. "Mac hated it, but I loved fixing things up. I went to design school that second summer after high school, and Dad loaned us the money for our first flip, a cottage in the woods that was practically falling down. We fixed it up and made a profit of fifty thousand dollars. That was five years ago, and my partner and I never looked back."

He glanced at her left hand. No ring. Not engaged, either. "And what's your decorating style?"

"It's a blend of coastal cottage and farmhouse. Think Joanna Gaines mixed with a blend of contemporary coastal touches and pops of chrome." She shrugged. "I do other designs for people, but that's what I tend to go for when we're flipping a house. And we always do a top-quality renovation with no cut corners."

"Sounds nice. I'm going to look around, but I'll try not to disturb you."

There was no way her sister was innocent. He had a hunch about these kinds of things, and he was rarely wrong.

Why did the guy bug her so much? Ellie walked out to the deck and into the crisp, clear air to get away from his presence. He was just so . . . big and overpowering. Her dad was big like him, and he'd made her feel unimportant and weak. And this Bradshaw guy seemed so set on Mac's guilt. He hadn't even investigated yet, but he was ready to handcuff her.

Ellie stepped across the yard past a glorious rambling rosebush that wafted its scent on the breeze, then turned to examine the house. The smooth cedar siding was in good shape. Terrance had kept it sealed, and she saw no sign of damage from the salt air, which was a bonus. The windows didn't need to be replaced, and the roof appeared sound. The yard was nicely landscaped too, so it would just be a matter of updating the inside and fixing the driveway.

She had no other excuse to loiter outside, so she moved slowly toward the back door again. Maybe he was done by now. She'd reached the seating area on the patio when her phone rang. Shauna Bannister's name flashed on the screen. "What are you doing calling on your honeymoon, Shauna? How was Hawaii?"

"It's gorgeous, and our Hawaiian cruise was . . . interesting. I'll tell you about it when I get home." There was a lilt in Shauna's voice. "But I need a favor."

They'd met when Ellie decorated the house Shauna and her first husband had built. Shauna had kept to herself after Jack died, but with her new marriage, she seemed to be herself again. It didn't sound like she'd heard about Mac.

Ellie welcomed the reprieve from being in the investigator's presence and walked over to drop into one of the comfy chairs overlooking the water. A gull swooped and squawked overhead, then landed on the deck handrail to peer at her with black eyes. "You know I'd do just about anything for you. Well, other than give up coffee. I wouldn't do that for anyone." Telling her about Mac could wait until she got back. No sense in ruining her honeymoon.

"Neither would I. This shouldn't be too hard because he's quite the hunk."

"Uh-oh. I've had it with blind dates. I swear, all you newlyweds are alike. You want everyone else to share in the glow."

"No, no, it's nothing like that. We've never really talked about this, but I had a brother and sister. I thought they died in the earthquake that killed my mother, but I found out they went into foster care. Zach found my brother here in Hope Beach!"

"You're kidding! That's wonderful. I bet you're enjoying quite the reunion. Does that mean you're not coming back on Saturday and you need me to keep Alex? No problem. I love that kid."

"You keep jumping ahead of me." Shauna laughed again. "No, my brother had to come to Lavender Tides on assignment. He's with the Coast Guard. I told him he could stay at my place. I wondered if you'd mind taking him under your wing a bit. He hasn't lived there since he was two and won't know anyone. You know my place pretty well and could show him where everything is. Maybe tell him where to get groceries, that kind of thing."

"Sure, I can do that. When's he hitting town and what's his name?"

"He should be there now. His name was Connor, but his adoptive parents named him Grayson. Grayson Bradshaw."

The blood drained from Ellie's head. "You've got to be kidding me. He's here now, poking around into Mac's disappearance."

Shauna's voice rose. "What's this about Mac? She's missing?"

Ellie told her everything she knew. "He's sure Mac took that cocaine, which is totally *insane*." Her voice trembled. "He's really your brother? He's a little—overpowering."

"I had no idea about all this. I'm so sorry, Ellie. Zach and I will be praying you find her safe. I can ask someone else to help out."

"Thanks." She exhaled and fisted her other hand in her lap.

"I'll do what I can for him. I don't want you to worry about anything on your honeymoon. I'll go talk to him now."

"Are you sure? I can easily call someone else."

"He's here now anyway. I can do it, no problem. See you soon." Ellie ended the call and stared out at a ferry chugging past. If it was anyone other than Shauna, Ellie might have found a way to get out of such an onerous favor.

She rose and entered the dining room, then stepped through to the kitchen. Grayson was nowhere to be found. Had he left? She glanced through the front-door window, but his SUV was still there. She walked through the living room to the laundry room, then saw the door to the basement standing open. A light glimmered from below.

She stepped to the top of the stairs. "Grayson?"

"Yo." He appeared in a swatch of light with cobwebs draped over his hair. "Found something interesting down here."

She hated basements. The dank smell, the damp chill, the drippy noises. She forced herself to plod down the stairs, and it was just as bad as his cobwebbed appearance indicated. The floor beams were only seven feet overhead, and she felt like she needed to duck under the debris hanging from them. She shuddered at the spider eggs swaying at her passage. Spiders were the worst.

She reached him where he stood at a wall covered with shelves containing old paint cans, cleaning supplies, and oily rags. "What is it?"

He shone a flashlight past the shelves to the wall. "Looks like a door back here. There's a ton of debris around it, so I don't think it's been used in a long time. Okay if I move this shelf and dig around back in there?"

"I guess. I'm not sure what you think you're going to find

here about the investigation, though. The Robb family lived here, not my sister. And she would have had no reason to be poking around in the basement."

"There's more to all of this than I'm at liberty to say."

That didn't make sense. She moved out of the way to allow him to get to the door.

Chapter 7

Rooms left abandoned quickly gather dust and cobwebs.
—HAMMER GIRL BLOG

The metal shelving unit scraped across the floor, and Grayson steadied a can of paint before it could topple to the concrete. The air was thick with the odor of damp and mold. He eyed the door. "It's not locked so maybe it's nothing important."

Ellie sidled closer, her face pale in the wash of light from the weak bulb overhead. Her eyes were huge behind her glasses, and her lips twisted with disgust. "Let's see what's back there and get out of here."

She was clearly scared of basements, and he didn't blame her in this case. This one was plenty creepy. The knob twisted under his fingers, and he pushed the door open. A light inside came on to reveal a room with several stools, a metal file cabinet, and a heavy wooden table with mismatched chairs. Heavy draperies covered the walls.

He let her in, then looked at the door. "The lock is on the inside, not on the outside. Whoever used this wanted to keep people out once he or she was inside."

He caught her sweet scent as she moved past him to examine the walls. Lavender maybe. He frowned as he peered behind one of the curtains. "Whoa, this wall is lined in cork." He looked at another wall, then another. "The whole room is sheathed in cork."

"What's that mean? Why would someone do that?"

"Probably to protect from listening devices. It was commonly used during the Cold War. How long has Terrance Robb owned the house?"

"Fifteen years. The home was built in the early sixties by a man who worked for President Kennedy, or so I've heard. This was his vacation home. I don't know much about him. The timing would be right, though." Her hand trailed along the back of one of the high-back chairs. "It's filthy in here. It's hard to say when it was last used."

He grunted. "Interesting."

"You think he held private meetings here?"

"It would make sense." He examined the furniture and walls for anything hidden. "Doesn't seem to be anything here worth noting."

"Good. I want some sunshine." She went past him out the door, and her steps pounded up the stairs in a quick staccato.

He shut the door, then went after her. There was nothing of interest here. Since discovering the link between her sister and Nasser, he'd hoped to find some kind of drugs stashed here. A crazy thought, maybe, but nothing in this case made sense. No matter what it took, he was going to make Tarek pay for what he'd done.

He shut the light to the basement off at the top of the stairs and closed the door. "I'm done here. I'm going to go get settled. Where would you recommend I grab dinner?"

She shuffled from foot to foot and didn't look him in the face for a moment. "I need to eat too. Follow me to town, and we'll go to Smokey's. They have the best ribs you've ever eaten."

Was she asking him on a *date*? He thought she was cute, but he didn't think she liked him.

She must have caught his expression. "Shauna called me and told me about you a few minutes ago. I promised to show you around and make sure you're settled. We're friends."

The disappointment rocketing up his spine perplexed him. Hadn't he just thought she was too forward? But he wasn't a child to be met at the airport by a guide. "I'm sure I can find my way."

"It's no trouble. The grocery store is across the street, and you can grab some things. We can run out to Shauna's, and I'll show you where to find everything. It's really nice. Quiet, with no close neighbors. How long are you staying?"

She wasn't taking no for an answer, and he didn't want to offend his new sister by being rude after she was trying to help him. "It depends on how long it takes to finish my investigation. I'd guess a couple of weeks, but that's a stab in the dark."

He followed her out the door, then turned to watch her lock up. "You don't like me very much."

Something flickered in her golden-brown eyes. Consternation perhaps?

She put her keys in her bag, a utilitarian leather satchel with multiple pockets. "I don't know you yet, but you're Shauna's brother, so that's enough. For now."

He watched her head for her truck and grinned. Such honesty was refreshing.

The atmosphere at Smokey's Ribs and More always felt like an embrace to Ellie. The rivets in the dark wood floors reflected the glimmer from the Edison lights overhead, and pictures of patrons over the years plastered the walls. Plus, the yummiest food aromas on the planet filled the place.

Felicia Burchell stopped her and took her hand. "How are you holding up, Ellie? I've been praying for you."

"Hanging in there." She could feel everyone's support and prayers. Everyone in town had gathered around her and tried their best to help out. It was the only way she'd gotten through.

Ellie had always liked the sheriff's young and beautiful wife who used to model in New York. Her half-Asian genes gave her an exotic look the camera loved, but she was even more beautiful inside.

Felicia released her hand. "I've been pestering Everett to death. The poor guy is so exhausted, but he's determined to find out what happened to Mac."

"I know he's doing his best. It's very puzzling."

Felicia slung her purse on her shoulder. "I have to run. I'll stop over with some cookies soon."

"Thanks, Felicia." Ellie walked to where Grayson was perusing a picture of Paul McCartney.

He raised his brows. "Impressive clientele."

She scanned the place. "Once you taste the ribs, you'll know why."

The hostess seated them at a booth in the corner by the window and took their drink order. The setting sun shone in Ellie's eyes, so the hostess lowered the blinds and left them.

Grayson flipped open his menu. "So what's good?"

She pushed her menu away. "Everything. I usually get the pulled pork plate with corn bread, fried okra, and fried pickles. My favorite sauce is the Texas one."

He shut his menu. "I'll have the same. Hey, a jukebox! What's your favorite music? I'll get this party started."

Why was he being so nice? She'd expected him to grill her about Mac over dinner. "Anything by Taylor Swift."

"You got it."

He went to the jukebox and dropped in some coins. Moments later "Fearless" began to play, and he rejoined her. "Did I do okay?"

"It's my favorite." The server had brought their iced teas while he was away, and she took a sip of hers. How did she fill the silence? She didn't know him very well and wasn't sure she wanted to, but she couldn't be rude, not to Shauna's brother.

"How'd you become an investigator, Grayson?"

"My dad was in the navy so I was taught from an early age to care about serving my country. Law enforcement was appealing, but I wanted to do it on a bigger scale than locally because I wanted to travel. Dad has a good friend who'd just retired from the Coast Guard, and he helped grease the skids a bit. I took criminal investigation in college and was lucky enough to get hired right after graduation five years ago."

"I'll bet luck didn't have much to do with it. You probably worked your tail off in college."

Grayson nodded. "True. I graduated at twenty-one by taking classes through the first two summers. And I did an internship the summer before my senior year and got to know some people who helped too."

His thick, muscular arms held her attention as he stirred sugar into his tea. He might be a jerk, but every single woman in the place was looking at him. Did he even see the covert smiles and glances sent his way? He didn't act like it, and she liked that about him.

"What do you think of Lavender Tides? Do you remember it at all?"

He shook his head. "Though I have a weird sense I have been here before, I can't point to any true memory. Nothing looks familiar. Have you lived here long?"

"Born and raised here. I went away to college in Savannah, but I missed the fields of lavender and the orcas breaching offshore. I missed the ferries chugging from island to island. I just plain missed home, so when Jason suggested we start our own business, I was all in. I didn't want to have to move away to afford to live."

"It sounds perfect. I haven't been here long enough to see what you're talking about, but I'm sure I will." His gaze went to the window, and he looked out onto the street. "Do you know where the earthquake happened, where my birth mother died?"

She nodded. "They razed the grocery store and made a parking lot. I can take you there after we eat. It's just two blocks over."

"Thanks. It's hard taking in everything. My whole life is turned upside down. I don't know what to think, really. You know Shauna well? And her husband?"

"She was a widow for over a year, then married her first

husband's best friend." It would serve no purpose to bring up how Zach had blamed himself for Jack's death. "Zach loves her boy, Alex. You haven't met him yet, have you?"

"No. My sister Isabelle is married and lives in Okinawa where we both grew up as military brats. She and her husband have two kids. I need to call her and tell her what's happened. I asked my parents to let me talk to her. We've always been close, and this news is going to rattle her too. It's incomprehensible that my parents didn't tell us I was adopted. It's going to be hard to get past that."

"To trust them, you mean?"

He took another sip of his iced tea. "Yeah." His blue eyes sharpened as he studied her. "What do you think happened to your sister?"

She'd known the interrogation would eventually begin, but she'd hoped to at least eat dinner first. "I don't know. There was a lot of blood. It's hard to believe she could live through losing that much blood."

"Blood from a head wound can look deceptive. She might not have lost as much as you think. When was the last time you spoke with her?"

"That morning. She'd been helping me paint our newest flip."

"How'd she act?"

Ellie went silent as she thought about Jason's comments about Mac. Maybe he was right. Mac had never before asked her to cut ties with Jason. "She's been a little moody lately, but I thought it was preoccupation with the tall ship flotilla she had been arranging to come here."

"Tall ship?"

She wiped the beaded moisture off her glass. "Mac loves history and sailing. She thought having a flotilla of tall ships here would bring in some tourism during our Dungeness crab and seafood festival."

"She's an Asian language professor, correct? Seems an odd hobby."

"She fell in love with sailing when we were kids."

"Tell me more about the picture the sheriff received."

"I don't know anything more. Only that someone sent him a picture of her in Hamhung, North Korea. I think it's a prank, though."

"It could be doctored. Few people have ever been to North Korea. Has she ever left the country?"

Her mouth gaped and she closed it. He was helping her construct a defense? "She often travels to Asian countries with students and on vacation. She loves Asian culture, food, language. Her best friend since they were three was a girl from Japan. She visited Japan when she was thirteen and seemed to have a natural talent for Asian languages. She speaks Japanese, Korean, and Mandarin. She went on a mission trip to Seoul last year with her best friend too."

"I think you're probably right and this picture is a prank. The sheriff will figure it out."

He saw a young couple with a child wave at Ellie, then head their way. It was probably the end of his probing. For now.

Chapter 8

When you have a vision for a house, you have to stay
true to it and not let every passing fancy lead you astray.
—HAMMER GIRL BLOG

G rayson masked his irritation as the other couple joined them. He'd hoped to learn a lot more about Mackenzie while Ellie's guard was down. He forced a smile during the introductions with Michelle and her husband, Jermaine.

"And this is Elijah." Michelle handed the little guy a straw. He chortled and began to chew on it. "Our oldest is with her grandmother for the night."

Cute kid with his mom's dark hair and his dad's unusual green eyes. Chatter paused while they placed their orders with the server. Ellie filled in the first awkward pause with the story of how Shauna had found Grayson. His face burned, and he sipped his tea to cool off. The entire town would know all about him by morning.

He forked up a bite of barbecue pork. "Wow, you weren't kidding. This is great." His stomach rumbled in approval at the reality that food was on its way. He hadn't eaten since breakfast, and he tucked into the mound of meat. The corn bread was good too.

Ellie washed down a bite with iced tea. "Michelle, you and Jermaine went to Seoul on the church mission trip with Mac, right?"

Michelle fed her son some barbecue, and he smacked his lips, then squealed for more. "Yes, we did."

"Did you spend much time with Mac?"

"The first week we did. She decided to do another excursion that was offered the second week. I think it was to Busan or somewhere. I can't remember for sure."

Grayson leaned forward. "You didn't see her at all for a week? Did she fly home with you?"

Michelle shook her head. "She sent me a text message and told me she'd been hung up and would see us back home."

Ellie put down her fork. "Did she say why she'd been delayed?"

"No, I just assumed there was more she wanted to see. Why, what's wrong?"

Grayson watched Michelle's expression as Ellie told her about the picture in North Korea.

Michelle was shaking her head before Ellie finished explaining. "The rumors are flying around town about Mac, but I don't believe a single one of them. Why would she go to North Korea? That doesn't even make any sense."

Ellie's fingers pleated her paper napkin. "It's probably something totally innocent."

Grayson glanced at Ellie, and their gazes locked. For the first time he saw uncertainty in the depths of her eyes. He might be able to figure it out by looking at the picture. It was something he'd have to talk to the sheriff about.

The dinner conversation turned to the upcoming festival, and he tuned it out as he thought about the job ahead of him. Mackenzie's disappearance and possible murder muddled everything. It was going to take a lot of work figuring this one out and retrieving the missing cocaine.

Elijah rubbed his eyes and whined, so his mother scooped him up. "My little foodie is getting tired so we'd better get him home to bed. It was nice meeting you, Grayson. I hope we see more of you."

"I'd like that."

Jermaine snatched up the bill as Grayson reached for it. "Our treat to welcome you to town. I don't suppose you kayak?"

"I do. One of my favorite sports."

Jermaine grinned and pulled out a card. "Give me a call if you have time to join some of us on Saturday. I've got an extra kayak." He tossed down some money for a tip, then hoisted the toddler in his arms. The little guy snuggled into his daddy's shoulder and popped a thumb into his mouth.

Grayson took the card. "I'll do that. Thanks." He watched them head for the cashier. "Nice people."

"Yes, they are." Ellie wore a worried frown. "I can't believe Mac would go off like that on her own in Korea and not tell me about it. She's not usually secretive." She slid out of the booth and stood.

"I think we talked about how impossible it is to know how someone will behave in every circumstance."

"That's not what I meant!" She stormed through the restaurant and out the door.

He followed at a slower pace to allow her time to cool down. She had good reason to be upset at her sister, and it was understandable to take it out on him. He was still reeling at finding out his parents had lied to him all these years. What did he do with that?

The streetlight cast glimmers of light on her hair, and the tears on her lashes shimmered. "Sorry, I didn't mean to bite your head off. This has been a hard week." She tilted a glance up at him. "Just because they didn't see her for a week doesn't mean she went to North Korea. And it doesn't mean she stole that cocaine. It doesn't mean a lot of anything."

He chose not to answer her. The truth would come out, and it wasn't his place to point out the holes in her thinking. "So where's this parking lot?"

"This way."

He fell into step beside her and walked through the charming downtown. Most of the Victorian storefronts wore colorful Painted Lady exteriors, and the brick sidewalks added a touch of nostalgia as well. Lavender scented the air from a place selling candles and essential oils. Its appeal was strong, but he still couldn't dredge up any memories.

Maybe standing at the site of where it all happened would be different.

The night swallowed up the last of the sunset before Ellie could blink. The streetlights cast a comforting glow as she walked beside Grayson toward the parking lot. She was still trying to process the likelihood that her sister had kept some secrets from her. But not mentioning straying during the Korean trip didn't mean Mac had stolen a seizure of cocaine.

Nothing could make Ellie believe it.

A Ford pickup slowed beside them, and the driver's window slid down. Stuart Ransom peered out. He was the fire chief for the volunteer fire department, and he owned a local gym. He was seventeen years older than Mac, but she'd always found him attractive and, at Mac's urging, had said yes to coffee dates a few times over the past month.

His blond hair was tousled, and his face was sunburned. "I was on my way to see you, Ellie. Any news?"

Her face heated at the warmth in his eyes. She wanted to hug him for his concern, but she settled for a grateful smile as she stepped off the curb to stand by his truck. "We still haven't found Mac."

A frown crouched between his eyes, and his gaze darted past her to Grayson. "I'll do whatever I can, Ellie."

"Um, this is Grayson Bradshaw." She paused, at a loss whether to say he was Shauna's long-lost brother or that he was with the Coast Guard and believed her sister had stolen millions of dollars' worth of cocaine.

Grayson stepped forward. "I'm a CGIS investigator. I'm here looking for some missing cocaine. Ellie was kind enough to take pity on a stranger in town and fed me dinner at Smokey's."

"Missing cocaine, you say? I hadn't heard anything about that, and I generally hear most everything. Good luck with your search." He returned his attention to Ellie. "What can I do to help?"

"There's nothing to do but wait for the sheriff to find her."

Stuart stared at Grayson, then nodded at Ellie and ran his window up before driving on down the street.

"Nice guy," Grayson said.

His tone shot her blood pressure up. "Don't sneer about it. He *is* a nice guy."

"A little old for you."

"Not that it's any of your business." It bugged her that he'd noticed there was something between her and Stuart, but then, he *was* an investigator. He didn't have to know she rarely dated. "Surely you can see no one believes Mac would do anything like you're saying. You're wrong."

"I doubt it." Shadows hid his expression, but nothing masked the weary tone in his voice. He stopped. "Is that the parking lot across the street?"

"Yes."

For a few minutes she'd forgotten how important this mission was to him tonight, and her sympathy stirred. While she'd lost her sister, he was facing something hard as well. What must it be like to find out your whole life had been a lie?

He continued to stand where he was and look across the dark street to the parking lot. The old drugstore building blocked most of the view and hid the space in shadow. Once they crossed the street and got past the line of stores, he'd be able to see it better.

"Would you rather come back in the daylight? It might be more familiar." She heard the click of his throat as he swallowed. "Are you okay?"

"Fine, I'm fine. Do you know much about the earthquake?"

"Just a few random memories. I was about two at the time also. I remember the house shaking and things falling from the shelves. I was crying for my mom, and that's about all I remember."

"I'm sure that was scary."

His monotone told her he wasn't really listening, but she pressed on anyway. "My mom told me she came rushing in to make sure I was okay. She took me outside, and we waited for my dad to get home. When he got there, he told her about the grocery store before grabbing an ax and a shovel to go back to help dig in the debris. The grade school had been hit too, and there was a preschool meeting going on so most people went to rescue the kids and adults trapped in there."

He blinked, then stuffed his hands in his pockets. "Were many buildings damaged?"

"Much of the downtown. These old brick storefronts weren't built to withstand the ground shaking. Many of them were repaired. Mom said some kids were sent to CPS until their parents could be found."

"There were more than just me?"

"Yes, I think there were two or three. You and your sister would be two of those. Mom said their parents had probably died too. They were small, too young to tell their names."

"I was two. My sister was a newborn."

Was he going to stand here all night?

He finally stepped off the curb and headed across the street. "I guess I'd better go see what I remember."

She tried to summon some sympathy for what he was going through, but she could hardly make herself follow him across the street when she felt such urgency to find her sister.

66

Chapter 9

A house holds the energy of the happy memories within its walls. It's important to find one you can bond with.
—HAMMER GIRL BLOG

Gravel crunched under Grayson's shoes, and he paused to look up and down the street. The view held all the charm of a Norman Rockwell picture with storefronts built in the last century illuminated by the soft glow of old-fashioned streetlamps.

A red-and-white barber pole caught his attention. "Has the barbershop always been there?"

Ellie was close enough for him to catch a whiff of her sweet scent.

"As far back as I can remember. Does it look familiar?"

"Sort of." He rubbed the back of his neck and wished he could actually remember something clearly.

He turned his attention back to the parking lot. As they

neared, the stench of pavement sealant burned his throat, and the gleam of the parking lot lights bounced off the sheen of the blacktop. Barricades blocked cars from driving onto the asphalt.

He stopped and rested his hand on the barricade. "Nothing left of the grocery store."

She pointed to his right. "The five-and-dime used to be there. They had the best root beer stick candy ever made."

"And gumballs in a machine for a penny." The memory popped out without any prompting. "I liked the blue ones."

"You're remembering."

He shoved the memory aside. "Just stuff that doesn't matter."

What was he doing here? His job was to find the missing cocaine and bring Nasser to justice, not wander the streets and dig up old memories about candy and haircuts. Keeping his footing amid such life-changing distractions was going to take all his concentration. This had been a mistake. His curiosity could wait until he did his duty.

"I think I'd like to go to Shauna's house now, if you don't mind."

"We should stop and get some food so the cupboards aren't empty."

"I can just eat out." He knew his clipped voice sounded unfriendly so he tried to soften it. "I appreciate your help, but I need to focus on finding that missing cocaine."

She put her hands on her hips and glared at him. "You don't really care about my sister, do you? Whether she's dead or alive. You just want to do your job and ignore what's happened to her."

"I didn't say that. Of course I hope she's fine." He ran his hand through his thick hair. "Look, this is all a little overwhelming, you know? I wish Shauna hadn't found me, at least not yet.

It's distracting me from my job. I'm sorry if that seems harsh, but I never asked for this kind of interruption in my life." Unable to look at the tears hovering on her lashes, he turned away. "I can find my own way there. I have the address."

He practically ran to the SUV he'd rented and climbed under the wheel. Running the window down so the ocean air could blow in his face helped clear the fuzziness from his brain. He could do this. Find the cocaine and keep the whole family thing at bay for now. Shauna wasn't going anywhere. There'd be time to figure out if he wanted a relationship with her later, *after* he did his job.

He told Siri to find the address and began to drive. His thoughts were a jumble until the app on his phone announced he'd arrived at the house. He glanced at the clock on his dash and realized he'd spent the last ten minutes barely aware of his surroundings. He pulled into the driveway, and the motion-sensor lights flooded the darkness. He used the flashlight app on his phone and punched the key into the lock, then stepped inside and disarmed the alarm.

The scent of some kind of pine cleaner wafted toward him. Shauna had said the house had been sitting empty, but she must have had someone come by and clean it. He flipped on the light and looked around the bright, airy space with its open floor plan and high ceilings. Nice. She'd said to use the master suite so he found it, then went back to his vehicle and hauled in his suitcase. He traveled light so it only took minutes to stash his clothes in the dresser and closet. The master bathroom was large with double sinks in a marble counter and a huge walk-in shower.

He washed his hands, then went back to the bedroom and

pulled out his computer and the files on the theft. The cocaine seizure had been a month ago off the coast of Vancouver and had been cut with Fentanyl, an opioid that often led to overdoses, which meant it should be easy to figure out when it hit the market here. The street value was worth twenty million dollars. Mac would be unlikely to get that much if she sold it to a dealer, but she'd certainly rake in enough to be able to live comfortably the rest of her life, even in a high-rent district like the United Arab Emirates.

If she was alive.

It might all begin with her Coast Guard boyfriend. Grayson launched his browser and looked up Dylan Trafford in the Coast Guard records. The guy had been confined to barracks twice on Article 15 infractions, and his pay had been reduced once as well. He had a smart mouth and a generally insolent attitude. Mackenzie's lack of good judgment in choosing her boyfriends didn't speak well of her.

Trafford was stationed at Station Port Angeles, and Grayson intended to talk to him first thing tomorrow. His buddies might shed some light on the situation as well. The station had intercepted the cocaine on a fishing vessel, and it appeared Trafford was on the intercept boat, which sent him to the top of Grayson's suspect list.

But Mackenzie had broken up with him. Was it to throw suspicion off her, or had she realized what he was up to and decided to jump ship while she could? He thought of Ellie's honest eyes and great love for her sister. It was possible Grayson was wrong about Mac, but he didn't think so.

Ellie slammed the door to her house behind her and threw the dead bolt with more force than necessary. If she never had to deal with Grayson Bradshaw again, it would be too soon. She'd tried to accommodate him and help out for Shauna's sake, but not even friendship could make up for the man's insufferable confidence in his own judgment.

If she waited for the Coast Guard and the sheriff's department to find out what had happened, they'd be blaming Mac for the missing drugs, and Ellie didn't believe it for a minute. It was beyond horrible that Mac might be dead, but Ellie couldn't sit back and let her sister be turned into some kind of criminal too.

After taking a few deep breaths, she lit a vanilla-lilac candle to help her distress and inhaled the sweet aroma. The tension began to ease from her neck. She'd bought this house five years ago and had redone it herself. She especially liked the pale aqua-blue walls and wood floors with a hint of gray in the stain. The master bedroom was on the first floor, near her office. Two more bedrooms, seldom used, were up the open stairway off the entry. The house brought her a sense of security and belonging, and even with Mac missing, she let that comfort envelop her.

She went to her office and retrieved her secondary laptop. Mac often used it, and she hoped to find some clue to what was going on. She sank onto the sofa, and with her legs curled up under her, she put the computer on her lap and opened the lid. It would take a minute to boot, so she got up to fix some decaf. While in the kitchen, she heard something at the back door, and her heart rate spiked until she recognized a faint mew. She peered through the door's window. A small white kitten sat on the mat outside the door. It looked pitiful with dirty, wet fur and what appeared to be blood on its ear.

She threw open the door. "Oh, you poor thing." The kitten had one blue eye and one golden eye. It curled around her ankle and mewed again. Did she have anything to feed it? She scooped it up, then shut the door and locked it again before heading to the refrigerator. An egg might work. She whisked the egg in a bowl, then set it down for the kitten. The little thing hunched over the bowl as if to defend it from anyone who might try to take its food, then attacked the egg like it hadn't eaten in days.

Ellie put water in another bowl and placed it beside the kitten too. She'd already made up her mind she was going to keep the little thing. Tomorrow she'd get some food for it and take it to the vet for a checkup. She could use the company.

Coffee in hand, she went back to the laptop and pulled it onto her lap. She knew her sister's email password so she checked Mac's email. This computer was synced in the cloud with Mac's main computer. There were a couple of emails from students still in the in-box, one dated today. The person must not have heard about Mac's disappearance. Ellie scanned the emails and found nothing remarkable—just students asking questions. There was nothing special in Mac's Documents folder either, just tests and scoring documents.

Next she opened the Applications folder and looked through a list of programs on the computer. Scrivener might have something. Mac sometimes used it to organize things. The familiar boxes appeared, and a folder opened. The folder was titled "EMP Bombs."

She inhaled, and her hand shook as she scanned the documents in the folder. Why would Mac be investigating *that*? First cocaine and now EMP bombs? What was going on with her sister?

Before she could take a look at the documents in the Scrivener folder, her doorbell rang. She'd been so immersed in the computer, she hadn't seen lights or anything. She closed the computer and rose to peer out the peephole.

Grayson's face looked straight ahead as if he was staring at her. Great, just great. She didn't want to deal with his surliness tonight. She'd had enough.

She unlocked the dead bolt and opened the door. "How'd you know where I live?"

He leaned against the door frame in a nonthreatening manner. "I asked the sheriff."

His placating smile did little to soothe her irritation. "What do you want?"

"To apologize for being a jerk. You had been gracious and helpful all afternoon, and I bit your head off. There was no excuse, and I'm sorry."

She blinked at the genuine apology. He didn't even try to excuse himself. "You'd had a rough day."

"You've had a rough week. I tried to go to bed—it's after one o'clock eastern time—but I couldn't until I told you I was sorry."

What kind of man did that? She opened the door a bit wider. "I just made some decaf if you want some." She longed to get back to that Scrivener folder, but she didn't want him to think she was holding a grudge.

"That sounds great. I won't stay long." He stepped inside and followed her to the kitchen. "Nice. I like the aqua with the gray."

"Me too." She poured him a cup of coffee and handed it to him.

"I wanted to tell you what I found out about Dylan Trafford." Without waiting for an invitation, he headed back to the living room.

A tiny mew came from under the kitchen table, and the little white cat sprang after him and attacked his shoelaces. He chuckled. "Looks like this little thing nearly drowned."

"I found it crying outside. I don't know if it's a boy or girl."

He scooped it up and flipped it over. "It's a girl." He let the kitten settle on his lap. "She's going to need a bath."

"Yes, I'll do that eventually." Her irritation sprang to life again. "I was more concerned about getting her fed." She settled in the chaise across from him. "What did you find out about Dylan?"

"He was working on the boat that seized the cocaine."

The breath left her lungs. "Maybe he took the drugs."

And maybe Mac suspected he might so she broke up with him. Maybe he took her.

Chapter 10

It can be as hard to let go of a much-loved
house as it is a closely held conviction.
—HAMMER GIRL BLOG

G rayson ran his fingers through the kitten's white fur. The
dank scent of mud rose from the small body, and he waited
for Ellie to say something. For a second he'd thought she might
even yell. Her face had reddened, and the muscles in her jaw
flexed.

She took a gulp of her coffee and choked. "Hot!" She fanned
her face with her hand. "Are you going to investigate him? What
if he took Mac? He'd have access to a boat, and he could have
transferred her from her ship to that vessel."

"I already thought of that. I'll talk to him tomorrow."

"What's wrong with tonight?"

The woman was worse than his physical therapist who was

determined to work the limp out of Grayson's leg. "He's still out to sea." He eyed her over the rim of his coffee cup. Her light-brown curls were in disarray, and she'd removed her glasses, which made her look even more attractive.

She rose and paced the fluffy aqua rug with her hands clenched. "But if he has Mac, we need to find her. There was all that blood . . ."

He should have realized her thoughts would head that direction. His eyes burned from the long day, and his neck ached from the flight. "I checked his schedule before I got here, and he's out on duty until tomorrow morning. We can both get some rest, and I'll talk to him as soon as he disembarks the boat."

Her shoulders drooped. "I guess we have no choice."

"I am trying to run down whether he owns any property around here, anywhere he might have stashed your sister. I should hear something tomorrow about that too."

"You talked to the sheriff?" She reached down to the table and snatched up her glasses, then slipped them on.

"Do you even need those things?" He waved his hand at the computer. "You weren't wearing them before when you were looking at the screen. I saw you through the window." Color rushed to her cheeks, and he realized he'd made much too personal of a remark. "Sorry, forget I said that. It's none of my business. And yes, I did speak to the sheriff. He has someone going through property tax records."

"Good." Her voice sounded strained, but she said nothing about the glasses. "Did you ask him about the picture and tell him what we found out about Korea?"

"I did. He didn't have much to say about it, but I think he

already suspects the picture is doctored. His technician will tell him soon."

More to break the ice, he grabbed her laptop and lifted the lid to do a search himself on property records. The screen popped up to the Scrivener program, and his gaze landed on the folder's title. "EMP bombs?" He stared at her. What was going on here?

Her face went a strangled shade of red. "Give me that computer!"

He silently passed it to her, but his suspicions rose. First stolen cocaine and now EMP bombs. Nasser sold drugs to support his terrorist organization. Was there more to Mackenzie's involvement than he'd suspected? The hackles rose on his back at the thought of a terrorist attack on American soil. Maybe he was overreacting, but he had to see where this led.

The color washed out of her face, and she exhaled. "Mac uses this laptop, so I thought I'd check to see if I could find anything on it. It's probably something to do with a lesson plan for her class."

She didn't meet his gaze, and he raised a brow. "What are you hiding?"

"Nothing! I haven't even looked at the files yet." She closed the computer. "I'll let you know if I find anything about the cocaine."

"Is there something you don't want me to see?"

Ellie reached for her coffee. "I don't know what all is on there yet, but I'm sure there's nothing about any stolen cocaine. A quick look showed only lesson plans. I think you'll need to look elsewhere for your missing cocaine. You surely have some idea who is behind this. If you knew Mac, you'd see how ludicrous it is. She's a professor, not a drug dealer."

She'd said something about Mac not even taking aspirin,

and her unwavering belief in her sister left him with confusion. He hadn't been able to find any evidence she was using drugs. Why *would* a language professor who didn't do drugs get involved in selling them? Money? He hadn't gotten a warrant yet to look at her bank account, but he would. There was more to this than met the eye.

He stared at her and felt a tug in his gut. She'd been through a lot this week. "You obviously love your sister a lot. Can you tell me about her? Do the two of you have any other siblings?"

She hesitated, then reached for the kitten. "We did, but our younger sister . . . died. Alicia drowned when she was four."

"I'm so sorry. That had to have been hard."

She gave a jerky nod. "I don't talk about it much, and I don't even know why I'm telling you now. Maybe so you understand how important Mac is to me. Sh-She's all I have left. Our mom killed herself after Alicia's death, and Dad just kind of checked out. He was there physically and taught us what he had to, but there was always something missing. Especially toward me, since it was my fault Alicia died."

"What happened?"

She didn't look at him and continued to focus on the kitten. "I was thirteen and babysitting Alicia. Mom had to run to the grocery store, and I was supposed to be keeping an eye on Alicia." Her head came up, and her mouth flattened. "And I *was*. One of my friends was there, and we'd gone into the house for a minute to grab a soft drink. I thought Alicia was behind us, but when we came back out, I saw her in the water. I dove in right away and pulled her out, but I couldn't get her to breathe. My friend went to call 911, and I kept trying to get her to wake up." Her voice broke, and she swallowed.

"I'm sorry. She didn't make it?"

Her fingers twisted a curl, and she shook her head. "The paramedics tried to revive her too. She was pronounced dead at the hospital. My mom went kind of crazy. She hated me and wouldn't talk to me. Two weeks later she killed herself."

He winced. Double guilt for her to swallow. "It wasn't your fault."

She bit her lip. "Yes, yes, it was. If I'd been playing with her, really *looking* after her, I could have kept her from jumping in."

"It was an accident, Ellie. Accidents happen."

The golden lights in her eyes shimmered through tears as she lifted her head and stared at him. "I feel like I failed Mac too. I should have noticed she wasn't herself."

He leaned forward. "What had she been doing?" Pushing her for answers felt wrong, but he had a feeling she was finally about to reveal something about Mackenzie's behavior.

She blinked and looked away. "Just what I said—not herself. Kind of irritable."

Which could mean nothing or everything.

He looked around the house. "Did Mackenzie stay here a lot?"

"Quite often. She has her own room here."

"Could I see it?" He saw the indecision in her eyes. "I can get a court order, Ellie."

She bit her lip. "There's nothing here to see, but I'll show you."

Ellie hadn't been upstairs in several days. Two bedrooms, one on either side, opened off the wide hallway. A bathroom at the end of the hall served both bedrooms.

She flipped on the light in the bedroom on the right, and the glow illuminated the queen bed with its new white quilt and aqua throw pillows. After pulling up all the old carpets, she'd refinished the oak floors to match the ones downstairs, then put down area rugs. The room still held the lingering scent of Mac's shampoo and favorite pumpkin candle.

Grayson followed her into the room and looked around. "It almost looks like she lived here."

"She left clothes here and some of her books." She indicated the white bookcase on the right side of the bed. "She's a big Stephen King fan as you can tell."

Seeing Mac's things here left a boulder lodged in her throat. Would her sister ever pull out her well-worn copy of *The Stand* again or curl up in the upholstered armchair with her computer? She stepped to the closet and opened the door to the small walk-in space. Floor-to-ceiling shelves lined the back wall, and clothing hung on either side of the closet.

"Mac's a neatnik, and she puts most everything in the closet."

She caught the scent of Mac's light floral perfume, Daisy, on her clothes, and her vision blurred. She blinked until she could see again, then moved to the shelving. Boxes, games, and more books resided back here as well as seldom-used toiletries like blue nail polish and a foot bath. Sometimes she wondered why Mac hadn't just moved in with her since she'd brought so many of her things. Her sister had a loft apartment in the downtown area, but Ellie had never liked the cold, featureless space. Mac evidently didn't either.

Grayson joined her in front of the shelves. "You mind if I look through the closet?"

It wouldn't do any good to object. "Go ahead."

She watched him step into the walk-in closet and look at the shelves. Her gaze was caught by the family treasure box. It was a large wooden box with an ornately carved picture of a tall ship on the lid. She reached for it and held it to her chest.

"What's that?"

She lifted her chin at the suspicion in his voice. "It holds our keepsakes. I thought I'd sift through it just to feel close to Mac."

"Mind if I have a look?"

She hugged it closer. "Absolutely not! It's just personal stuff."

"You never know where your sister might have hidden something important. Unless you're afraid she's really guilty?"

Even though she knew he was manipulating her, she thrust it at him. "Fine, take a look through old family pictures and keepsakes. Maybe you'll see Mac would never do anything illegal."

He took the box and carried it out of the closet to the bedroom. After setting it on the bed, he lifted the lid and looked inside, then lifted out the jumble of contents. An old locket of their mother's, their grandfather's pocket watch, both of their diaries from when they were teenagers, tickets to various music venues over the years, and pictures of them together from childhood.

Nothing seemed out of the ordinary until he got down to the bottom of the box.

Several yellowed newspapers were folded up in the bottom. Ellie picked up the top one and unfolded it. The front page of the *Lavender Tides Journal* featured a picture of her and her little sister at the park. She was swinging Alicia, and the four-year-old wore a wide smile and an expression of bliss. Ellie's breath seized in her lungs at the unexpected snapshot of a time long past.

Though she wanted to thrust it back in the box, she forced

herself to scan the article about her sister's death. It wasn't anything she didn't relive every day.

Grayson inhaled as he was reading the article over her shoulder. "When did your parents get back?"

She forced herself to answer. "I can't really remember. Hours later. Mom was gone to the store much longer than I'd thought, and I never asked where Dad was, but he didn't get home until after she did. One of the neighbors drove me to the hospital and then back home to wait on them. I tried calling the grocery store, but the clerk didn't seem to know who she was. It was a new employee, I think. I didn't know who to call to find my dad, so I called his best friend, but no one answered. I can't remember the time, but I know it was dark by the time they got home."

"You were by yourself while you waited?"

She shook her head. "My best friend and her parents stayed with me and Mac." The horror of that entire day stole the strength from her voice. "Mom about went crazy when she got home. I knew I deserved every bit of her anger, though."

She put the papers back inside the box, then reached for the other items. "There's nothing here, like I said."

Nothing but the pain of her worst memory.

Chapter 11

Home remodeling can show you what you're
made of. It can bring out the worst in people.
—Hammer Girl Blog

The one they called Wang—which meant "king" in Korean—
stood in the deep shadow of the oak tree on the west side
of the driveway and watched the lit windows in the upstairs bedroom. Why was Ellie roaming upstairs with that man? He kept
seeing them pass back and forth in front of the window, but he
couldn't tell what they were doing.

And who was that man anyway? Was this a new threat?

Another shadow moved, and Tarek Nasser joined him. "About
time you got here," he told Nasser. "If you'd come earlier, you
could have snatched her before the big guy got here."

Nasser's face couldn't be seen in the darkness, and his voice
came out in a low hiss. "What's he doing here?"

"You know the man with her? Who is he?"

"Grayson Bradshaw. He's been dogging every move I make. What's he doing with Ellie Blackmore?"

"I don't know. He's as big as a football player, though, and I think we're going to have to scratch tonight's plan. I don't want to risk alerting them and then not taking her. We've got a little time before I need the picture."

"He's probably here looking into the stolen cocaine. I can call some more men. We can take him down, then grab her. I've been wanting to get him off my back."

Wang shook his head, then realized Nasser wouldn't be able to see him. "No, things are at too crucial a point. I don't want them realizing what we're doing. You can take him out after it's done."

"He's smart. He showed up at the barn, and I barely got out first. Don't underestimate him. He could stop us."

"I never underestimate anything, Tarek."

"With him on this investigation, things just got a little dicier. Are you sure everything is in place?"

"With Mackenzie out of the way, nothing can go wrong."

There was a long pause, and when Nasser spoke again, his tone was as cold as the night breeze. "I hope you are right. If you mess this up, you will regret it."

A shiver ran down his back. Wang had always assumed he could control Nasser, but maybe that was like thinking you could control a pet tiger. You never knew when the big cat would turn on you and rip you to shreds.

He turned and moved toward his car parked down the road. "I'll see what I can find out about her whereabouts tomorrow." He headed into the tree line.

It was only when he was behind the wheel that he looked back toward the house and saw a shadow slipping around the side of the house. Nasser was still there. He cursed and slammed his palm against the steering wheel. Nasser had better not derail all his careful planning.

Ellie's steps lagged as they went down the stairs to the living room. She'd rather go to bed and pull the covers over her head than continue to think about those articles in the treasure box. Stirring up the pain from so many years ago felt like undergoing surgery with no anesthetic. She'd managed to lock most of that pain and guilt away in a dark closet, but it came surging back into the light, bringing more horror than she liked to deal with.

Hadn't she endured enough this week? And why had her sister kept that old newspaper article?

Grayson followed her. "Look, I know you want to protect your sister, but if she's innocent, why not let me look at her computer?"

"I'm sure there's personal stuff on there too. I don't want to invade her privacy."

"Ellie, you're not facing facts. I hate to say it, but do you really think she's still alive?"

A weight settled on her chest. "I can't give up hope. Not until I'm sure. And what if she turns up alive and I've helped you build a case against her? I'd never be able to live with myself."

"How about if I agree not to use anything on the computer in any charges? I just want to get at the truth. If Mackenzie isn't involved, then I can quit wasting my time in that direction."

He had a point. She hated drugs and would love for the Coast Guard to get that cocaine back off the streets. "Do I have your word you won't use anything on the computer as evidence against Mac?"

His eyes held hers in a long gaze. "You have my word. And I never break my promise."

She squared her shoulders and reached for the computer, double clicking on the file titled "EMP Bomb."

Grayson's shoulder snugged against hers as he leaned in to look too. His warm breath touched her ear, and she struggled to ignore the heat spreading in her chest. There was no way to move away without looking rude, so she forced herself to relax. Why was she so prickly around him?

They began to read through the files together. There was a link that looked like a technical article on the damage a nuclear EMP bomb might cause. A nuclear one detonated high in the air would cause the most widespread damage to people while an electromagnetic bomb would cause more localized knockouts of technology. There were numerous articles about Kim Jong-un and his threats against the United States. And one article about how to build an EMP bomb.

Grayson sat back. "Any idea why she'd be researching North Korea?"

"For her class maybe? She's interested in everything about Asian culture."

His mouth twisted. "Nothing about the cocaine she stole."

"She didn't steal the cocaine! You have found nothing on this laptop linking her to that theft, have you?"

"No. But if she did take it, what if she's part of a terrorist organization planning to detonate an EMP device?"

Where did he come up with such a weird leap of logic? "That's ridiculous! It's just research on North Korea for her class."

"What if it's not? What if we ignore all this and there's a huge loss of life? Could you live with that?"

His expression told her he knew she couldn't. A widespread EMP device would shut down the grid so much that people would die of starvation. Normal life would come to a screeching halt as people struggled for daily necessities. There would also be radiation fallout to deal with. While she didn't believe Mac could be involved in anything evil like this, she couldn't just walk away from it. There was some reason Mac had these technical files.

"Look, just think about it, okay?" He yawned. "I think I'd better get home and go to bed. You know as well as I do that we can't ignore this."

She shook her head. "I guess we can't. I'm not sure where to look for answers, though."

"First we track the cocaine and see where it leads." He rose and headed for the door.

She followed him to the door and opened it, then stood aside for him to exit. "Mac doesn't have your cocaine."

His broad shoulders barely passed through the door frame. "We'll find out."

She shut the door and threw the dead bolt. "Find Mac and find the cocaine" seemed to be his mantra. She was reluctant to trust him to search for the truth.

Only the streetlights and a few house lights lit the darkness as Grayson drove through Lavender Tides after leaving Ellie's. He should be exhausted since it was the wee hours on eastern time, but he was wide awake. He drove down to the ferry pier and parked in the lot, then walked down to the water's edge.

Omar's belongings had yielded no new leads, and he wasn't sure where to look for Tarek next. He was here somewhere, though.

Waves collided against the sides of the ferry, and he felt cocooned by the darkness and solitude. The brilliant canopy of stars overhead filled him with awe, and he settled on the pier to dangle his legs over the edge. The October air held the sting of a cold forty-degree breeze, but he felt warm enough in his jacket. His sister was probably sitting down to dinner in Okinawa, but he ached to hear her voice to bring normalcy to a life that had suddenly careened off course. He pulled out his phone and called her.

Isabelle answered on the first ring. "I was just thinking about you."

"I don't hear the girls. Am I interrupting dinner?"

"No, we're eating late tonight. Shinji took the girls to Cape Manza for the day, and they are stopping for dinner on the way home. I had a deadline looming, and he wanted me to have time to finish. And I did."

His sister was a novelist and nearly always on deadline. She'd married his best friend growing up, and he knew she was happy, which made up for only seeing her every couple of years. Living in Okinawa had shaped both of them. He loved the courtly way his brother-in-law treated his sister, and he sought to be that kind of man himself.

Cape Manza, with its elephant rock, was one of his favorite spots, and he wished he could close his eyes and be there without all this drama hanging over his head. "I should plan a trip out to see you. I miss you, Izzy."

"I miss you too. You sound sad. What's going on? Where are you? It's crazy early there."

"I'm back in Washington. You talk to Mom or Dad lately?" He'd asked them to let him tell Isabelle, but he wasn't sure they'd honored his request.

"Not in a couple of weeks, now that you mention it. Mom usually calls every Friday, but she hasn't. Something's up, isn't it? What's going on?"

"They're fine, but I've had some pretty earthshaking news. I'm adopted." He let the long pause linger as he could almost hear the wheels turning in her head.

"That's not possible. You look so much like Mom. Where'd you get a crazy idea like that?"

"Believe me, it wasn't something I came up with on my own. Mom and Dad confessed as soon as I told them my biological sister had contacted me." He launched into the story of how Shauna had found him and told him of his origins.

"Oh, Gray, how are you handling this? I can't quite wrap my head around it." Her voice wobbled.

"It's a lot to take in. I'm in the town where I was born now. I keep getting flashes of familiarity but no real memories. I just needed to hear your voice to ground me."

"Well, it changes *nothing*. Mom and Dad love you, and so do I. That's just past history. No matter how you became a Bradshaw, you *are* one. Nothing can change that."

"I don't quite know who I am anymore, sis. I hardly know what's real and what isn't."

"*We're* real, Gray. Me, Mom and Dad, you. I'm not saying

don't get to know your other family, but your identity is with us. You belong to us and always will. The memories we share and the love we have for each other is real. Mom and Dad should have told you instead of letting you be blindsided like this. Do you know why they didn't?"

"I guess Mom thought it would confuse me or something. I don't really know. Dad wanted to tell me, but she didn't."

Isabelle gave a sound of disgust. "I love her, but I've never liked how remote she's always been. She's never been good at sharing her feelings, not with either of us."

His mother's reserve was something he was used to, but now that Izzy mentioned it, it all made sense. No wonder she held him at arm's length—she never forgot he wasn't hers.

"Maybe I should come see you. I just hit Send on this manuscript, and I have a month before I start a new book."

"The kids need you and so does Shinji. I'll be all right. I just needed to hear your voice."

"You saying you don't want to see me?" Her voice held a teasing lilt.

"I always love to see you, but I can fly there when I finish this case. It would be an easy trip from this side of the country."

"I'll hold you to that. Tell me about this new sister."

"Jealous? No one could ever take your place. Shauna is nice, though. She has a five-year-old boy I haven't met yet. Her first husband died, and she remarried a couple of weeks ago. Zach seems like a stand-up guy. I liked both of them. I think she hoped I'd throw my arms around her and just accept everything. But I couldn't do that."

"Wow, another kid in the family too. I can see why you're shaken. What about your birth parents and any other siblings?"

He told her what he knew about his dead parents and the still-missing sister. "It sounds like my dad was a real piece of work. I'm kind of glad I don't have to face him."

"I've got a little time now. Let me see if I can dig up anything on Brenna."

She was a master at research. "Thanks, that would be great. Zach is looking too." They talked a few more minutes, then his eyelids began to droop. "I guess I'd better get some sleep. It's been quite the day."

"Love you, Gray."

"Love you too, Izzy. Thanks for talking me down. I'll let you know how things go here."

He ended the call and slid his phone back into his pocket. Isabelle was right—he was a Bradshaw at his core and always would be.

Chapter 12

Well-built doors and windows are the bones of
security in a house. Never skimp on them.
—HAMMER GIRL BLOG

The sound of the bedside clock ticking seemed unusually loud. Ellie stirred and threw off the covers, then wiped her damp forehead. She'd been having a nightmare where she ran through a maze with a black Taurus following her. Crazy. Probably from that car she'd seen a few times.

She glanced at the clock and saw it was just after two. She had only been asleep a few minutes, but she was wide awake. Maybe she should get up and make some chamomile tea, do some research while she waited to get drowsy again. Her tummy rumbled too, so there was no going back to sleep for now.

A soft sound she couldn't identify at first set her nerves

jangling. She sat up and swung her legs to the side of the bed and listened, hardly daring to breathe. The hair rose on the back of her neck, and she clutched her hands together. Surely her panic was a remnant of the nightmare. Then the noise came again, a scraping, sinister sound right outside her window.

She willed her muscles to move. She'd always assumed she would take charge in any situation, and the reality of how fear froze her in place was unwelcome. She swallowed hard and glanced around the room to see what she could use as a weapon.

The heavy brass lamp might work.

She slowed her breathing until the pressure eased in her chest. She could do this. She vaulted to her feet and reached for the table lamp, one her grandmother had given her when she got her own place. She followed the cord down to the outlet and unplugged it, then hefted the base in her hand and made a test arc with it. The balance of it felt good, and the head of it was heavy enough to do some damage.

Was that a knife cutting through the screen? She needed to call for help, but her phone was charging in the kitchen, and she would have to pass the windows in the living room. Moonlight was likely streaming into the space and she'd be seen, but what were her choices? She couldn't stay cowering in her bedroom.

She tiptoed to the door and eased it open, then slid along the hallway wall to the living room. As she suspected, moonlight poked silvery beams into her great room. From her vantage point she could see the blinking light on her phone. She could race for it and have 911 on the line in moments.

A squeak sounded behind her, and was that a breeze? He must have the window open. She ran back to her bedroom door to see the curtains blowing.

"I've already called 911! They'll be here any minute."

As if on cue the distant wail of a siren floated in the air followed by the sound of running and the slamming of a car door. She ran back down the hall to the entry and peeked out the door window in time to see a dark car speeding away with no lights.

The black Taurus? Maybe not. It could have been any dark color. Her heart was still in her throat when she went back to her bedroom to examine the window. The screen was sliced open, and the window was up about four inches. She tugged on it, but it refused to budge up or down, which was probably why he hadn't come on in.

Her phone. She could retrieve it now. She rushed into the kitchen and grabbed it. Her hands shook as she dialed 911 and reported the attempted break-in. The dispatcher had her stay on the line until the deputies arrived, and she was thankful for the connection to a sympathetic person.

While she waited, she checked the locks on the front and back doors, then examined the rest of the windows. Her bedroom window seemed to be the only one that had been disturbed.

The bubble light from the deputy's car strobed through her front window, and she hurried to unlock the door and step out onto the porch as two officers came up the walk. The kitten wound between her feet, and she scooped her up.

"You had a break-in?" The female deputy was Mac's good friend Rosa Seymour. In her early thirties, she wore her black hair nearly as short as a man's, but it suited her high cheekbones and dark-brown eyes. Few women looked good in law enforcement uniforms, but the tucked-in shirt accentuated Rosa's slim curves. She'd been married several years to one of Jason's buddies, and they had no children, which was probably a good thing with all her odd hours.

"Oh, Rosa, thank goodness you're here. I didn't see the intruder—well, would-be intruder—but he slit the screen and had the window partway up." Still carrying the kitten, Ellie led Rosa and her partner through the house to her bedroom to show them the damaged window.

Rosa turned to her partner, a blond young man in his early twenties. "Check outside." He hurried out and Rosa looked around. "Did the intruder awaken you?"

"I think so." Ellie told her about the nightmare and waking up in a sweat. "I saw a car without its lights on pull away. It looked like it might have been black or some other dark color."

"So it might have been the driver of the black Taurus?"

"I'm not sure. I can't tell car models very well, and it was dark. It could have been the black Taurus that ran me off the road this morning."

Rosa jotted something in her notebook. "I can check on black Tauruses in the area."

Her partner shouted through the window. "Better see this, Rosa. Footprints out here. Big ones. A man for sure."

Ellie's gut clenched. Could it be Mac's attacker? But even if it was, why would he be targeting her now?

Grayson had woken up at six, wide awake and ready to see Trafford. By the time he worked out with an exercise band, showered, and grabbed coffee and an egg sandwich on the way, it was eight. The Coast Guard boat cruised toward the dock where he waited, inhaling the familiar scent of seawater and diesel fuel. He'd familiarized himself with Trafford's appearance and stood off to one side as the crewmen took care of final docking and disembarked.

There he was. Trafford was whistling as he walked jauntily down the pier. According to his records his mother had been born in Turkey. Trafford had been born in the US. There were no flags on his record about radicalization, either online or from a visit to the Middle East. As far as Grayson could tell, he'd never been out of the country. His parents lived in Ohio after his father retired from the navy. A good military family didn't mean this guy was lily white, though.

As Trafford started past him, Grayson stepped out of the shadows. "Lieutenant Trafford, I'm an investigator with the CGIS. Grayson Bradshaw. I'd like to speak with you."

Trafford stopped and looked him over with dark eyes. His olive complexion looked yellow in the glare of lights overhead. "Intelligence officer? What's this about?"

Grayson didn't like the lack of respect in the guy's tone. "It's just routine." He jerked his head toward the parking lot. "I'd suggest we take this discussion to a private location."

Trafford glanced around and saw they had the attention of several other crewmen. He muttered to himself as he followed Grayson, but Grayson couldn't make out anything except the man was irritated at the interruption. They reached Grayson's SUV in the parking lot, and he unlocked it with the key fob, then slid behind the wheel while Trafford went around the front of the vehicle and climbed into the passenger seat.

"I've been out all night, Bradshaw, and I'd like to get to bed, sir. Can this wait until I've had some sleep?"

At least he'd thrown in a *sir.* "I'm afraid it can't, Lieutenant, but it won't take long." Grayson eyed him.

About six feet tall, he obviously worked out and prided himself on the biceps bulging under his blue uniform. His insolent manner rankled Grayson, and he could see why the guy had racked up some disciplinary action.

The man's overpowering cologne reeked and gave Grayson a sudden headache. He opened his iPad. "You were on the boat that seized a large stash of cocaine about a month ago."

Trafford straightened and smiled. "Sure was. In fact, I spotted it trying to evade us. It darted into a small inlet, and I just knew there was something illegal on it. Not that my superiors noticed my initiative."

Grayson jotted down Trafford's answer. "Where was the seizure the last time you saw it?"

Trafford frowned. "What are you talking about? It's in the secure hangar where it's always been."

Grayson had a hard time believing Trafford wouldn't have heard of the cocaine's disappearance, but maybe scuttlebutt didn't travel here as fast as it did at other stations, and he *had* been out to sea. "It's missing."

"All of it?"

"Yep. A pallet of Styrofoam blocks was left in its place. Someone knew what it looked like and planned it well."

Trafford snorted. "And you think I'm involved somehow?"

"Just gathering information. Did you hear anyone talking about how easy it would be to take it?"

"If I had, I would have turned him in."

The guy was saying all the right things, but Grayson sniffed something else under his denials. "A man could do a lot with that kind of money."

"I wouldn't know." Trafford yawned. "Look, is that all, sir? I want to get some sleep."

"Did Mackenzie Blackmore question you about the seizure?"

Trafford blinked and pushed his cap back off his forehead. "What's Mackenzie got to do with this?"

"We have information she may have been involved in the cocaine's disappearance."

He scowled. "Look, that's total garbage. What kind of information? She wouldn't even begin to know how to do something like that. Just go talk to her."

So he hadn't heard that news either. "Her sister arrived to go to dinner for Ms. Blackmore's birthday and found a large amount of blood on her ship. There was no sign of a body."

The color leached out of his face. "I-I don't know what to say. She's a nice girl."

"What happened between you two?"

"That's none of your business. *Sir.*"

Poor guy had been caught off guard. Grayson's initial dislike softened a bit. "It is when it might affect property seized by the Coast Guard."

Trafford's dark eyes flashed, but he shrugged. "She broke up with me about a couple of weeks ago."

"Why?"

Trafford shrugged. "Jealousy, I guess. Every time I so much as talked to another woman, she got all bent out of shape."

"Did you try to talk her out of it?"

"Heck no. If a woman doesn't want to be with me, I don't want her."

"Did you ever talk about the cocaine seizure with her?"

Trafford chewed on a thumb hangnail. "Well, yeah, just general stuff. Like the weight and likely street value. We were all pretty elated, you know?"

Grayson did know. Victory was meant to be shared. "Did she know where it was stored?"

Trafford fell silent as he looked out the window for a moment before meeting Grayson's gaze. "I sneaked her in one night and showed it to her."

Grayson curled his left hand into a fist. Just great. "Did she say anything to you about EMP bombs?"

"Good grief, that's a random question. No, she didn't mention bombs of any kind. I can't see her having any interest in that kind of thing." Trafford yawned again. "I'm beat, sir."

"You can go."

He didn't want to tell Ellie her sister's guilt was looking more and more likely.

Chapter 13

You know a forever house when you
see it. It's like part of your soul.
—HAMMER GIRL BLOG

A storm had rolled in overnight, and the overcast skies lowered Ellie's mood even more than awakening to the knowledge her sister had been keeping secrets from her. Nothing would stop her search for Mac, though. She inhaled the scent of wet loam as she went to the front door of the House at Saltwater Point.

Jason's truck was outside, and the door was already unlocked. She smelled the unmistakable odor of demolition, a mixture of old mold and dirt, when she stepped inside. "Hello?"

"In the kitchen." Jason's voice was nearly drowned out by the sounds of hammering.

She veered left and found him standing in the middle of splintered two-by-fours and broken plaster attached to lath. The kitchen was nearly totally demolished. The old cabinets were in a heap where a wall used to be. Clint Parker, a blond college student who worked for them part time, was with him.

The place already felt more open and airy. "You've gotten a lot done already."

"Time is money. The longer it takes us to finish, the more our carrying costs will be."

Her own dithering about Grayson came to mind. What would delaying a search for the truth accomplish? She thought he was closed-minded, but at least he had skills and resources. If she worked with him, they would likely find the truth sooner than if she dug in her heels and refused to work with him.

She put her hands on her hips and looked around. "You're here early. I fed Mia, then came straight here."

Jason wiped the perspiration from his forehead. His sun-streaked hair glistened with moisture too. "Who's Mia?"

"My new cat." She told him about finding the bedraggled kitten. "I gave her a bath before I left this morning. She wasn't a fan."

Jason chuckled. "You're ever the rescuer." He stooped and gathered an armload of debris. "Any news about Mac?"

"Do you care?" She pressed her lips together as she gathered debris and followed him out the door to the Dumpster.

He tossed his load. "Of course I care. She might hate me, but I don't hate her. I see her faults, unlike you, but I didn't wish her dead."

She dropped her load into the green Dumpster. "We don't know she's dead!"

He raised a brow. "Ellie, I know it's hard to live in limbo, but you have to face the fact we may never find her body. The fish—" He broke off and swallowed hard. "It's hard to think about, but even the coroner is saying she's likely dead. He took a look at the blood evidence."

"Where did you hear that? The sheriff hasn't said anything about it."

"I talked to him myself. I ran into him at Harvey's Pier and asked him for his opinion. He said it was possible she survived that kind of blood loss if she got immediate medical attention, but he didn't think she'd lived through it."

Her throat went tight, and she gulped. "That's his opinion, not fact."

"He's basing it on his years of experience, Ellie. We have to accept what's happened and move on." He stomped off back to the house.

She stood by the Dumpster gathering her composure. Five days without her sister had been agony. How was she supposed to get through the rest of her life without Mac? Her sister was all the family she had left.

Grayson will get to the bottom of it all.

She was going to work with him. It was the only way she'd have closure. If she knew for sure what had truly happened to Mac, maybe she could accept it and grieve. If she'd been involved in something illegal that led to her death, Ellie had to know it.

She rubbed her dusty hands on her jeans and walked back inside. Today she would focus on her work.

Jason hammered out the last two-by-four in the wall. He saw her watching and stopped. "I'm sorry, Ellie. I know how much you loved her."

She nodded, unable to get any words past the constriction in her throat. After reaching for a bottle of water from the cooler, she gulped down half of it and inhaled. "What would you think if I told you I wanted to keep this house?"

Surprise flickered in his brown eyes. "But you love your house."

"I do, but this place is special, don't you think? I keep imagining myself living here and seeing the water."

"I'm okay with it. We won't make a profit on it, but I don't mind. You've worked hard, and you deserve it. Besides, your house probably holds a lot of memories. This will give you a fresh start."

A fresh start wasn't something she wanted. She longed to hear her sister's voice and hug her. She wanted to spend evenings watching Hallmark movies and sipping cocoa with Mac.

She turned away before Jason could see the tears in her eyes. One day at a time. Just as she moved forward on the house day by day, she'd move forward without Mac. Somehow.

The Rainshadow Brewhouse was packed. The building looked like it had been a bar once back in the gold rush days, and the wide plank floors underfoot were a bit uneven. Tin ceilings soared to sixteen feet, and the polished wood bar top looked like it still had the original mirrors behind it. Big drum roasters squatted in the west window.

Grayson saw an empty table for one in the back corner and carried his black coffee and breakfast sandwich through the throng to snag it. Even though he'd only gotten three hours of sleep last night, he felt surprisingly alert, though he wasn't sure where to go next with the investigation.

College students with backpacks, mothers with toddlers, and businessmen talking animatedly on their phones while ordering their drinks held his attention for a few moments. He'd been born in this nice little town, which was still hard to wrap his mind around.

The enticing aroma of coffee and cinnamon sparked his appetite, and he took a bite of his sandwich as he looked around. Did any of them know him as a little boy? Some of the grandmotherly types would be old enough. Maybe he wouldn't feel so adrift once Shauna and Zach got back later today. He'd thought about going over and introducing himself to his new nephew, but he wasn't quite ready for that yet. At least not without Shauna there.

He had his breakfast and was about to leave when he heard a woman mention Mackenzie's name. He glanced around as if looking for someone so he could get a glimpse of the two women and a man who sat sipping mochas and eating cinnamon rolls. One was a white-haired woman with a surprisingly unlined face dressed in khaki slacks and a red top. The other woman had red hair and was as round as a cue ball. She wore a shapeless dress splashed with gold flowers. The blond guy was much younger and probably a student.

He held his breath and leaned toward them.

The red-haired one waved her hands in the air. "If you ask me, I think Mackenzie's boyfriend killed her. I ran into him right after she dumped him, and he was nearly incoherent. He kept yelling about making her pay and that no one dumps him. It gave me the willies."

The young man spoke. "I heard he was out to sea when she went missing. It's a good idea to look at him, though. Those military types are capable of any kind of violence."

Red Hair nodded. "He has friends. Those military types stick together."

White Hair took a sip of her drink. "I don't know what to make of the accusation that she took that cocaine. It seems so out of character. But Trafford is another matter. He's capable of just about anything, even murder."

"I sure miss her at the university."

A lightbulb went off in Grayson's head. These women must be teachers who worked with Mackenzie. The legs on his metal chair scraped as he pushed back from the table and turned toward them. "Excuse me, could I ask you a few questions?"

White Hair fixed him with a stern look in her blue eyes. "Who are you?"

He dug for his badge. "Grayson Bradshaw with Coast Guard Investigative Services. I'm investigating some missing cocaine, and I couldn't help but overhear you."

A blush ran up both women's necks. Red Hair glanced at White Hair. "We shouldn't have been gossiping."

He moved his chair over to their table. "You don't think much of Dylan Trafford. May I ask why?"

Red Hair snorted. "He's a sleazebag. Mac caught him out with another girl. He was all over her, and Mac followed them back to the girl's place. He tried to turn it around like it was all Mac's fault for being a prude. Piece of trash." Her hazel eyes studied him. "I guess we should introduce ourselves too. I'm Darcy Farrow, and this is Penny Dreamer. We both worked with Mac at the university. Clint Parker here is a student majoring in political science. We all know Mac. She didn't take your cocaine."

"So everyone keeps telling me." He smiled to soften his sarcastic tone. "How did Mac seem the past few weeks?"

Darcy glanced at Penny and shrugged. "Distracted, uneasy. We thought it was because she was hurt over Dylan's behavior, but now I'm not so sure. She was looking up a lot of stuff online, and she'd close the tab whenever anyone got close."

"You don't know what she was investigating?"

Penny ran a perfectly manicured finger around the top of her cup. "I'll admit I checked her history one day when she was out of the office."

Darcy gasped. "Penny, you didn't!"

Penny's chin came up. "I was worried about her, okay? I thought maybe it was something I could help with." She returned her attention to Grayson. Color ran up her neck again, and she looked down at her half-eaten breakfast. "There were pictures she'd saved of a Coast Guard pier."

His gut clenched. "The hangar where the cocaine was stored?"

"I don't know where it was stored."

"But she did."

Penny's blue eyes narrowed. "How do you know that?"

He shouldn't have blurted that out. "Anything else?"

"That's it," Penny said.

"Do you know where Mackenzie might have stashed something important? A locker, a safety deposit box, anything?"

Darcy frowned and shook her head. "The sheriff took away everything in her desk. Her computer too."

So the sheriff's department would see what she'd been researching. Would they be as uneasy as he was?

Chapter 14

Buy quality materials right from the start. What you save
when buying cheap items costs much more in the long run.
—HAMMER GIRL BLOG

It was nearly noon when Ellie parked on the street a few store-fronts down from the sheriff's office. She'd circled the block, and most of the spots were taken for setup for the Dungeness crab and seafood festival on Saturday. Workers hung banners from streetlights and others banged together street-side booths along Main Street.

She was still a little shaken from her discussion with Jason. She had to stay focused if she wanted to find out what had happened to her sister.

The wind blew the sweet scents of vanilla, cinnamon, and lilac from the candle shop to her nose as she hurried to the sheriff's office. Someone called her name as she started up the steps, and she turned to see Grayson exiting the coffee shop. The wind ruffled his thick blond hair, and as he neared, she realized again how big he was. His hands could about encompass her waist.

In spite of his size, she didn't fear him the way she had initially. Maybe it was because he showed so much care about the pain she was feeling about Mac. He was nothing like her dad.

She pushed the baseball cap off her forehead a bit and smiled up at him as he reached her. "I see you found the coffee shop."

"Would you believe there was no coffee in Shauna's house? Only a few grounds in the bottom of the canister. Sad state of affairs so I had to make a stop to get some supplies. Who lives like that?"

"I should have sent a few groceries home with you last night. I doubt there was anything for breakfast either."

"I had a sandwich at the coffee shop and ended up working there all morning." He fell into step with her, and they went up the stairs. "We might as well talk to the sheriff together. I'm sure we have similar questions."

"I actually thought I'd talk to Rosa, Mac's friend who is a deputy here."

"You know her? Good call."

As she was talking to Grayson, a homeless man caught her attention. He was pushing a basket containing a sleeping bag, water, and all sorts of belongings, and he stood looking at the food truck selling crab Rangoon.

"Hang on a sec." She walked past Grayson toward the food truck. She bought some food, then took it to the man, who thanked her with his hand on her shoulder.

She noticed Grayson staring at her as she jogged back to join him. "Nice thing to do."

"That's Ned. He's had a hard life since he got out of the military. Any of us could be in his shoes."

He held open the door for her, and she went past him into the cool wash of air-conditioning. Rosa was looking at a clipboard behind the desk, and she gave a little wave when she saw Ellie. She put down the clipboard and came around to hug her. "How you holding up?" She released her and shook her head. "Forget I said that. Did you get any sleep after the break-in?"

Grayson straightened. "Someone broke in last night?"

Ellie wished she could have warned Rosa not to say anything. She wanted the focus to stay on finding Mac. "Probably a Peeping Tom. He left as soon as he realized he'd been seen."

Rosa glanced from him to Ellie. "You're here to see the sheriff? He's out right now."

"I actually came to see you." Ellie introduced Grayson to her. "Is there a room where we can talk?"

"Sure, this way." Rosa led her down a hall to a small room on the left. She shut the door behind them and indicated the chairs around the table. "Have a seat. What can I do for you?"

Ellie slid into a chair and waited until Grayson settled too. "I found some interesting files on a computer at my house that Mac often used."

Rosa's dark eyes sparkled. "You brought it?"

Of course she should have thought of that. Ellie shook her head. "I didn't. Anyway, it appears she'd been researching North Korea's threat to use a nuclear EMP bomb. She ever talk to you about her interest?"

Rosa blanched. "A few weeks back she asked me how prepared we were for an EMP strike. It had been in the news so I thought that's what triggered her question. You're thinking it was more than that?"

"She had files on how to build them on the laptop. It seemed strange."

"Very strange. I guess we'll never know."

Ellie flinched. "You think she's dead, don't you?"

Rosa sat back in her chair. "I don't know, honey, but there was a lot of blood on that ship deck. If she's not dead, she's in pretty bad shape. I don't know how to tell you this, but the sheriff decided to take some cadaver dogs out into the woods outside town after a tip came in about someone dumping something out there."

A roaring started in Ellie's head, and her vision blurred. "H-He found her?" She took a few deep breaths to calm herself.

"I haven't heard yet, but he thought it was possible. He's going to call you as soon as he's done."

Ellie felt faint. She'd thought she was ready for closure, but not if it meant finding Mac's dead body.

Grayson leaned forward. "Has the sheriff taken a look at Dylan Trafford? I spoke to him early this morning, and I think he's capable of taking her."

"We're looking at everything. You must have grabbed him the minute he hit land."

"I did. He told me he took Mackenzie to the storage unit where they'd stashed the cocaine. She knew where it was."

Ellie curled her hands into fists. "You can't still be thinking she took it, Grayson!"

He held her gaze in a long look. "If we want to find what happened to her, we have to follow up every lead, Ellie."

Was he right? Her throat was tight, and she swallowed down

the lump forming there. If only they knew for sure which lead to follow.

Grayson touched her shoulder. "Let's go get some lunch. I have things to tell you too."

The Crabby Pot food truck line moved quickly, and Grayson ordered two bowls of crab chowder, then carried them to where Ellie sat waiting at a picnic table with a million-dollar view of the bay. Gulls squawked and wheeled over his head, and several kayakers paddled by in the calm water.

Ellie, her face pale, stared blankly out at the bay. She looked cute in that baseball cap with her chestnut ponytail dangling out the back keyhole. The muscles in her smooth, tanned arms showed definition with her hands clasped together under her chin.

He slid a bowl of chowder her way. "Here you go."

"Thanks." She lowered her hands and reached for the bowl. "I'm not sure what to do next. Do you think the sheriff has found her body?" Her voice was choked, and her eyes glimmered with moisture behind her glasses.

"He'll let us know as soon as he checks out that lead." He sat across from her. "You really need closure, Ellie. Living with the not knowing is hard. I've seen it tear people apart." She didn't want to face where everything pointed, but then, he hadn't been totally forthcoming with her.

She took the lid off her chowder and blew on it. "It doesn't look like Dylan took her since he was out of the port."

"We're still waiting on authentication of that picture of her in North Korea. She might be there."

"She isn't. After losing that much blood, she never would have been able to travel that far."

"DNA isn't back yet, so we don't know for sure if the blood is hers," he pointed out.

Her eyes widened. "Do you think there's a possibility it's not hers? That maybe she's actually just missing and not likely dead?"

He shouldn't have said that. "I'm trying to make no assumptions. Without DNA there's no confirmation."

Maybe he shouldn't have given her that glimmer of hope. He suspected Mackenzie had gotten mixed up with the wrong people, then was killed. They'd dumped her in the water so there was no chance of finding the attacker's DNA on her body. Ellie didn't need to dwell on that, though.

Her large amber eyes studied him over the rim of her glasses. "There's one thing you haven't told me. What evidence do you have that she's even involved with the cocaine's disappearance?"

"That's what I wanted to talk to you about." The truth was likely to upset her even more, but maybe it was time she understood this wasn't just something the Coast Guard pulled out of a hat. She'd never believe in Mackenzie's guilt until she saw all the evidence. "There were surveillance cameras in the storage room. We have her on camera directing several men as they carried out the cocaine."

She inhaled. "There has to be some kind of explanation."

"I'm sorry. I know you don't want to believe your sister would do something like that, but the video is proof positive."

"Could I see it? The video?"

"I don't know what purpose that would serve other than to upset you more."

"Please."

It was impossible to ignore the plea in her beautiful eyes. "We'll have to get my computer. It's back at Shauna's house."

She rose. "Let's go now."

He shrugged and grabbed his chowder, but before he could stand, the sheriff waved and headed their way. Ellie's mouth tightened, but she sat back down as the sheriff sat beside her at the picnic table.

His black hair was damp, and he mopped his forehead with a red bandana. "It's going to be another scorcher. I thought I might find you here. Rosa told me she'd spoken with you." His dark-blue eyes stayed focused on Ellie.

"Did you find a-a body?"

"We did, but it was just a dead deer. False alarm." He stroked a long black sideburn. "I warned Rosa not to be running her mouth off again."

"Is she in trouble for telling me?" Ellie asked.

Sheriff Burchell shook his head. "We got the DNA back on the blood. It's Mackenzie's."

Grayson winced. "Was there an estimate on how much blood she lost?"

"Three to four pints."

"Not likely survivable."

The sheriff nodded. "That's what the coroner said. If she got an immediate blood transfusion, maybe she could, but it's not very likely considering where she was attacked."

It was unlikely the attacker would provide any medical assistance anyway. Ellie was staring intently at the sheriff and gave a slight nod. "What about the picture?"

"Got that back too. The picture is doctored, so we can't go by that."

"What does that mean?" Grayson asked.

"It appears she wasn't really in North Korea. My expert thinks she was actually standing in front of the Bomun Pavilion."

"Who would doctor it and why?" Grayson asked.

"I think it was likely her attacker, and he was trying to get us off his tail."

"I knew all along she wasn't there," Ellie said. "What's next?"

Grayson caught and held her gaze. He hadn't shared the video with the sheriff, but maybe he should. They could pool their resources. "I'm still pursuing the cocaine. I think it will lead us to Mackenzie."

Ellie sent him a pleading look and gave a slight shake to her head, so he gave a quick nod. He could wait until she'd seen it first, but she needed to face facts. Her sister was involved in this up to her neck.

Chapter 15

I look for a solid foundation first. If the floors slope,
you'll never succeed in restoring that dream house.
—HAMMER GIRL BLOG

Shauna's house had been Ellie's favorite project. She loved the big, open windows and high ceilings and the layout. Grayson shut the door behind them and moved to the living room where he reached for his laptop.

She pulled off her baseball cap. "Let's get this over with."

He opened his computer and clicked on a video file. "Here you go."

She took the laptop and curled up on the sofa with it on her lap. It was hard to concentrate with him looking at her. His eyes looked bluer as the light flooded into the room from the floor-to-ceiling windows. A swatch of blond hair fell across his forehead, and he looked at home as he dropped into the chair opposite her.

The video showed a dark space with several pallets covered in shrink-wrap. The door opened, and a shaft of light illuminated the room more. Overhead lights came on, and she watched the figures step into the room. Two men headed for the pallets, and the woman stood near the door. One of the men was blond and the other had dark hair. Ellie didn't recognize either of them, but there was no mistaking Mac.

Her sister took a step closer to the men. "Let's get that stuff and get out of here. Hurry!"

She wished she had an answer, but nothing about this situation made sense. "Maybe she was forced into doing this, and she wants someone to track the cocaine. That would explain the tears and sad expression."

"You see anyone holding a gun to her head? And I think you're reading into her expression what you want to see."

She pressed her lips together and watched through to the end of the video in silence. Mac seemed to be the one in charge as she directed the men to carry the stacks of cocaine outside. Another camera showed them loading the cocaine into a box truck. Once it had all been moved, she shut off the light, plunging the room into shadows again.

"I think there's more going on than we know," Ellie said.

He sighed. "You're a hard one to convince. There's no duress. She seems to be the mastermind and orchestrates the theft every step of the way. There's really no defense for her actions."

"I know my sister." Ellie shook her head and handed back the laptop. She couldn't bear to watch it again. "There's something behind all this."

"Money." He closed the laptop lid with a snap. "Maybe she was in trouble of some kind, and this seemed the only way out. It's hard to tell what drove her. Do you know anything about her finances?"

"She's thrifty and often buys things from garage sales. She drives a secondhand Toyota and doesn't have any bills except for routine things like utilities and rent. You can ask the sheriff. I'm sure he's checked out her finances."

No matter how hard she tried, she'd never convince him. He had his mind made up about Mac, and she couldn't really blame him now that she'd seen the video. Anyone who didn't know her sister would assume the worst.

"It's true she has no bills that I could see. I'd hoped you might know something more secret. Gambling debts, that kind of thing."

"She hates gambling. She's never even bought a lottery ticket."

"There has to be some reason. Maybe she wanted to start a new life somewhere else?"

"She would never do that." She blew out a frustrated breath that stirred her bangs. "If you only knew her, you'd realize how impossible this is."

"It's not impossible. You saw the proof with your own eyes."

She couldn't deny it. "I saw her, but we need to figure out why she did it. Who was making her do it and why? There's someone else we didn't see in the video. Maybe she had a good reason for taking it, and it's not about the money or the drugs. What about Dylan?"

"What about him?"

"He's the one who showed her the cocaine. Why would he do that?"

"Bragging, I think." But for the first time, a frown crouched between his eyes as if he was rethinking it. "He was onshore during the time the cocaine came up missing, so it's possible he was involved. But there's no sign of him."

"Maybe he's waiting to deliver it to a new location."

"He could be an accomplice, but she's clearly not being forced to be there, Ellie."

She pressed her lips together and rubbed her forehead. "Please keep an open mind. I think there's more going on than you realize. We have to figure out what it is. It might lead us to Mac."

"I'd sure like to have you on my side in a pinch." Smiling, he set the computer over on the end table. "When you believe in someone, nothing shakes your faith."

She knew too well what it was like to have someone you love doubt everything you were. Her mother had done that when Alicia died, and Ellie never wanted to desert someone she loved.

Zach pulled his truck in behind a big black SUV in the driveway of Shauna's house. "Looks like he's here. That's Ellie's car too, isn't it?"

Shauna leaned forward with her hand on the door release. "Looks like it."

She could barely wait for the truck to stop. She wanted to see Grayson again, drink in his familiar blue eyes and blond hair. It had taken all her strength to let him come back to Lavender Tides without her. Zach had cut the final days of their honeymoon short because he saw how she was pining to see her brother.

It was still hard to wrap her head around his new name after all these years.

Zach put his hand on hers. "Calm down, honey. He's not going anywhere."

"I'm so eager to get to know him, to find out about his childhood. There's so much to catch up on." She sent a smile her husband's way. Zach was so wonderful. They'd spent lazy days walking the beach and talking about the future. They wanted more children, and he had all kinds of plans about making Hurricane Roost a full-service regional airport. The current expansion was just the first step.

It still thrilled her to look at his broad shoulders and easy smile and to know they had a future together. She put her other hand on top of his. "Thanks for finding him for me."

"Now to find Brenna."

Her mood took a detour at the reminder of her missing sister. "There seems to be no trace of her, Zach. How can that be? There isn't even a reference to a baby being found at the grocery store in the debris. But she was there—I held her."

"Maybe Grayson remembers something."

"I doubt it. He doesn't even remember me."

"Getting back here might stir some memories." He squeezed her hand and released it. "Let's go in."

She shoved open her door and jumped out. Her heart hammered in her chest, and she grabbed Zach's hand to hurry up the walk to the front door. "Looks like the yard needs to be mowed."

"I'll get to it tomorrow." Zach paused with his finger on the doorbell. "I suppose we should ring the bell. We're not living here now, but he is."

"You think of everything."

He pressed the bell, and she heard it ding from inside. Through the big windows she saw Ellie and Grayson talking. They looked friendly and almost cozy. Grayson, clad in khaki shorts and a red T-shirt, had his long legs stretched out in front of him and watched Ellie with a lazy smile.

Grayson's head turned at the doorbell, then he rose and came their way. He smiled when he saw them through the window and opened the door. "You didn't have to ring the bell."

What was the proper thing to do now? She wanted to grab him in a tight hug, but their relationship was still awkward. There was no textbook on how to begin a relationship with a long-lost sibling.

He took the decision out of her hands when he gave her a quick sideways hug, then released her before she had a chance to respond. They were both navigating unknown waters.

Ellie rose as they came in. "Hey, let me make coffee. You two are a sight for sore eyes! I don't even have to ask if you had a great time. You're both tanned and glowing. Where's Alex?"

"We haven't seen him yet. We came straight here from the airport. Marilyn was taking him to Seattle for the day today, and I don't expect them back before seven."

Shauna glanced at Grayson and studied his good looks. He looked a lot like their father when he was younger. Muscles bulged under his shirt, and in khaki shorts, his legs looked tanned and ropy with exercise. She hadn't missed the glances flying between him and Ellie. She'd like nothing better than for a romance to develop there, but she was probably getting ahead of herself.

Ellie went to make coffee, and Shauna sat down on the sofa. "You're getting settled, Con—I mean Grayson?"

"It's a nice town, and I like your house."

"Did you remember anything once you got here?" She winced at the eagerness in her voice.

"Not memories exactly, but some sense of familiarity I can't quite put my finger on. Is the house where we lived still around? Maybe seeing it would trigger something."

The aroma of coffee wafted toward her, and her stomach rumbled when the scent of cinnamon rolls joined it after the microwave dinged. "It is. We can go there anytime you like."

He nodded. "I'm not sure how I'm supposed to feel about all this, Shauna. I hope you'll give me time to adjust. We're still strangers."

Her vision blurred and she looked away, then took Zach's hand for comfort. "I've had a lifetime to miss you, but I understand it's going to take some time for you. I-I want us to be close if we can."

"I'd like you to meet my sister Isabelle too. She wants to come visit."

Jealousy stabbed at Shauna, an emotion she wasn't used to feeling. "I'd love to meet her." This family reunion wasn't quite what she'd envisioned, but she'd make room for another sister. But would this Isabelle allow Shauna into Grayson's life, or would she make her feel like an interloper? Shauna prayed there was room for all of them.

Ellie came back in with a tray of coffee and cinnamon rolls. "The rolls are a day old but I warmed them up, and I think they're edible. I know how plane food is, so I thought you were probably hungry. I can order a pizza if you want more."

"This is great." Zach scooped up a roll, then took a mug of coffee. "The coffee on the plane was barely drinkable."

Ellie looked cute, but then, she always did. She wore a blue T-shirt over slim-fitting jeans, and her chestnut hair was on her shoulders in a shining curtain. Shauna had always wondered why she'd never been married. Though she was around twenty-six or twenty-seven, she looked about twenty-one with her fresh skin and big, golden-brown eyes behind the oversized glasses. Shauna often caught her doing things without her glasses, and Shauna even looked through them once. If there was a prescription to them, it wasn't much of a correction. Maybe Ellie used them to hide behind, but Shauna didn't get it. She was cute, sweet, and would give you the shirt off her back.

Shauna glanced at Grayson and found him looking at Ellie too. He could do a lot worse.

Chapter 16

You never forget the place where you grew up. It takes on mythical proportions, and we unconsciously look for something in our home to bring back that same warmth.
—HAMMER GIRL BLOG

The pizza for dinner had been ordered, and Shauna had texted Marilyn to let her know they were back in town. If she wanted to talk to Grayson about Brenna, it needed to be before Alex arrived. It was so surreal to see the brother she thought was dead sitting on the sofa in her living room. If she closed her eyes, she could see him as a small boy, his hair sticking up at the back from a swipe with a sticky hand. He used to wear Teenage Mutant Ninja Turtle shirts, and the TV show constantly played at the house.

Did he even remember that now? Shauna curled her fingers around her warm coffee mug and went to sit in a chair across from the sofa. Zach was making a fresh pot of coffee, and Ellie was looking at some computer files with Grayson on the sofa.

"I'm so glad you're here, Grayson." She struggled to speak past the choking sensation in her throat. "I was just remembering your Teenage Mutant Ninja Turtle shirts you used to wear."

His eyes held a quizzical light. "Funny you should say that. I still like them, and I'm the first in line to see one of their movies." He glanced at Ellie. "Ellie took me to the parking lot where the grocery store used to be."

"Did you remember anything?"

He shook his head. "I wondered if you'd mind telling me everything you remember."

"I was about eight." She launched into her memories of that terrible day.

"Mommy, I want to go play." Shauna tugged her hand out of her mother's grip and took hold of Connor's hand. "I'll look out for Connor." It was her responsibility to take care of her baby brother, who was six years younger.

The market had tables with blocks and other toys in the back corner of the building, and it was the best way to keep Connor happy. He liked to grab boxes off the shelves.

Her mother was the most beautiful person in the world, even with her belly sticking out. Her hair was the color of the night, and she was always smiling. Shauna sometimes put her ear on Mommy's tummy to see if the new baby would talk to her, but she never heard anything other than gurgling. Little Peanut was supposed to be here any time, and Shauna was hoping for a baby sister just because she didn't have one.

Mommy touched her head. "Okay, stay in the play enclosure.

I'll come get you when I'm ready to check out. I have to get a lot of groceries so it might be a little while."

That was just fine with Shauna. She led Connor through the aisles of canned goods and bags of chips and somehow kept him from throwing himself to the floor in a temper tantrum. Mommy said all kids who were two had those temper tantrums, but Shauna hated it when he did it in the store.

She and her brother hopped onto the small, plastic teeter-totter. He shrieked with laughter as Shauna bounced down and lifted his small rear end into the air.

But in the next moment, she went catapulting off the end. She bounced to her feet. "You pushed too hard."

But Connor was on the floor too. And the carpet was *moving*. There was some kind of low rumble that made Shauna want to hide under the small table covered with puzzles. Was it a T rex about to come eat them? She wasn't supposed to watch scary movies, but she'd seen a little bit of *Jurassic Park* last week at a friend's house. The shaking intensified and threw her and Connor to the ground.

She hugged her brother as Connor began to cry. "Mommy!" His scream hurt Shauna's ear.

Then their mother was there. She covered them both with her body and tried to soothe them. "It's going to be okay. Stay still."

Connor's sobs began to calm until the ceiling came down in big chunks. Shauna peeked past her mother's arm and saw blue sky above. What was happening? She was too frightened to even cry. Pieces of the ceiling hung over them like some kind of tent, and there were only small tunnels here and there.

Her mother gave a strange *oomph* sound, then didn't move. Shauna tried to shake her, but she didn't respond.

"Mommy, Mommy!" Connor's wails sounded weak, and Shauna saw red on his forehead.

"Mommy!" She tried again to get her mother to open her eyes, and finally Mommy stirred a little and looked at her. "Mommy, you scared me."

Mommy licked a bit of blood away at the corner of her mouth. "My good girl. Lie still. It's an earthquake. Someone will come to help us soon."

The rumbling that seemed to last forever finally stopped. "Can I get up, Mommy?"

Her mother winced as she moved her arm far enough for Shauna to crawl out. She turned and helped her brother up too. He had white dust in his hair, and the blood on his forehead caked it.

Her mother's eyes started to close again. "I can't move, honey. There is something on top of me. We have to wait for help."

"I'll get help!" Shauna climbed through the tunnels formed by the concrete and fallen beams, sometimes coming to a dead end until she retraced her path and found another way. She saw a man with a green shirt lying motionless on the floor with blood on his head. She was afraid to get closer, and her chest started to feel tight. She had to find help.

She crawled through the tunnels until she found a woman seated in the crumbled concrete with her head cradled in her arms. Shauna touched her wrist. "My mommy is trapped. Can you help her?"

The woman had blonde hair and looked friendly, and she put her hand on Shauna's arm. "Where is she, honey? I'm a paramedic."

Shauna pointed. "Back in the play area with my little brother. It's not easy to get there, though. I can show you."

The woman peered through the tunnel Shauna had exited. "I

think the worst of it is over, but there might be aftershocks. We're trapped here until help comes."

Shauna led the way back and only went down the wrong tunnel once before emerging into the small, cramped space where her mother lay with Connor.

Shauna pointed out her mother, who wasn't moving. "There she is."

The paramedic lady made her way to Mommy and touched her shoulder. "Let me see if I can get this beam off your legs."

She grabbed another broken piece of wood and propped it under the big beam on a piece of concrete. Grunting, she pushed on the thing until the big beam rolled off Mommy.

Shauna's mommy cried out a little and put her hand to her tummy. "I think the baby's coming."

Shauna backed away and reached for Connor's hand. He didn't move his fingers. Maybe he was sleeping. It was dark by the time she heard a baby cry. The paramedic lady soothed the baby, then everything fell silent.

Shauna blinked and looked into her brother's face. "We were stuck there for two days. I think our mom died as soon as Brenna was born. I named her and held her, but Mom never spoke. The paramedic found some formula and bottles in the debris and managed to feed Brenna. I heard her cry a couple of times. There were some other earthquakes, aftershocks, and another beam fell on you. I stayed with you until help came. I thought you would die before anyone got there. You didn't cry, just moaned. Dad found me at the triage center, but he never found you and Brenna. I told him you both died, but I didn't see it. I just felt it."

His face was unreadable, but she knew this had to hit him hard.

Listening to his sister recount the details of the night their mother died brought the tragedy closer, and Grayson could almost feel the plaster dust choking his throat and the pain in his stomach.

"I-I sort of remember my stomach hurting. And the taste of blood."

Shauna's green eyes widened. "You had blood coming from your mouth, and you held your stomach and moaned."

Zach brought in the coffee carafe and refilled her cup. "I'd forgotten what you said about the paramedic who helped when Brenna was born. Do you remember her holding the baby? It sounds like maybe she took care of her after the birth."

"She did. I wanted to hold her, but she only let me for a minute, then she took her back. She said she was too fragile."

Grayson could almost hear a baby crying. "I don't really remember being at the hospital or even when my parents took me home with them. You'd think I'd have some kind of memory of that, wouldn't you? You haven't said much about our dad."

Shauna didn't meet his eyes. "H-He wasn't much of a father. And a few weeks ago I found out he caused the earthquake."

Grayson's gut roiled as he listened to Shauna recount the discovery of what their father had done. "He sounds like a horrible person."

Shauna's eyes filled. "I pretty much raised myself. I can't tell you how happy it makes me to know you had good parents."

Did good parents lie to their kid for years? Grayson needed

to examine how he felt about what they'd done. It explained so much about his mother in particular. Approval from his dad had come readily, but his mother's praise had been sparing, and he always felt he didn't quite measure up to her expectations. Izzy had been her darling, the smart, beautiful daughter. He suspected his mother had never fully accepted him as her son. Had his dad been the one insistent on adopting him? He wished he could ask, but he wouldn't want to drive a wedge between his parents.

Ellie held up her mug for a refill. "There's no record of Brenna being taken to the hospital?"

Zach shook his head. "I've talked to every possible official out there. That's how I found Grayson, but no one seems to have seen or even heard of Brenna. Now I'm wondering about the paramedic. I need to find her. She should know what happened to Brenna."

"How will you do that?" Having one new sister was more than Grayson could handle right now. He wasn't sure if he wanted to meet a sister who had no memories of either of them.

Zach shrugged. "I can get a list of paramedics working that year. I should be able to tell by ages and appearance. Someone has to know of her. She was blonde, right?" He headed to the kitchen and put down the carafe before rejoining them.

Shauna nodded. "I thought she was a little older than Mom, who was about thirty, so she was maybe in her midthirties." She rubbed her head. "She wore a black uniform, and I saw the patch on the shirt that said Lavender Tides EMS."

Zach dropped into the empty chair. "That gives me a lot to go on if you remember she worked for Lavender Tides EMS. I thought maybe I'd have to check Port Townsend and Port Angeles."

The topic was making Grayson more and more uncomfortable. There was so much of his background that he didn't know. Did he even want to? Maybe it would have been better if Shauna had never found him. Did they have the right to disrupt Brenna's life too?

Grayson shifted on the sofa. "What if she's perfectly happy the way she is? Brenna, I mean. She could be married and happy. Have you thought of the disruption you'll be bringing to her if you find her?"

Shauna's green eyes looked a little sad. "Do you wish we'd never found you, Grayson?"

"I don't know," he admitted. "My life is pretty topsy-turvy right now."

She looked down at her hands. "If we find her, we'll check out her situation before we talk to her. Just like we did with you."

He knew she was hurt, but he wasn't sure how to heal the sudden awkward silence. "I think I need some air." He rose and rushed for the door. He snatched his laptop off the counter on his way out.

Chapter 17

The kitchen is still the heart of the home. Good
food, laughter, and warmth never go out of style.
—HAMMER GIRL BLOG

The sea breeze lifted Ellie's hair as she stepped out onto the back deck and followed Grayson down toward the water. Maybe she should have let Shauna go after him, but after all the intense time they'd spent together, she had reacted on instinct.

Poor guy. Ellie had heard most of the story, and she tried to imagine how she would feel to hear such a horrific tale and not able to remember it.

He stood under the shade of a tree and skipped a rock out over the calm waves. A seagull scolded him overhead, and several passengers waved from the ferry chugging by. She automatically waved back as she moved to join him at the gently lapping water.

She let the salty scent of the sea wash over her and relax the muscles in her shoulders. "You okay?"

He shrugged and tossed another rock. "Just something I have to get used to. Every time I think I've accepted all of it, I get hit with something new. Hearing Shauna recount that day made me feel like I had a boulder on my chest."

"Or a piece of concrete."

He turned to stare at her again. "You think it was a memory?"

"Shauna said you were trapped. It would make sense."

"I guess so." He ran his hand through his hair, and it stood on end. "So now I guess I meet a new nephew. I'm not sure I'm up to all this unknown family."

"Shauna will understand if you ask her to postpone it."

"He's probably already on his way. I like kids. It's not that." He settled on a rock and stretched out his long legs. A gull landed nearby, then hopped closer to see if he had any food. He finally looked up. "You have a calming way about you, Ellie. Thanks for coming out here with me. I didn't really want to be alone, but I didn't know how to tell Shauna how it all made me feel."

Heat ran up her neck. "You're welcome." The gull swooped away when Ellie joined him on the sand. She sat cross-legged, then picked up a stick and threw it into the water. "Is there anything I can do to help?"

He shook his head. "Coming out here to listen was enough. There's really nothing anyone can do. It's a new world I have to get used to. And I'm fine, really. Shauna is great. I can see how much she loves me, but it feels so odd not to love her back. I think I can, but it's going to take some time." He picked up a small pebble off the sand and rolled it around in his fingers. "So much about my life growing up is clearer now. It explains the distance I always felt from my mother. She treated Izzy with so much more warmth. I always thought it was because I was male, but it wasn't."

"How about your dad?"

"He was great—when he was home. Being in the navy meant he was out to sea a lot. When he was home we'd go fishing, play ball in the yard, go to the beach. He tried to make up for his absence with lots of fun."

"Have you talked to your sister about this?"

He nodded. "She didn't believe it at first. She offered to come here, but she's got kids and a writing career. I can handle it, but it's been a shock."

"Does it make it worse to stay here? I've got a house we just finished and it's on the market. Even if it sells immediately, you'd be able to stay there for at least another month by the time all the financing and inspections are done."

"Good of you to offer, but it's not the house. It's just everything. I need to be concentrating on finding the cocaine and your sister, but the personal stuff keeps inserting itself. I have to focus."

She nodded. "And nothing is easy about all of it. I happened to think of something, though." She told him about the confrontation with the woman over the mah-jongg tiles. "I haven't opened the box of tiles yet."

She told him about her slashed tires after the sale. "It's probably not related, but I'm trying to look at everything."

"I don't like it. You also had that break-in. For all we know, it's all related to Mac's death."

Her throat closed, and she looked away. "We don't know she's dead."

"Ellie—"

She shook her head when he reached toward her. "I know I'm being ridiculous to cling to hope, but I can't just give up on her."

His big hand came down on hers. "If anyone understands this, it's you. We're kind of in this together."

His touch sent warmth up her arm to lodge in her neck. "I guess we are." It was difficult to step away from the intensity in his blue eyes.

He wiped his hands on his shorts and turned to where he'd set his laptop down. "I wanted to take a look at the whole EMP bomb thing." He opened his computer. "I've been on the trail of a terrorist who sells drugs to fund his organization. He's here in the area, and we think Mac took the drugs for him. I want to see if he's been implicated in any kind of EMP threat. His name is Tarek Nasser. Ever heard of him or met him?"

Terrorist? "Y-You think Mac was part of a terrorist cell?" Bile tinged the back of her throat. "Mac is not a terrorist! I've never heard of this guy."

"Good, because he's a bad dude—brutal and likes torture."

He must have realized how the news hit her because he looked up quickly. "There's no doubt she took the drugs. At first I assumed it was for the money, but the files about the bomb add another layer to investigate. I have to look at everything. I'm sorry."

She struggled to catch her breath. "You're wrong, Grayson. You have to be."

"I hope so." He looked back at his computer and began to type.

She watched him scroll through pages of information and tried to think of anything Mac might have said that would indicate she'd gotten involved with terrorists, but there was nothing. She loved her job and her students. She was passionate about sailing. Mac had shown no signs of being interested in some kind of radical theology.

"Ah." Grayson straightened.

"What is it?"

"One of the CIA operatives in Korea said he suspects North Korea of partnering with Nasser's group to set off a coordinated attack. He suspects they intend to use an EMP bomb."

The words fell like a boulder on her heart. "You're thinking it makes sense because of Mac's visit to Korea. And her specialty in Asian language and culture."

"You can see it too, can't you?"

She shook her head. "I can't believe Mac would do that."

"I know it's hard to accept, and I could be wrong."

"But you don't think you are."

He shook his head. "Could we go to your house and look at those mah-jongg tiles when we're done here?"

She managed to nod, but she wanted to bolt for the house. What had Mac gotten involved with? She couldn't deny any longer that her sister had taken the drugs. What other secrets did Mac have?

How did an uncle talk to a nephew he'd never seen? Grayson eyed the five-year-old, who had followed him into the kitchen. Grayson set down the pizza boxes and opened the first one. The scent of tomatoes, cheese, and garlic made his mouth water.

The boy's grandmother had brought him over an hour ago,

and she'd been curious but kind. She'd left Alex with his mom and had gone home to get the dogs and cat. It was about to be a circus. Maybe he should reconsider Ellie's offer to use one of her houses, but he was too far into this to back out now.

"Plain cheese, buddy?"

Alex nodded, his turquoise eyes somber. "Are you going to live here forever?"

Cute kid, and he looked a lot like the picture of his dad on the fireplace mantel. Grayson slid a slice of cheese pizza onto a plate. "Well, it's hard to say how long I'll be here. I work for the Coast Guard, and they tell me where to go and for how long. You probably know that, right?"

Alex nodded and accepted the paper plate holding the pizza slice. "You don't look like Mommy."

"No, I don't."

"I look like my dad. Maybe you look like your mom or dad."

"That's probably true." Gosh, the kid had him scrambling for answers. Grayson hadn't even seen pictures of his birth parents. Maybe Shauna had some. The things he didn't know kept slamming into him.

Ellie's smile was wide as she came to help him. "I'll fix drinks." She touched Alex's head. "Hey, little man, you've grown a foot since I saw you last."

He stood taller. "I'm going to be tall like Daddy and Zachster."

"I'll bet you are."

"Do you think I should call Zachster Dad? He's going to be my dad now, isn't he?"

Grayson suppressed a grin as his gaze locked with Ellie's. Let her be in the hot seat for a while.

She wrinkled her nose, a very cute nose, at him before

smiling down at the boy. "I think you need to talk to your mom and Zach about that."

"Okay." He wandered back to the seating area where his mom and Zach sat with their pizza and iced tea.

Grayson handed her a slice of pizza. "You handled that well."

"Always refer questions to the parents." Her bright smile flashed before she bit into the pizza. "I'm starving. Have you tried it yet? It's wood-fired, and it's better than any other pizza I've ever had."

He grinned and took a bite. The Italian spices and Canadian bacon hit his taste buds at the same time as the tasty, wood-fired crust. "It's pretty good." Something about the flavor brought a vision of a ferry moving past in the sound. "How long has this pizza place been around?"

"As long as I can remember. I think it opened in the sixties."

It was like being two people. He knew who he was—Grayson Bradshaw. Son of a navy officer, older brother of Isabelle, and Coast Guard criminal investigator. The path of his life had run back to Japan, then forward to a series of places in the US. He knew what he wanted from his career, and he thought he knew his family inside and out.

He'd been wrong.

Life wasn't one long ribbon of known events. There were frayed areas he didn't understand, and he wasn't sure he wanted to try to tie them all up in a neat bow. It had been easier before Shauna showed up.

"Could we go talk to Dylan tonight?"

He lifted a brow. "We? I'd rather you didn't get involved in this. He could be dangerous."

"I thought you doubted he was guilty of anything."

"I do, but I'd rather not take any chances with your life."
He frowned as something Rosa said came to mind. "What's
this about a break-in last night? You never told me exactly what
happened. Did you see anyone at all?"

Her golden eyes lost their teasing light. "I heard someone outside my house last night. Splitting the screen with a knife."

He tried to cover his alarm. "Did you call Burchell?"

"No, but I called 911. A couple of deputies, Rosa included,
checked things out. They found a set of footprints outside my
window and the cut window screen." She took another bite of
pizza. "I would guess the sheriff got a report on it, though he
didn't say anything when we talked to him today. It's probably not
related to Mac's disappearance. Just some random Peeping Tom."

"You can't know that. You should stay with a friend for a
while."

"I could ask Jason to come stay. He'd do it."

A startling sensation swirled in his chest. *Jealousy.* He managed to push it away. "One man without a gun is hardly likely
to deter terrorists."

Her chin came up. "No, but I'm not helpless either. I want
to follow any trail Mac left. While I don't think my sister was
part of any terrorist plot, I have to know the truth."

"I'll keep you informed of anything I find out."

She lifted a brow. "I don't like the way you said that. You
trying to get me out of your hair?"

"Of course not." He grinned and reached for another slice
of pizza.

"Liar." She smiled. "It would kill me to sit on the sidelines
while you try to implicate Mac in a major crime. There has to
be someone on my sister's side. I've heard of way too many cases

where law enforcement gets fixated on a certain line of investigation and convicts the wrong person."

"I wouldn't do that, Ellie." He poured himself a cup of coffee. "I believe there are more layers to this than we realize. Who did your sister take the cocaine for? Nasser, like I suspect, or someone else? It hasn't hit the streets yet, and no one has seen it since it was stolen."

"How do you know it hasn't hit the streets yet?"

"It was cut with Fentanyl, which is an opioid that greatly increases the risk of overdose. And we haven't seen those kinds of deaths yet. Maybe Mackenzie took it to keep it out of Dylan's hands. Maybe it was for another reason, but I need to start thinking outside the box."

"I agree!"

He held up his hand. "That includes you too, Ellie. You're too quick to excuse your sister. Let's both agree to assess every angle. We both have had tunnel vision in our theories. Chances are, we're both wrong. Deal?"

When she nodded, he had to resist the urge to hug her. Where had that impulse come from?

Chapter 18

*One of my favorite things to run across during
construction is old newspapers inside the walls.
It's a peek into the people's lives from that era.*
—HAMMER GIRL BLOG

Grayson couldn't remember the last time he'd been at a
woman's house this often. Most dates he'd been on through
the years were dinner and a movie. Ellie's place with its soothing
colors was beginning to feel a bit like home.

Ellie came through the garage door holding a box. "Here
are the mah-jongg tiles. I put them in the toolbox in my truck
and forgot to take them out."

She joined him on the sofa and handed the box to him. "Mah-
jongg is Mac's favorite game."

"I've never played it." He turned the box over and examined
it before he lifted the lid. The tiles looked similar to dominoes in

shape and material, but instead of dots, the graphic on each tile was Chinese characters and symbols in red, green, and blue on an off-white background.

"Bingo." He reached for a paper folded in half and taped to the inside of the top of the box. "I hope this isn't just instructions." When he unfolded it, his heart rate picked up.

Ellie lifted a brow. "A Peanuts cartoon?"

"I suspect it's steganography. A message encrypted into a picture." He smoothed out the paper, then snapped a picture and uploaded it. "I'm sending it in to be looked at. The FBI has a program that will decipher it. I think we're on to something, though. Steganography is often used by terrorist cells. Most people would have looked at the cartoon and laughed. If we had the pass code to decipher it, we'd know something sooner."

Ellie's eyes widened. "Wait a second. Mac taught me a lot about these tiles, and the top row is a little unusual, almost deliberate." A frown crouched between her eyes. "Mandarin is read from right to left and often runs vertically, then to the left." She touched a green tile at the upper right. "This is the green dragon, which means 'to begin.'" She ran her finger down to the next tile, a red one. "This is the red dragon. It often represents hitting a target or achievement."

"So the first two tiles might mean 'begin hitting the target.'" This felt important, almost momentous, like they'd stumbled into something huge.

Ellie continued to frown and study the tiles. "The next ones are the duck and peacock bamboo tiles. They stand for an enduring partnership and success."

"Between North Korea and ISIS?"

"There's no way of knowing that." She touched the next tile.

"This is the pine tree circle tile. It means 'firmness' or 'strength.' This next tile is the insect circle tile for 'busyness' or 'a short time.'"

"Short time? Like maybe whatever they are planning will be soon?" He knew he was guessing, but headquarters would know more. He snapped a picture of the tiles and the way they were laid out, then sent it off too. "Anything else? This might be an indication of their intent, but I'd sure like to find a pass code."

She took off her glasses and set them aside, then continued to study the tiles. "Have them try 'east wind heaven' in some combos. There's a blank tile, then those two and another blank. It might mean something or it might be nothing."

"Will do." He shot off the request, then put his phone away. "You're really something, you know. I wouldn't have even thought to look at the combo of tiles."

"It might not lead to anything," she warned him.

"I know, but we have somewhere to start at least."

She caught her full lower lip between her teeth. "I've been trying to think of what we can do to investigate Mac's activities lately. She became really interested in ham radio and has been learning about it from our former coroner. I don't know what triggered her interest because it came out of the blue about three months ago."

"It's a place to start. How about you talk to him tomorrow?" Ham radio might be something the terrorists used to communicate in cryptic messages. "I'd go with you, but I have a conference call with headquarters, and I'm hoping they'll have some information about the mah-jongg tiles."

"It's probably nothing anyway."

He yawned. "This time change is kicking my butt. I spent too much time in North Carolina."

He didn't want to leave, though, not with her looking at him with those blue eyes. He liked being around her. He'd never known a carpenter, let alone a female one. He hoped to have enough time to learn her different layers and depths. She was just plain interesting.

"So this probably explains why that woman was so adamant about getting the mah-jongg tiles," she said. "And if we find out it's a message between terrorists, it would also explain why I was run off the road, and the break-in too." She glanced at the clock on the wall. "It's ten, and we've had a busy day. Go on home and get some rest."

Her mention of the attacks on her sent a chill up his spine. "Did you talk to Jason yet about staying with you?"

"When would I have had time? I'm fine to be here by myself. I'll keep my can of bear spray on my bedside table."

It wasn't safe. "I'm going to stay. I can sleep on the sofa. It looks comfy."

She shook her head. "Don't be silly. There hasn't been anything else since Tuesday night. Nothing last night or today. Maybe they got their message through another way, or maybe it was all a coincidence."

"I can't take that chance. Where do I find an extra pillow?"

She chewed on her bottom lip. "If you're determined to stay, you can sleep in the guest room. There are clean sheets on the bed."

And it was upstairs, while her bedroom was down here. "I'd better stay down here. It might take too long to get to you if someone tries to break in. I'm fine on the sofa."

Amusement lit her amber eyes. "Your feet will hang off the end."

He grinned back. "Won't be the first time."

He put the mah-jongg box into his computer bag for safe-keeping. He wouldn't get much sleep anyway, not with all the thoughts whirling in his head.

Ellie parked on the street at the former coroner's home. He lived in a tree-lined subdivision that had been built in the sixties. Most were sprawling ranches, but Monte Bennet's cute cottage had a front porch reminiscent of a Craftsman style. Roses bloomed in the flower beds and sent their sweet fragrance out over the walk to the door.

No one answered the doorbell, and she started to leave when she heard voices in the back. She went around the side yard with its bed of purple pansies and black-eyed Susans. The flowers would hang around until the first frost in November, and they appeared to be trying to make the most of their last few weeks of blooms. The backyard wasn't fenced, and a large deck took full advantage of the trees lining the back of the property.

Monte sat at a table with a coffee mug. A woman Ellie assumed was Mrs. Bennet bent over the flower bed by the steps to the deck. She had stylish gray hair and wore a blue-and-white top over navy capris.

"I told you these flowers would take over the bed. I shouldn't have planted them," the woman said.

"I was trying to help," Monte said. "I thought a ground cover would make you need less mulch."

"Next time let me buy the plants, Monte." She looked up, and her bright-blue eyes widened. "Well, hello."

Monte straightened and looked her direction too. In his seventies now, he had an erect posture and hair that used to be red but had dulled to brown with gray wings at the temples. His mustache and eyebrows were completely white. "Ellie, isn't it? Nelson and Lora's girl."

She advanced a few more steps into the perfectly manicured grass. "That's right. I hope I'm not interrupting."

"You're only interrupting coffee, and I have plenty to share. Doris, would you mind getting our guest a cup?"

Doris wiped her hands on a towel she had around her waist. "Would you like some breakfast, young lady?"

"No, thanks. My name is Ellie. Ellie Blackmore."

"I used to play golf with your mama, Ellie. You've grown up since I saw you last." The screen door banged behind Doris as she went into the kitchen.

"Have a seat, young lady." The coroner pointed to the blue flowered chair across the table from him.

"Thanks." Ellie pulled it out and sank down as Doris came out with a mug of coffee that smelled wonderful.

Doris set the mug down in front of her. "Monte and I like Guatemalan coffee. I brought some cream and sugar in case you take it that way."

Ellie poured in a bit of cream and took a sip. "Wonderful, thank you."

"If you don't need me, I'll get back to yanking out that dratted ground cover Monte bought me." She went down the steps and bent over her plants.

"Now, what can I do for you, young lady?" Monte asked.

"I wanted to ask you some questions about my sister, Mackenzie. You'd been teaching her all about ham radio."

His rheumy eyes brightened. "Yep, I was her Elmer."

"Elmer?"

"What we call a mentor in our world. Her enthusiasm inspired me. I've been involved in ham radio so long, I'd forgotten how exciting it is when you're first learning."

"Did she say why she was so interested in learning?"

He sipped his coffee. "I think she wanted to use it when sailing her tall ship. Other mariners do it too, and the fun thing about ham radio is you can talk to people from all over the world." He frowned. "Though now that I think about it, she was here the first night because I kind of coerced her. I ran into her in the market and told her she should learn it. I promised her some of Doris's famous coconut cream pie if she came over. That first night hooked her. She heard two men jabbering in an Asian language and got really excited. I think she said it was Korean."

"Did she say what they talked about? She knows Korean well."

He shook his head. "She was listening intently, though. She was so into it that she looked a little pale and tired when they stopped. She asked if she could come back and learn more. I'd guess she showed up three nights a week or so for more than three months. We'd turn the dial to listen in to all kinds of countries."

"Did she ever talk with anyone?"

"Yeah, the Koreans. She said they were talking about things to see and do in Korea, but she sure got animated about it."

Ellie decided to go with her gut. Hopefully she could trust Monte. "Listen, you've probably heard the rumor that she stole millions of dollars' worth of cocaine."

"I've heard that. Didn't believe it, though."

"It's true. I saw the video. I found stuff on a computer she used about making an EMP bomb. The Coast Guard investigator I'm working with thinks she might have been involved with terrorists."

Monte snorted. "I don't believe it, and I have to wonder if the video you saw was doctored. That isn't like Mac at all."

"I didn't believe it until I saw the video. I think it's real. Did she ever say anything about EMP bombs or terrorists? Anything?"

"Nope."

"That's not exactly true." Doris mounted the steps and wiped perspiration from her forehead with the back of a grubby hand. "I overheard her on her cell phone one night when you were in the bathroom, Monte."

Ellie's pulse jumped. "What did you hear?"

"She was arguing with someone. I heard her say the delivery should prove her devotion and loyalty. I didn't know what she meant, but it makes sense now. *Devotion* and *loyalty* seemed odd words to tie with *delivery*, but I didn't ask her, of course."

"Do you know who she was talking to?"

"She called him Omar."

Omar was a Middle Eastern name. Ellie felt faint. Could it all be true? She struggled to hold on to her faith in Mac. Maybe there was another explanation.

She sipped her coffee to wet her suddenly dry mouth. "Anything else?"

"Not that I can think of." Doris smiled at her. "You look so much like your mother."

"I'm not nearly as beautiful as she was. You said you played golf with her?"

Doris's blue eyes went soft. She tucked her hair behind one ear and nodded. "I was so sorry not to be here for her when your sister died. I was visiting my mother who'd had a heart attack the week before. All that happened when I was out of town, including her suicide. I blamed myself for a long time. I think I could have helped Lora get through her grief if I'd been home."

"Thank you. I'm glad you loved her."

Doris swallowed and sniffled. "She was a good woman."

"It was such a terrible tragedy." Ellie managed to speak past the constriction in her throat. "It was my fault, and it's been hard to deal with."

"It wasn't your fault." She shook her head. "I'm just glad your mother isn't here now to live through losing another child. She doted on Alicia."

Ellie ducked her head, her face burning with guilt. "Thank you for the information."

"Any time," Monte said. "You might talk to old Ralph Hodges. He builds ham radios, and Mackenzie wanted to talk to him about electronics."

Electronics, as in building bombs?

Chapter 19

On your first house restoration, you discover what
you're really made of. You're going to run into
trouble. Will you quit or learn from your mistakes?
—Hammer Girl Blog

The ferry steamed by out on the incredible blue of the water. Ellie sat on the park hillside. Her thoughts were a chaotic mess, and she couldn't even corral them enough to know how she felt. Tears gathered in the corners of her eyes, and she took off her glasses, then wiped at her cheeks. She'd like to lie back on the green grass and stare at the clouds going by so she didn't examine the screaming that was building inside her chest.

"I thought that was your car."

She turned to see Grayson walking along the water's edge. "How'd you know I was here?"

"I didn't. I was driving by on my way to talk to Dylan, and I saw your vehicle. It's hard to miss that blue pickup."

"You had something to tell me?" She heard the distance in her voice, but she couldn't change it. It felt like she was swimming in a mud flat right now.

"I thought I'd see if you wanted to have some lunch and come with me." He dropped down beside her on the soft grass. "What's wrong?" His long legs clad in khaki shorts stretched out, tanned and muscular, in front of him as he leaned back on his palms.

She quickly wiped her face and put her glasses back on. "I'm fine."

"No, you're not. You're pale and shaking, plus you've been crying. Talk to me."

"This has nothing to do with finding the cocaine."

"Whoa, where'd that hostility come from? I consider you a friend, Ellie. I don't want to force you to talk if you don't want to, but I'm here if you do." He got back up and started down the hillside.

Her hand shook as she passed it over her forehead. "Wait. I-I'm sorry. Hearing Doris talk about how upset my mother was after Alicia died brought it all back in such a real way."

He turned back toward her, and she couldn't help but notice the way the sun gleamed in his blond hair. He had shoulders big enough to carry the weight of the world. She watched him again lower his bulk to the grass beside her. Children squealed on the other side of the hillside in the fenced play area, but there was no one near them.

His large, warm hand settled on her upper back. "I'm sorry, Ellie. You were a kid yourself. You can't carry that guilt forever."

She dashed a tear away from her eye. "If I could only go back and do things differently."

His hand continued to rub her back gently, and she had to fight an urge to turn and bury her face in his chest, which was so unlike her. She'd always stood on her own two feet, and she'd do it now.

She straightened and forced the melancholy from her voice. "There's more about Mac too. She got interested in ham radio after hearing some Koreans talking the first night Monte was teaching her. And Monte's wife overheard her talking to someone named Omar." She told him what Doris had said.

Grayson's hand stopped its movement and gripped her shoulder. "Omar was Nasser's second in command."

"Was?"

"He's dead, killed in a raid my first day here."

She struggled to take it all in. "So there's a definite tie between Mac and Tarek Nasser."

"Looks like it. I just got Mackenzie's call records. Maybe we can see who else she talked to. If this really is a planned attack that's happening soon, we have to find out the details."

"What did you learn from your conference call?"

He removed his hand from her shoulder. "They're still working on the photo decryption, but I was ordered to stand down."

"Stand down? What's that mean?"

"My superiors said they'd take it from here, and I was off the case." He bit off the words as if they tasted bad. "I've still got vacation due me, though, and I'm taking it. I'm not letting this go."

"They can't do that! And why would they want to?"

"They're turning the case over to the FBI, but that makes

no sense either. I've worked with the FBI before. The different agencies all work together when we're confronting a terrorist plot. I don't get it."

Listening to his calm, deep voice brought her head up and pushed away the panic beating against her chest. She turned to look at him, and the compassion in his face warmed her. "There's someone else to talk to too." She told him about Ralph Hodges.

He glanced at his watch. "It's only one. We have plenty of time to drive out there and track him down."

"Let's take my pickup. We're liable to run into bad roads, and my four-wheel drive can handle it."

He grinned and stood, reaching out to help her up. "I bet that truck has a name."

Her hand closed around his, and he pulled her up as if she weighed nothing. "I call him Jaws. He can chew through any road you give him."

He kept her hand in his as they went down the hillside. "Okay, but I get to drive that behemoth."

Wang tossed the last of his crab roll to the squawking gulls and brushed the crumbs from his slacks. The rocky beach was deserted as usual. The perfect place for a private meeting. The bay was gray today from the overcast skies, though there was no rain yet. But he could smell it. He glanced at his watch. He'd give Nasser five more minutes, though he loathed tardiness.

Nasser's big, black SUV pulled into the grass along the side of the road, and Wang crossed his arms over his chest as he waited. Nasser wore a worried frown as he hurried down the path to the beach. Good. He should be worried.

"Well?" Wang demanded as soon as Nasser came within hailing distance. "Did you find it?"

Nasser stopped five feet away and shook his head. "We haven't found it. Bradshaw stayed there last night, but we checked every place in the house as soon as they both left this morning. It's not there."

He had just over a week to get that picture scanned and decrypted. "We'll have to grab her and make her tell us where it is."

"I'd have had the Blackmore woman already if you hadn't stopped me. I think it's time to eliminate her."

Wang considered Nasser's request. "I have to have the tiles." The North Koreans would blame him if he let those tiles get to the FBI.

"Maybe she has already given the tiles to Bradshaw. She's working with him to find out what happened to her sister. They might have stumbled onto the picture in the tiles. Bradshaw would probably know what it was the minute he saw it."

"Most people have no idea messages can be hidden in pictures."

Nasser's face twisted in a snarl. "Bradshaw isn't just anyone. He's got a grudge to settle with me, so he's especially tenacious."

"Maybe he's the one who should be eliminated. Get him out of the way first, then we can grab her and make her give us that box of tiles."

Nasser's grin held menace. "I'd be okay with that."

"Get rid of him then. If you still don't have the box by Monday, she's next."

"You got it, boss."

The old blue truck held its own on the deep ruts and narrow back roads up into the mountain's forests. Grayson whipped the wheel to the right to go around a tight curve, then straightened out the vehicle as the green metal roof on a log home peeked through the trees ahead.

"That has to be it," Ellie said.

Grayson parked by the small porch and opened his door to the whine of a chainsaw bouncing off the treetops. He caught a glimpse of a gray-haired man in a plaid shirt cutting down a tall spruce tree. The wind carried the pine scent to them.

Grayson reached out and caught Ellie by the arm as she headed that direction. "Wait here. That tree is about to fall." He pulled her back against him. She fit nicely, her head just reaching the middle of his chest. Her hair smelled of vanilla or something sweet.

A crackle rent the air, then the tree collapsed onto some shrubs and the whine of the saw cut off. The man shaded his eyes with his hand as he saw them, then he set down the chainsaw and came toward them. His gray hair curled at the nape of his neck and fell shaggily over his ears. His gray beard was just as unkempt and in need of a trim. There was mud on his knees, and he wore sneakers that used to be white.

He stopped a few feet away and looked them over. "Do I know you?"

Ellie took a step toward him with her hand outstretched. "Ralph Hodges?"

"That's me." He eyed her hand, then shook his head. "No offense, miss, but I just shoveled manure out of the goat pen, and I don't think you'd take kindly to a smear of that mess." He reeked a bit of manure.

She pulled her hand back and smiled. "I'm Ellie Blackmore, and this is Officer Grayson Bradshaw, an investigator with the Coast Guard. We have a few questions for you."

"Coast Guard, eh? I haven't even seen the ocean in six months, kids. I doubt there's anything I can shed light on. Most days I can barely remember my name." He wiped his filthy hands on his jeans and jerked his head toward his house. "Let me wash up, and I'll share my lemonade with you. Have a seat on the porch, and I'll be right back."

Ellie glanced at Grayson and shrugged as the old man went into the house. "What's your take?"

"He's a lot sharper than he wants you to believe." He took her elbow and steered her to the steps.

By the time they were seated on the porch swing, the old man was back with a tray of three glasses of lemonade and a plate of Girl Scout peanut butter cookies. He set it on the table in front of the swing, then settled into the rocker close to them.

He took a big swig of lemonade, then smacked his lips. "That hits the spot. So, Miss Ellie Blackmore, what can I do for you? Is this about your sister's death?"

Grayson suppressed a smile. He'd been right. The old guy was sharper than his chainsaw.

Ellie sipped her lemonade, then ran her finger around the sweating rim of the glass. "I spoke with Monte Bennet this morning. He told me how to find you and that Mac had been talking to you about building ham radios."

"I thought old Monte would drop dead in the traces. How's

he enjoying retirement? He should come see me, and I could show him the best fishing he's ever experienced."

"I'm sure he'd love that. Why would Mac be interested in building a radio? Couldn't she just buy one?"

He blinked, then reached for a cookie. After popping it into his mouth, he chewed slowly, his gaze looking off into the dark shadows of the trees. "Well, sure. But when you build one, you can make it special. And it's cheaper."

Ellie leaned forward. "Did she ever mention an interest in North Korea?"

His muddy brown eyes went wary. "The FBI already talked to me. I suggest you have a chat with them. I'm not supposed to talk about it."

"The FBI told us to back off, but she's my sister. I have to help her."

Hodges stared at her. "Okay, yeah, she talked about Kim Jong-un. I got the impression he scared her, and she was trying to convince herself the danger from him that the news is always blathering on about wasn't real."

Grayson opened his mouth, then shut it again. Ellie had a bit of a rapport with the old guy, probably because of Mac. He'd let her run with it.

"You've heard the rumor about her stealing cocaine, right?" Ellie asked.

The old man nodded. "Can't say I was surprised. That girl was running scared from something, but she wouldn't talk about it."

"Did the FBI tell you anything that might help us?"

"You want me to end up in jail, girl? I shouldn't have even told you they came to see me."

Ellie took a sip of her drink. "Did she ever mention anyone's name to you? Someone else we could talk to?"

"She often talked to someone she called Wang, which was a nickname meaning he was the boss or king of the operation. It's Korean, she said."

"Not a real king?"

"I don't think so."

He squinted toward the woods, and in the next second Grayson heard a bullet whiz past his head and saw it hit the old man, who slumped in his chair. "Get down!" He yanked Ellie from her chair and onto the porch floor, then pulled his gun out. "Stay here."

He saw a glint in the woods, which was probably what had alerted Hodges. In a crouched position, he started down the steps to the yard, but he heard the distant sound of a vehicle roaring away. He reversed his steps and went back to check on Hodges.

Ellie was kneeling by his side, and tears streaked her cheeks when he joined her. "He's dead, shot through the head."

"I'll call the sheriff."

He probably should call the FBI too, but they'd know he was still investigating. If they threw him in jail, he wouldn't be able to protect Ellie.

It was hours later by the time they'd briefed law enforcement and were on their way back. Had Hodges been the target or had the shooter been aiming for Ellie? She was so clueless of truly evil people.

He glanced over at her and found her staring out her window at the fall color in the trees. "Looks like your sofa and I are going to be best friends."

"I can't stay home." She turned her head to stare at him, and myriad emotions streamed through her eyes: curiosity, fear, resolve. "Someone doesn't want us investigating. We were followed today." She sat up straighter. "I know—I'll camp out at the Saltwater Point house. I've got tons to do there anyway. I'll stay in the apartment over the garage. I can let the sheriff know, and he can post a deputy."

At least she wouldn't be at her remote house. "I'll let the sheriff know myself."

And Grayson could camp out in his vehicle as well. She had no idea how determined these people were.

Chapter 20

*If a good foundation is the most important part of
a structure, the roofing is a close second. It does
no good to fix things inside if the roof is bad.*
—Hammer Girl Blog

The next morning Jason was waiting for her in the main house when she came through the back door with her backpack slung over her shoulder. The crashing of walls coming down and the banging of hammers told her demolition was still in progress. She coughed at the dust in the air.

Jason wore a tool belt slung low over his dust-covered jeans, and he motioned for her to join him at the wall between the kitchen and dining room. "You wanted this one down, right? What else?"

Ellie retrieved her blueprints from her backpack and rolled them out on the Formica counter in the kitchen. "That wall too." She pointed to an adjacent wall that adjoined the living room.

Jason nodded. "I checked the attic, and we're going to need a support beam."

"I assumed we would. I also want to join the two smaller bedrooms down the hall to make a master. And we can make a second guest master upstairs with the full bath next to the smallest room. We can put another half bath under the stairs." She pointed out her plans on the blueprint.

"Looks good. Nice and airy." He slid the hammer in his hand back into his tool belt.

She knelt and examined the floors. "These look like solid oak. I think we can save them. I know where to get lookalikes to fill in where the gaps are after we take down the walls."

"That's what I thought." Jason paused and studied her face. "Any updates about Mac yet?"

"No, they have no leads on what happened to her." She reached up and brushed drywall dust from his hair.

He frowned. "You said you were investigating. What have you found out?"

She couldn't tell him about the terrorist angle. He'd been too ready to believe the worst about Mac, and she didn't have the strength to defend her sister.

"What about the missing cocaine? Is the Coast Guard still fingering Mac for that?"

She looked away at his eager expression. All he wanted to hear was dirt about Mac. "Well, yes. There's a video that shows her directing two other men where to load it. There's not much doubt she took it, but I'm sure there was a good reason. I just have to find out what it was."

"I'm not surprised. She pulled the wool over your eyes for years. She wasn't the Girl Scout you've always thought she was."

He was talking about Mac like she was dead, and Ellie wasn't ready to accept that. "I think someone made her take it."

He took his cap off and ran his hand through his sun-streaked brown hair. "You have the evidence right in front of you, but you refuse to see it. I don't even know what to say to you."

She touched his arm. "You loved her once. How can you be so hard-hearted?"

"I have known her since we were in school, Ellie. She always wanted more. When you redid your bedroom with new paint and linens, she talked your parents into getting that big canopy bed that cost twice as much. When you were asked to the prom by that one boy, she worked on him until he withdrew his invitation and asked her."

Ellie took a step back. "I never held it against her."

His dark brows drew together. "You should have. Everything had to be about her, and she couldn't stand it when attention landed on you. You have never seen it, though." He jerked his hammer out again and slammed it against the next wall to come down.

Ellie rolled up her blueprints and went to get her tools. She'd always considered Mac her best friend, not just her sister. Mac depended on her. Before she ever made a decision, she called to talk it over with Ellie. Before she took the university job, she asked Ellie's opinion.

Was everything about her life a lie? Even though Jason disliked Mac, the things he'd pointed out were true. Mac had needed attention like a baby needed milk. Ellie had always assumed it was because Mac was the youngest. It was understandable.

Her head throbbed, and she rubbed her temple. She hated conflict, especially with people she loved. With her work she was in her element. Take down that wall, open up that space, raise that ceiling, and put a window in there. Design a house the way she wanted it, and she had a sense of satisfaction as she walked around and looked at her handiwork.

Why didn't life cooperate like that?

She glanced at the time on her phone. There was a meeting about the festival at three, and she needed to be there. If she was going to probe everything Mac was involved with, she needed to look at the tall ship flotilla coming to town. Mac had been obsessed with it. There might be a clue there.

City Hall used to be a mercantile back in the last century. The committee overseeing the festival met in a space in the back of the basement, cramped quarters with no windows. It always had a musty smell. Ellie looked through the tiny pane in the door and saw everyone was there.

Isaac Cohen noticed her and motioned for her to come in. She pulled open the door and stepped into the room. "I hope you don't mind my visit."

Isaac shook his head. "If this is about what happened to Mac, any one of us would do anything we could to help."

"It is." She advanced to the front of the room and turned to face the group of six.

She knew all of them: Isaac, Felicia Burchell, attorney Kristy Gillings, Stuart Ransom, and Michelle Diskin, whose eyes filled the moment she saw Ellie. The person she was most surprised to see was her employee, Clint, but she shouldn't have been. He was very interested in politics.

Ellie focused her attention on the most sympathetic face in the group—Michelle's. "I'm sure you've all heard the rumor about Mac stealing a seizure of cocaine from the Coast Guard."

Fire flashed in Michelle's eyes. "It's ludicrous."

She'd talk to Michelle privately and tell her what she knew, but right now Ellie didn't want to feed the rumor mill more. "I'm trying to re-create Mac's last weeks. She was very passionate about the tall ship flotilla coming. What can you tell me about the progress of it?"

Isaac pulled a chair up for her. "Have a seat, Ellie. I know it's been a hard week."

"Thanks." It felt a little cozier sitting at the same level as the rest of them.

Kristy Gillings tucked a graying strand of hair behind her ear. She looked like a frumpy housewife, but she had one of the finest legal minds in the state. "The fleet will be here a week from tomorrow. The festival is on Saturday, but they're getting in a few days early. The Parade of Sail wraps up the event on Sunday morning, then the boats will dock for tours through end of day Monday. Twenty tall ships from three countries will be here. Mac's idea was really genius. We've already sold three times the tickets we expected. I'm glad we didn't cancel it."

Ellie frowned. "Cancel it?"

Felicia looked stunning in a deep-red sheath dress. When she rose to get a glass of water, the men in the room watched her. She handed the glass to Ellie. "You know Mac was passionate about the tall ship plan. Did you know she changed her mind the day before her death?"

Ellie curled her fingers around the cup. "I-I don't under-stand. Mac talked of nothing else for weeks and weeks. Why would she want to cancel it? She never said anything about it to me."

Felicia settled back in her chair and crossed shapely legs. "It surprised all of us too. We'd gone too far and had actually paid the organizers in full by the time she made her request. We couldn't pull out."

"But she had to talk you all into it."

Felicia nodded. "I know. She didn't have a good reason for why she wanted to cancel it. She kept saying something about it being dangerous. I don't know if she thought one of the ships would run aground or what. She rushed out of our meeting quite upset, almost desperate." Felicia's dark-brown eyes held compassion.

"I'm stunned. That's all I can say. Is there anything else?"

Stuart leaned forward. "She said something about having to talk to Terrance Robb. You might ask him if he knows why she wanted to cancel it. We were all surprised."

"He's already gone."

"No, he's still in town for a birthday party for his wife. It's next Friday night at her parents' house. You might try to contact him then."

"Thank you, I'll do that." Ellie tossed back the small cup of water, then crumpled it in her hand. "I'd better let you get on with your meeting."

Isaac walked her to the door and took her hand. "Let me know if there's anything else you need. Mac was important to all of us."

"I will." She rushed out of the musty room and up the stairs to push through the door into the sunshine. The fresh air cleared the dankness from her lungs.

Why would Mac have wanted to cancel the big coup she'd worked so hard for? Ellie pulled out her phone and called Grayson.

"I was about to call you. Are you done for the day? I just saw Dylan heading into Harvey's Pier."

"I can come now. I was wondering if you could get an invitation to a birthday party next Friday." She explained what she'd found out. "Candace Robb's dad is a Coastie, and I thought they'd probably be in attendance at their daughter's party so maybe you could get an invitation. I need to talk to Terrance Robb."

"I think I can manage that. When is it?"

"On Friday night."

"I'll see what I can do. Meet you at Harvey's Pier."

Things were spiraling out of control. With all the information being tossed at her head, Ellie had no idea what to believe about her sister.

Chapter 21

Repairing doors and locks is like riding a bike.
Once you learn how, you never forget.
—HAMMER GIRL BLOG

When Mackenzie opened her eyes, she saw nothing. Total blackness pressed in on her from every side. She bit back a groan as she struggled to sit up. Her head throbbed in time with her heartbeat, and she touched a warm, sticky substance at her temple and found the skin stitched together at her hairline.

The springs underneath her squeaked a protest as she swung her legs over the side, and she ran her fingers along the surface of the mattress and down the bed frame. She appeared to be lying on a narrow metal cot. How long had she been here? Days or hours? She thought it might be days.

She forced herself to stand and groped along the wall in the dark. She smashed her shin against cold porcelain. A toilet.

She skirted it and continued around the next corner where she came to a door. She tugged on the knob, but she was so weak she could barely turn it. By her calculations the space seemed to be the size of a small bedroom, but the lack of windows and the dank smell told her she was likely in a basement.

This wasn't the way it was supposed to happen. She and Tarek were supposed to be together, and she'd intended to talk him out of his plans. But the attack had come out of the blue. Had he found out what she'd done?

Her throat and chest tightened, and she forced herself to take slow breaths. Calmer, she ran her fingers over the latch and door-knob, both old and crusty with rust. She pressed her ear to the latch and heard the faint trickle of water. No amount of screaming would lift her voice out of this deep hole, so she didn't waste her strength.

She touched the wall on the other side of the door and felt a light switch. She flipped it on, and light flooded the room. She flinched and closed her eyes until they began to adjust, then lifted her lids and peered around the room. A bare bulb swung from an open socket above her head. Cracks spidered across the concrete floor, and the only furnishings in the space were the cot and the old, stained toilet.

Only then did she look down at herself. She wore a hospital gown, but there were still traces of blood on her skin. Her arm ached, and she saw a puncture and the stickiness left by IV tape. Her head swam a bit, and she tottered to the cot and sat down with a *thump*, then put her head between her legs until her vision cleared.

Did she have anything she could use to pick the lock? When the dizziness abated, she stood and saw her jeans hanging over the end of the bed. She stuck her hands into the pockets of her jeans but came up with only lint. The cot felt a long way down as she dropped back onto its hard, lumpy surface. She had to get out of here.

Her head continued to throb, but the light-headedness began to ease. She slid off the cot onto her knees and looked the bed over. The legs screwed onto the frame, and she tried to twist the one at the bottom right side. The rust had it stuck fast, so she tried the other bottom one. It moved slightly under her fingers, but before she could get it loose, she heard footsteps outside the door.

She scrambled back to the cot and sat waiting with her pulse galloping in her chest. Her vision blurred again, and she put her head between her legs for a moment. When the hinges on the door screeched, she lifted her head. She clutched her hands together in her lap and tried to compose herself as a beautiful Asian woman entered the room.

She wore a deep-blue dress that complemented her figure. "Your meal." She spoke English but with a slight Korean accent, and her gaze flickered over Mac and dismissed her.

Mac staggered to her feet. "Please, I need medical attention. I've lost a lot of blood."

The woman shook her head and backed toward the door. "You aren't dying, if that's what you think. You've received the best of care, a transfusion and IV nutrition. It's not up to me what is done with you."

What is done with you. Mac swallowed, then wet her lips. Could she rush the woman and overpower her? Even as her muscles tensed for an attack, a fresh wave of dizziness blurred her vision, and she sank back onto the mattress. "Who are you? My name is Mackenzie."

"I know who you are. And why you're here."

Mac switched to Korean. "Why am I here? I don't know you. Are you Hyun?"

The woman Wang loved answered in Korean. "Ah, you've heard of me. I know what you tried to do to us, to Wang. He was wise to your ways, and I'll do anything I can to make sure you don't hurt him." She clamped her lips shut and stepped through the door, then slammed it behind her. The lock clicked into place.

Mac exhaled and blinked back the moisture in her eyes. Crying wouldn't help her now. Her worst fears were realized, and she was helpless to warn the authorities.

A Beatles tune blared from the jukebox as Grayson held open the door for Ellie at Harvey's Pier. The place was along the waterfront, and from the scent of fish and lobster inside, the food was going to be good and fresh. For a second he wished he could just sit across the table and look at Ellie rather than talk to a dirtbag like Trafford. He liked catching the expressions that flitted across her expressive face. He thought about hiding her glasses from her way too often.

He did a quick scan of the place. Fishnets draped from the wood walls painted the color of driftwood, and the wide plank floors underfoot made him feel as if he were on a boat. Through the expansive windows, he could see the blue water of Rainshadow Bay.

Ellie tugged on his arm. "There he is."

He followed her gaze to the pool table against the back wall.

Dylan was cuing up with another Coastie, a young man about the same age with hair so blond it was almost white.

He glanced down at her and wished he hadn't brought her. Something about the confrontation felt dangerous. Trafford was a hothead, and Grayson wouldn't be surprised to see the guy swing a pool stick at one of them, especially if he'd been drinking.

He watched Trafford take a swig from a beer. "You could grab us a table while I talk to him."

She shook her head. "He might talk to me. I think he really did care about Mac."

She might be right, but he didn't have to like it. He took her arm and steered her through the packed tables.

Trafford straightened as they approached, and his wary gaze flitted to Ellie, then back to Grayson. "Did you find Mac's body?"

Ellie shook her head. "We still don't know what happened to her. I was hoping you might help us."

"She dumped me, remember?" He bent over the pool table and cued up, then took his shot. A blue ball thumped into the left corner pocket.

His partner eyed them. "Talk to you later, Dylan." He put down his pool stick and fled.

Ellie took a step closer. "I saw the video, Dylan. We know she was involved in removing the cocaine from the Coast Guard hangar. Do you have any idea where she intended to take it? Were you in on it too?"

He jerked around with the pool stick in his hand. "That's a lie! I had nothing to do with it, and I don't believe Mac did either. That would mean . . ." He swallowed hard.

"Mean what?" Grayson prompted.

"That she only went out with me to locate the cocaine."

Grayson hadn't looked at how long they'd dated. "You only went out after the cocaine seizure?"

Trafford grabbed the neck of his beer bottle and took another swig. "She introduced herself in that booth right there." He pointed to a booth near the jukebox. "I was sitting by myself, and she came up to congratulate me. Said she'd heard about the seizure and wanted to meet the man instrumental in it."

"Were you? Instrumental, I mean?" Ellie asked.

"Not really, but she was all wide eyed and admiring so I couldn't burst her bubble." His shoulders slumped, and he laid the pool stick down on the table. "Looking back, I have to wonder, you know?"

Grayson examined the misery in Trafford's face. Poor guy really did seem to care about Mackenzie, and Grayson was beginning to believe the young woman didn't deserve Ellie's loyalty. She had dark depths. He'd hoped he was wrong, but it wasn't looking that way.

"Where might she have taken the cocaine?"

"I would think she'd sell it. I assume it hasn't hit the street yet?"

"Not that we can tell. I suppose it could have gotten out of the country, but we've been watching smuggling routes pretty closely. I think she took it somewhere here."

Ellie's chin jutted out. "I think she was forced to do it."

Trafford barked out a derisive laugh. "No one coerces your sister into anything."

Color swept up Ellie's neck and lodged in her cheeks. "You don't know her as well as I do."

Trafford lifted a brow. "I think maybe you don't know

Mackenzie as well as you think you do. That girl had dark layers. Lots of them."

Ellie opened her mouth, then closed it again with a scowl. Grayson knew she wanted to argue but didn't have any proof to offer. Was any of this getting through to her? It was one thing to be loyal and another thing to be stubbornly blind. She needed to realize her sister wasn't who she thought she was.

Grayson would have to handle this now. "Any sign she might be part of a terror cell?"

Trafford rolled his eyes. "Get real. She was no terrorist."

Grayson watched him shift from foot to foot and glance toward the door. "Thanks for your help. If you think of anything else, would you give me a call?" He passed his card to Trafford, then took Ellie's arm and steered her to an empty booth.

Chapter 22

Not just any hammer will do. Select
the right one for the job.
—HAMMER GIRL BLOG

E llie flung herself into the booth and wished she could throw
something. "Why does everyone say such terrible things
about Mac? You could tell by talking to him that he had something to do with this. He doesn't want you to be suspicious of
him, so he's making sure you believe Mac did it on her own."

Grayson's blue eyes held a dark shadow. "Ellie, I think he was
telling the truth. He seemed genuinely hurt at the thought that
Mac was using him to get to the cocaine."

The words slammed into her heart. "Gray, you said you'd
keep an open mind, that you'd look at all the options."

He smiled. "Only my sister calls me Gray. It sounds good
coming from you." He reached across the table to take her hand.

"I've been doing that. And you promised you'd keep an open mind too. I don't think you want to face Mac's true character."

The warm press of his fingers did something funny to her pulse, and she pulled her hand away. "Where is my sister? Or at the very least, her body?"

"I wish I knew, honey."

The endearment threw her for a moment. She liked this guy with his broad shoulders and caring manner way too much. It was hard to believe she'd only met him a week ago. "Nothing makes sense."

"Maybe it doesn't." His gaze softened, and he shrugged. "I don't see how all the dots connect, not yet. I don't like how I was taken off the case. That points to something bigger than we might realize."

"An EMP bomb?"

"Maybe." A troubled frown settled on his forehead. "I wouldn't want anything to happen to you. Maybe I should follow orders and back off."

Warmth spread into her chest, and she couldn't look away. "I-I'm sure I'll be fine. Even if you back off, I'm not going to. They can't make me. Mac is my sister."

"I worry about you."

"I don't want someone hovering over me. I can take care of myself. If nothing else, I have my hammer."

He grinned. "Hammer Girl. That's a good nickname for you. I've yet to see you swing a hammer with intent."

"I have a blog by that name. It's got a pretty good following. Come out to the House at Saltwater Point and watch me. You wouldn't believe all we've got done."

"I'll have to do that." His phone dinged, and he pulled it

from his pocket to view it. "Looks like my date and I are invited to the Robb birthday bash next weekend. Black tie." He glanced up from the phone and grinned. "I wouldn't wear a monkey suit for just anyone. I'll have to rent a tux, and you'll have to buy a new dress."

Her chest squeezed. "I don't think I've ever gone shopping for a new dress without Mac's advice."

He waggled a brow at her. "My sister Izzy would tell you I have an accurate eye for what looks good on her. I could go with you. How about we head to Seattle tomorrow? We could talk Shauna into flying us in her chopper."

It was an appealing idea, and she could no more say no than she could stop breathing. "Okay." Her voice sounded a little breathless. "If she's busy, we could go to Port Townsend. They have a few shops."

"Nope, we're going to Seattle. Only the best for this shindig. If Shauna is busy, Zach would probably fly us. Let me check." He bent his head over the phone as he texted Shauna and Zach.

What kind of guy offered to go dress shopping? Not a single one of her friends had ever talked about their husbands taking them shopping for clothes. Most men wouldn't be caught dead in a women's department.

He looked up and caught her gaze. "What?"

"Just wondering if you have an ulterior motive. You're going to toss me out of the chopper to shut me up, right?"

His mouth eased into a grin. "You figured it out." His phone dinged again, and he pumped his fist in a triumphant gesture. "Yes! Shauna is snickering about it, but for your sake I'll endure her mockery."

A chuckle erupted from her, and she put her hand over her

mouth. "I think we should record tomorrow's events. No one will believe it if I tell them."

"I hope you're not telling anyone. My reputation as a big, bad dude might be compromised." His grin widened. "Want to go for a run after dinner? I haven't had any exercise since I got here."

"You might have to carry me."

"I'm game."

She smiled back. "Okay, let's give it a try."

The server arrived with menus and Ellie took one, then peeked over it at Gray. She liked him way too much for her own peace of mind.

Mackenzie's headache had finally subsided to a dull roar instead of a full-on scream, and she wasn't quite as dizzy. She hoped she was beginning to recover. Her fingers throbbed from unscrewing the bed leg. She sat on the cold, hard floor and studied the metal appendage she'd managed to obtain after hours and hours of weak effort. What had she thought to do with it? It was only six inches long and had no sharp edges.

She palmed the end that connected to the frame and brought up the smaller tip in a swooping arc. It might work as a weapon if she managed to thrust it into someone's eye. The thought of doing that made her stomach roil. She started to discard the bolt, then thought better of it and stuck it in her pocket.

The soup the woman had brought had congealed in the bowl, but Mac reached over and pulled the tray closer. She had to be strong enough to attack. She forced herself to slurp down the nasty mess, then tossed back the tepid water. Her stomach rebelled a bit, and she swallowed hard to keep it down. The nausea gradually subsided, and she felt stronger when she rose and went to the door.

There was no sound on the other side. How long before someone came to check on her again? Hours probably. She dug the bolt out of her pocket. It might not fit through the keyhole. She squatted in front of the door and inserted the bolt. It didn't go in at first, and she maneuvered it until it scraped through, but it needed to have a bend in it to unlock the door.

She and Ellie had helped their dad around the house many times over the years, and she'd helped Ellie and Jason often enough with their remodeling business. Though they'd never come up against an antique lock like this, she knew how it worked by principle. What else could she use to pick the lock?

She glanced at the tray the woman had brought in. The spoon handle might work if she could bend it. She grabbed it, then lifted the cot and placed the tip of the spoon under one leg. Sitting on the cot for weight and leverage, she bent down and pulled on the spoon. It was flimsy and bent easily. This just might work.

Heartened, she went back to the door and began to manipulate the bent end of the spoon in the skeleton keyhole. The click reverberated through the metal, and she tried the door. It opened easily, but the squeak and scrape of the hinges froze her in place for a minute. When no one came thumping down the steps, she slipped out of the room and looked around in the dark space.

A dirty window let in a bit of light in spite of the cobwebs covering it. She didn't think she could squeeze through the opening if she broke the glass pane. She went past the rickety steps to a door on the back wall. When she heard no sound on the other side, she pushed it open to find a dank space filled with boxes and another tiny, dirty window. No escape there, but maybe she could summon help through one of the windows.

She walked toward the window farthest away from the steps and stepped onto some boxes. The broken glass looked out onto an empty parking lot overgrown with weeds. The area didn't seem familiar, and scraggly pine trees pressed close to the perimeter of the cracked concrete. How far had they brought her? She went to the room with the steps and peered through the window, only to be greeted with the same view.

She turned and stared at the steps. It was her only way out. Was anyone upstairs? She hadn't heard any noise since the woman had brought down lunch. Only one way to find out. The first step creaked when she put her weight on it, and she froze. The door remained closed, and she heard no steps. She braved another step, then another until she reached the top of the steps and touched the doorknob. Was it locked?

But no, the knob turned easily under her fingers, and she stepped out of the stairwell into what appeared to be a deserted office building. Debris littered the floor, and bullet holes and broken panes let in light past the dirt. Where was this place and how did she get to civilization?

Before she could decide what to do, the sound of tires crunching on pavement near the front door set her rushing for the back door. She had to get out of here before they came in and discovered her gone. The door wasn't locked, and she walked outside into the late-afternoon sunlight.

The forest was a good two hundred feet away, but she ran

that way, gasping with weakness. It would take several minutes for them to go downstairs and find out she'd flown the coop. With any luck, they wouldn't realize she had just escaped.

The coolness of the forest was like a balm. She plunged through the trees, then spared a glance back at the building. The back door was still shut, and no one was racing after her. Not yet. Maybe she'd escape this after all. She picked her way through the tangle of fallen limbs and tangled vines. Could she be tracked? She looked behind and saw her footprints in the damp weeds as clearly as if she'd walked through cement.

Maybe there would be a stream up ahead where she could mask her path. She rushed on, trying to ignore how the thumping in her head had resumed. At times she felt so weak and dizzy she had to stop and bend over at the waist until her sight cleared. Her path grew darker as the large trees blocked out more of the sunlight. She reached a run-down fence topped with barbed wire. There was no way she could climb it without getting entangled. She gave it a violent shake. There had to be a way. She hadn't come this far just to be captured again.

The bottom of the fence was loose in spots. Maybe she could scoot under. She fell to her knees, then army crawled under the fence. That wasn't so hard. She staggered to her feet, then back into the forest. There seemed to be a deer path or something. Reeling like a drunken person from fatigue and light-headedness, she followed it to a knoll and looked down into a clearing where a charming cottage sat. An old pickup was parked in the drive as well as a motorcycle. Surely they'd help her.

She hurried down the slope to the back door and peeked through the window into the kitchen. It appeared empty, but surely someone was here. There was that truck.

A hard hand gripped her forearm. "There you are, Mac. I thought we'd have to get dogs to track you, but you came right home to me."

She whirled to stare into the face of the handsome man sporting a thick mass of black curls on his head. Tarek Nasser himself. No amount of yanking and squirming could tug her arm out of his powerful grasp.

The run was just what Grayson needed. He could almost feel the blood pumping through his veins. When was the last time he'd seen a sunset like this? Maybe never.

The road ran along the top of a cliff overlooking Rainshadow Bay, then veered through tall stands of Sitka spruce, maple, and Douglas fir that shielded an understory of lady fern and stair-step moss. A black-tailed deer darted across the road in front of them, and a bald eagle soared overhead.

A sharp cramp hit his wounded leg, and Grayson bent over and gasped for air, then massaged his left calf muscle. "Cramp. Go ahead without me. I'll catch up."

She stopped and wiped her forehead. "I need to catch my breath. I'm not used to jogging."

He rubbed his knotted muscles. A thrush peered at them from a huckleberry bush, and he wished they had some bread to throw to it. They were deep in the Olympic Forest, and the quiet of the woods was like an embrace. He really liked it here.

A black Taurus idled toward them. The windows were tinted, but he had a vague impression of a man with his face obscured by a ball cap. Adrenaline shot up his spine as the car slowed to a stop.

Hadn't Ellie said something about her truck being rear-ended by a black Taurus?

He knew when she caught sight of it because her amber eyes went wide, and she stepped farther into the ditch. "Grayson . . ."

"I see it. Get down." He yanked out his Sig Sauer and planted his feet.

She dove for the weeds in the ditch as the darkened window lowered on the driver's side and the barrel of a gun appeared. The first bullet came his way, not hers, and he returned fire as he dove into the ditch too. There was water in the weeds, and he was soaked instantly.

"Stay down." Keeping his head below the top of the ditch, he crawled through the weeds toward the front of the car. He wanted to catch this guy. He aimed at the tires first and fired at the front driver's side. His angle was bad from here, and the bullet ricocheted off the fender.

In the next moment the car engine revved and the vehicle peeled away, spitting gravel into Grayson's face. He leaped out of the ditch and fired after it. He might have hit a rear tire, but the car sped out of sight.

He helped Ellie up. She was pale, and scratches marred her beautiful face from her tumble into the ditch. Grayson wished he'd had the opportunity to grab the dirtbag.

He pulled out his phone to make notes. "Did you get a look at him?"

Ellie quit rubbing her wrists for a moment. "I didn't see his face. He was wearing a black baseball cap. He was brown skinned, though. I saw a black T-shirt."

"I saw him, but his cap shaded his face and I mostly saw his nose, mouth, and chin. He was clean shaven with a square jaw.

His nose was a little on the big side. Thin lips. Late twenties maybe."

Her dry throat clicked when she swallowed. "I'm so tired of this. Who is following us, and what did he do to my sister?"

"He seemed to be aiming at me."

"You're right. I assumed I was the target after the way the car ran me off the road. Why you?"

"Maybe one of Nasser's henchmen." Grayson rose. "I'll go with you to your house. There's no one there, right?"

"No, Jason is working. I'd appreciate the support." She stood too.

"I need coffee."

"Me too."

He wished they didn't have to jog back. They were sitting ducks out here. He kept his gun out and ready as they ran back to her place. It would be a long night by the time they made a report to the sheriff.

No matter how hard he tried, Grayson was no closer to finding who had taken the cocaine or Mackenzie. Waiting for the next shoe to drop felt like a gathering storm, electric with brooding danger.

Nasser must be getting desperate to get rid of him. He'd have to stay on alert every second.

Chapter 23

*The right clothing is always important, and never
more so than when engaging in construction. Sturdy
denim and long sleeves help protect you from injury.*
—Hammer Girl Blog

Several women glanced at Gray as his long legs sprawled halfway into the aisle where he sat in an armchair near the dressing room. Ellie could see the admiration on their faces as they eyed him, then glanced at her with quizzical looks as if to ask what he saw in her.

She had to agree. It was no use getting herself in a tizzy over him because he wasn't going to be here long, and she wasn't the glamour girl a man like him would be likely to gravitate to. Especially not with last night's scratches on her face.

She forced her gaze away from him and looked around. The boutique had an understated elegance that made her worry before glancing at the prices, but luckily the dresses she'd grabbed to try on were on sale and something she could afford.

Shauna, dressed in white capris and a red top, had four dresses slung over her arm too. "I'll go in with you to button you up if you want."

Felicia held up her phone. "I've got the camera and I'm recording it." Shauna had suggested inviting her, and Ellie had been quick to agree. Felicia had the best taste in town. And she was fun to be around.

Gray sat up. "Camera? I think I'm in trouble."

Ellie smiled at him. "Told you I wanted proof of this. You sure you don't want to go across the street and get some coffee?"

He quirked an eyebrow. "Nope. I have an eye for what looks good. I'm sitting right here so you don't make a mistake. Besides, one of the clerks is already bringing me coffee and a muffin."

Ellie had seen the beautiful brunette dancing attendance on him. "Well, if you're sure. I'll be out in a minute."

Felicia entered the large dressing room and hung up the gowns on her arm, then stepped aside for Shauna to hang the four she carried. Disrobing in front of Shauna felt a little awkward, but her friend turned her back to ready the first dress. Ellie slipped out of her capris and shirt, then ducked her head for Shauna to drop the cocktail dress over her head.

Ellie had asked for neutral colors in this first batch, and she tried on the beige one first. Felicia frowned when she came out in it but said nothing as she recorded the moment.

Gray shook his head. "Too bland."

She went back for the next dress and the next. With every dress Gray frowned and shook his head. "Too boring" or "too shapeless" were the most common remarks from everyone.

Felicia's dimple emerged, and she put down the phone a moment. "This man has a good eye. Think you can do better than me, Grayson? I'll pick one and you pick one."

"You're on." He rose and flexed his fingers, then dove into the rows of dresses and surfaced with three—a deep-blue off-the-shoulder mermaid dress with a daring back, a pink one with a lace overlay, and a flirty number with a flared organza skirt.

None of them were anything she would have chosen herself.

Felicia had two slinky numbers over her arm, one green and one turquoise. "Try these."

Ellie thought all of them were much too flashy, but she exhaled and nodded. "Let me try them on."

Felicia whipped out her phone again. "Wait, I have to record this. It might encourage Everett to come shopping with me sometime." She recorded Grayson handing Ellie the dresses he'd chosen.

Ellie wrinkled her nose as she took them. "Really? Your fashion judgment is about to go down in flames."

Felicia snickered. "I'm still recording. You should see your face." She tucked her phone away again. "Let's see how they look on you."

"I'm not sure I want to."

Shauna tugged on her arm. "He might know what he's talking about, and I'm sure Felicia does." She held open the curtain for Ellie to enter the room again, then closed it behind them.

Ellie shucked the last dress, a white lace number that had little shape and washed out her skin. "I guess I didn't do so well myself." She bent her head for Shauna to drop the blue over her shoulders first.

"Turn around and I'll zip it. I love that color." Shauna's

cool fingers pulled on the zipper and slid it up to the nape of Ellie's neck.

Ellie stared in the mirror, hardly recognizing herself. The deep blue made her eyes look bigger and mysterious behind her glasses, and her light-brown hair glowed with blonde lights. She actually had curves in this dress too, and a slit up the side showed flirty glimpses of her leg.

"Ooh, I love it. Go see what Grayson says." Shauna pulled back the curtain on the dressing room for her.

Ellie's stomach fluttered at the prospect of facing Gray in this dress. It seemed too revealing, though it was modest by most standards.

Shauna gave her a little push. "Go on."

There was no getting out of it now. She walked on bare feet in front of all the mirrors as well as Gray's gaze and Felicia's ever-present phone camera.

His blue eyes widened when he saw her, and he sat up straighter. "That's a keeper. You look beautiful."

She almost choked. Beautiful? No one had ever told her she was beautiful.

"Don't even try on anything else. That's the dress." Felicia smiled at Grayson. "I might take you shopping with me next time."

Ellie smoothed her palms over the fabric at her hips. "Isn't it a little too, um . . . I don't know the word."

"Sexy?" he suggested. "I might have to fight off the other guys at the party, but I'm up to the challenge even with a bum leg. I think Felicia is right, and you don't even need to try on the others. This is the one I liked the best anyway. Go change, and I'll take you ladies to lunch. I hear Dick's is a Seattle icon and has the best burgers and milkshakes in the state. I vote for that."

Did she dare buy this dress? She liked seeing the light in his eyes when he looked at her, but it made her self-conscious at the same time. The beige dress with a concealing jacket would be safer. And this one was probably expensive.

Gray's eyes narrowed. "What's going through that pretty head? Don't even think about getting one of the other dresses."

Trapped. She glanced at Shauna and Felicia and saw no allies there. It was only one evening. She could wear this dress to the party, then hang it up in her closet and forget about it.

"If you're sure." She ducked back into the dressing room and pulled on her safe capris and top. It was like Cinderella returning to her torn and dirty clothing. With the blue dress hanging over her arm, she emerged to find Gray handing over his debit card at the register.

"You can't do that!" She tried to grab his card back, but he blocked her move, and the clerk came around to get the dress and bag it.

"You wouldn't have bought it if not for me, and I'm not positive you'll wear it if you spend your own money on it." He scribbled his signature on the receipt. "This is insurance."

In a daze she followed him out into a light Seattle drizzle. There was no stopping him.

Mackenzie's head pounded as Tarek shoved her through the cabin to a couch in front of a massive stone fireplace. The scent of old smoke still lingered in the worn furniture. Her legs wobbled, and she nearly fell onto the sofa cushion, which sank under her weight.

Tarek Nasser wasn't anyone to mess with, but she tried to

tamp down the fear. He could smell it like a tiger stalking prey. Why had she once thought he was so wonderful?

She wet her lips and stared up at him as he paced back and forth across the faded rug. "C–Could I have some water?"

He stopped and shook his head. "Only someone as foolish as you would think I would offer any comforts like water."

She didn't like his derisive tone or the way he studied her. "Why did you do this to me? I thought you loved me."

"Love?" He quirked a brow. "I'm sure you know why you're here."

She shuffled on the sofa and tried to see any weapon in her peripheral vision, but the room didn't hold much, just the sofa, a chair, and the rug. No tables with any heavy ashtrays. "I don't, actually."

He snorted, and his face reddened. "I have an incompetent team. Why wasn't your sister at your boat? They were supposed to take both of you."

It felt like a giant hand took hold of her heart. She'd done what she did to save Ellie and so many others, not to draw her in deeper. "Leave Ellie out of this."

His mouth twisted, and his dark eyes narrowed. "Don't play dumb with me. You told her to grab that mah-jongg tile set, didn't you?"

"What are you talking about?"

"Your sister is meddling in my business. She's going to have to be eliminated."

"No!"

His grin held no real mirth. "You shouldn't have crossed me, Mackenzie. Who have you told about our plans?"

"No one! Not even Ellie." Why hadn't the FBI stopped this?

Now Ellie was mixed up in this too, and Mac had no idea how to get her away from this maniac. "Why do you even care about Ellie?"

"I can't run the risk that she'll turn the mah-jongg tiles over to the authorities."

"So take the tiles. You don't have to take her."

He grimaced. "We can't find them. Bradshaw may have even gotten hold of them by now. My men tried to eliminate him yesterday, but he got away. He always seems to get away, like a snake growing another head."

He pulled a phone from the pocket of his khaki slacks and held it toward her. "Text her and ask her to meet you."

She took a step back. "Absolutely not!"

"You'll do what I say, or I'll kill you now myself."

"You'll have to do it then. I'm not going to text her." Goading him wouldn't gain her any ground, but she couldn't help herself.

"I'll do it myself."

"No!" She darted forward and grabbed the phone from his hand, then turned and threw it with all her might against the fireplace stones. It shattered into pieces.

His hard fingers bit into her arm. "I should strangle you now."

She smiled into his face. "Go ahead."

He hesitated, then threw her to the ground. "You're going back to the basement, and I'll make sure you don't escape again."

She'd blown her one attempt at escape, and all she could do was pray that Ellie figured out what was going on before it was too late for both of them.

Chapter 24

Living spaces for an extended family member are always handy. A good spot to build one is over the garage.
—HAMMER GIRL BLOG

The dark sky glittered with stars in a beautiful canopy overhead that Grayson could see through the windshield of his SUV. He glanced at his phone. Midnight. The lights at the Saltwater Point house had just gone out, so he hoped Ellie was able to get some rest. Man, she had looked so beautiful in that dress. He grinned and laid his seat back a bit to get more comfortable. The deputy's car was on the other side of the street and down about half a car length.

He turned the key on and ran both front windows down a few inches. The night temperature hovered around forty-five, and the ventilation would be enough to keep him cool. Ellie would be embarrassed to find him camped out here, but he'd felt uneasy knowing she was in there by herself. Maybe he should crash in a sleeping bag in the garage. He'd be able to stretch out his bum leg. She'd really flip out if she knew he'd camped out here both nights since she'd stayed here.

His iPad rested on the passenger seat, and he grabbed it to go over his notes. A shadow flitted across the yard, and he grinned when moonlight illuminated Ellie's face. She'd seen him out here and had marched out to confront him.

He opened his door and got out. "I thought you were asleep by now."

She wore a silky aqua nightgown decorated with lace around the neck. Her hair was down around her shoulders, and those glasses were nowhere in sight. He shoved his hands in his pockets to take them out of temptation's way. For an instant he had imagined testing the softness of the fabric billowing around her.

Crazy thoughts.

She put her hands on her hips and glared at him. "You can't stay out here all night."

He made a show of looking up and down the street. "Isn't this a public street? I don't see any deputy coming out to tell me to mosey on my way."

"You know what I mean, Grayson. The deputy is there." She pointed.

"Uh-oh, I'm really in trouble if you're not calling me Gray."

A smile emerged, albeit a feeble one. "I hate that you're not getting any rest."

His grin died. "One deputy was all the office could spare, and he's nearly retirement age. I don't think he's up to the challenge of dealing with this kind of threat. I don't want you to be unprotected when that time comes."

She sighed and tucked a lock of hair behind her ear. "You can't stand guard every night."

He folded his arms across his chest. "I'm not leaving you unprotected."

She folded her arms across her chest to mirror his action. "You're stubborn, you know that, right?"

"So my sister has told me. Isabelle, I mean."

She tipped her head to one side. "What does she have to say about all this change in your life?"

"She was taken aback too. I really should call my parents. I haven't talked to them since I left." His mother had texted a couple of times and he'd responded, but things were strained.

"Are you mad at them?"

He shrugged and looked away from her perceptive stare. "A little. I need to get over it."

Her gaze linked with his for a long moment before she moved away. "Well, I guess I'd better go inside. I wish you'd go home."

"Not gonna happen. I can sleep right here in the SUV. I'm a light sleeper. If you hear anything, just call or text me and I'll be right there."

"I know you're right—I just hate being dependent on anyone." She hesitated. "It's a mess in there, but there's another air mattress in the basement. I could throw it down for you."

Something about her pulled him like no other woman he'd ever been around. Her loyalty and sweet spirit combined in an enticing physical package to make her nearly irresistible. Maybe once this was all over he could think about getting to know her better.

"I wouldn't say no to a bed in the garage. I'd be right there if anyone tried to go up those steps."

She huffed, then smiled. "I guess I'll get that bed set up. I hate being someone who needs to be taken care of."

"Believe me, anyone up against these terrorists needs help." He grabbed his laptop and bag from his vehicle and followed her inside.

"What's with the shadows under your eyes?" Shauna stirred the spaghetti sauce on the stove and speared Grayson with a concerned stare.

Grayson liked looking at his new sister and figuring out if they had any similarities. Their coloring was different, but he thought he could see himself in the shape of her lips and the widow's peak in her black hair. He had one of those himself. She was very short and he was tall, but her fingers were long like his.

"You're staring at me." She wiped her hands on her jeans and gave him a cheeky grin. "Is that supposed to distract me from the way you're not answering my question?"

He sent her an answering grin. "Sorry, lost in thought. I camped out in the garage of the Saltwater Point house to make sure Ellie was all right last night. I don't like her staying alone."

"I don't either. We've got a spare room, but it's not furnished yet. Let me get some furniture for it tomorrow, and she can stay with us. Alex will be staying with his grandmother this week."

"Can I sleep on your sofa?"

She grinned. "What, you don't trust Zach and me to protect her?"

"It's this control thing I have."

"Zach is the same way. I was only teasing."

"And she hates having to ask for help."

Zach entered the kitchen and dropped a kiss on her head. "Sounds like someone I know."

She made a face at him, then lifted the spoon for him to taste the sauce. He gave it a thumbs-up, then went to make a fresh pot of coffee.

A slight smile played at Shauna's lips. "I've seen the way you look at her."

He rolled his eyes at her. "I admit I like her. She's spirited and fun, and she's pretty darn cute too."

"She is." Shauna wound her long black hair on top of her head and stuck a pencil in it. "Thanks for being so patient in church today when I introduced you as my long-lost brother."

After church all Shauna's friends had crowded around to shake his hand and introduce themselves. He couldn't remember a single name after they walked out, but he'd started to get to know them. "I enjoyed it. It's fun to get to know this place. I like it."

"I thought we might go out to the old cabin after we eat. If you want to, of course. You said you'd like to see where we used to live."

"That would be great."

Ellie entered the kitchen with Alex in tow. "What would be great?"

She'd changed from her pretty peach dress to jeans and a lacy green top. She was entirely too beautiful.

He got up from the stool at the kitchen bar to pour a cup of coffee. "We thought we'd go out to the place where Shauna and I lived as kids. I was hoping I might remember something."

She glanced at Shauna. "You want me to stay behind with Alex?"

He didn't want anything of the kind. "No, I'd like you to go." When she brightened, he looked away. He needed to rein in his growing feelings for her and remember the job he came here to do.

Zach ruffled Alex's hair. "I can stay here with Alex. We've got a Pac-Man game calling our names, don't we, buddy?"

"Yay! I was hoping you'd say that, *Dad*." Alex grinned as he emphasized the word *Dad*. "It's sad to go to Grandpa's house. I miss him."

Shauna and Zach must have given him the go-ahead to call Zach Dad. A good decision in Grayson's opinion.

Shauna finished the last touches on the pasta and carried it to the table, a wooden farm-style type that had a few scratches and crayon marks. "Let's eat. Alex, you can say grace."

They chatted about different people Grayson had met that morning as they ate, and he caught himself stealing glances at Ellie, who sat beside him. The night had gone quietly, and he'd driven home to grab breakfast and change for church before she came out to shoo him away again.

"I saw you talking to the sheriff and Felicia this morning," he said between mouthfuls. "Anything new to report?"

Ellie shook her head. "I asked him about Hodges' murder, but he was pretty tight-lipped."

"The FBI probably got to him."

Shauna rose and began to clear the table. "If we're all done, we can head out to the cabin."

"Alex and I will take care of the dishes." Zach took the plates out of her hands. "After our Pac-Man marathon, he and I will whip up sandwiches for supper."

Shauna kissed him. "You're wonderful. We'll be back in a few hours." She glanced at Grayson. "You want to drive?"

"Sure. My Tahoe will eat up the miles with no trouble." Did it make Ellie uncomfortable to realize he wanted her with him?

She didn't seem to think anything about it as Shauna climbed into the back seat and told her to take the front one. She fastened her seat belt and stared out the window.

The drive out to the cabin was quiet. Shauna tried to keep up a conversation, but she soon went silent when he only answered in short replies. His stomach tensed more and more as he drove along the rutted track that meandered through hills and valleys and over rocky soil.

He sucked in his breath when he first spied the cabin with its mossy roof. A tree swing still clung to its fraying rope, and he spied the remains of a tree house in the branches of the same large oak. He braked without thinking, then sat back and stared.

Shauna leaned forward. "You remember something?"

What did he remember? The soft sound of a woman's voice maybe. "A little. You used to swing me, didn't you?"

"It was your favorite. You want to get out and walk around?"

After coming all this way he could hardly say no, but he wanted to turn around and go the other direction. He turned off the engine and pocketed his key, then got out. His gut clenched as he approached the cabin, but the inside was nearly empty now, both of belongings and memories.

He needed to call his parents, but every time he started to place the call, he couldn't do it. The betrayal was too great. He wasn't sure what to say.

Chapter 25

Most construction workers aren't big, but they're strong.
We women get around that by using the proper tools.
—HAMMER GIRL BLOG

Monday morning Ellie had spied Gray's black SUV pulling away while she was making coffee. It was still dark outside. She'd planned to invite him in for breakfast, but he'd been too fast. She couldn't believe he had been there the last three nights. She couldn't continue to let him do that. A man that big couldn't be comfortable sleeping on the concrete floor of her garage.

They'd both stay at Shauna's tonight, though.

"Hey, Ells." Jason called to her from the front door, then clomped through the drywall dust and scattered nails to join her in the kitchen where she had perched the coffeepot on a piece of plywood. "What the heck is going on? You're not even dressed."

She looked down at her gauzy nightgown. "I slept in the garage suite." She told him about the man slicing her screen and trying to get in. And Ralph Hodges' murder. "With what happened to Mac, Gray didn't want me to stay there."

"I could stay with you. Why didn't you ask? You never want anyone to help you, and it ticks me off." He put his hands on his hips and glared at her. "I'm your friend. You can turn to me when you need help."

Shocked, all she could do was stand there with her mouth dangling open and stare into his angry face. He rarely got mad at her, but he was furious today. "I'm sorry. I should have talked to you about it."

His scowl lessened slightly, and he ran his hand through his hair. "I can't believe you'd really be in danger, though. Whatever happened to Mac, she brought it on herself."

It was an old argument, and one she wasn't going to win no matter how much she tried to change his mind. When he got like this, it was better to change the subject. "I'm going to tell the sheriff about the hidden room in this house and maybe have his techs search it."

"What hidden room?"

"In the basement. Let me show you."

She led the way to the dingy basement and showed him how a door was concealed in the paneling of the far wall. When she opened it, a sickly sweet odor wafted toward her. A dead rat maybe? She flipped on the light and blinked at the sight of a bloated body lying on the floor. Part of her tried to scream, but her throat locked up and not a sound made it past. Jason made a choking sound behind her. He grabbed her arm and rushed her up the stairs.

He clawed his phone out of his pocket. "I have to call the sheriff!"

She could tell from his side of the conversation that the dispatcher wanted him to stay on the line until the deputies arrived, but he refused and ended the call.

"They're on their way." His voice was subdued. "D–Did you recognize the body in that room?"

She shook her head. "I couldn't bear to look at him. He had black hair. That's all I saw."

"Yeah, I didn't know him either." He put his hand on her shoulder. "I'm sorry I doubted you, Ells. I should have known you well enough to realize you'd never overreact. I'd tell you to stay at my place, but you'd have to sleep on the couch, or I could take the couch and you could have my bed."

"Shauna has offered up her spare room, so I'm going there tonight. You're sweet to offer, though."

The sound of sirens grew louder. She opened the door and started to step out, but he caught her arm and stared at the porch. "Wait a minute, what's that?"

He darted past her and scooped up an old Pepsi bottle with a piece of paper sticking out of it. Turning with it in his hand, he yanked the paper from the top.

"Be careful. It could be booby-trapped."

"It's just a note." His expression was grim when he looked up. "Addressed to you."

A shiver made its way down her back. "You read it. I don't want to touch it."

"'Ellie, it's about time we meet. Get ready to die.'"

She gulped. "Well, that's pretty scary."

"He sounds crazy. The sheriff will want to see this." He

nodded down the street where a deputy's car rushed toward them. "I shouldn't have touched it, but I wasn't thinking."

From here she could see the block letters spelling out the letter, and she took a step back. *Get ready to die.* Like Mac and that poor man in the basement? Ralph Hodges too. She shuddered.

Grayson had spent the morning talking to possible witnesses to the cocaine theft. He'd gotten nowhere, but he was beginning to feel more and more at home in this place, and he appreciated the natural beauty of the mountains looming over the blue sea. For the first time he began to think about making this place his home base.

His phone sounded with a call from his mother as he parked in front of the sheriff's office. He clenched his fists and stared at her picture on his phone. Part of him wanted to let it go to voice mail, but that was the cowardly way out.

He took a calming breath and answered it. "Hey, Mom, I was just about to call you."

"You were never going to call." Her voice vibrated with anger. "You're being childish, Grayson. Your sister would never treat us this way. Anger is a useless emotion."

Mom always threw Izzy in his face, but he'd never blamed his sweet sister. This was all on their mother. "How did you think I'd feel when I found out you've lied to me all these years? This is why you've always held me at arm's length, isn't it? I've never been as good as Izzy in your eyes."

"That's not true, Grayson. I love you both equally."

The lack of conviction in her voice told him everything he needed to know. "Is Dad there?"

"No, he's deep-sea fishing."

He exhaled and drummed his fingers on the steering wheel. "I don't really know what to say to you, Mom. You haven't even said you're sorry." There was only silence on the other end of the line. "You're not sorry, are you? You'd do it all again."

"I-I didn't know if I could bond to you if you were always asking questions about your birth parents."

"And the sad truth is that you never bonded anyway. Don't try to convince me otherwise. I lived it."

"Don't shut us out, Gray." Her voice wobbled. "Isabelle is thinking about visiting us in a few weeks. You could come too, and we could talk all this out. We're still a family."

That much was true, but he wasn't ready to see her face-to-face. "I'll think about it. Listen, I have to go. Tell Dad I'll give him a call soon." At least Dad had wanted to tell him.

He got out of his SUV and headed into the sheriff's office, which was buzzing with activity instead of giving off its usual sleepy vibe. Rosa caught his wave, and she came to greet him at the counter.

"Busy day."

Her dark eyes were somber. "You haven't heard?"

"Heard what?"

"Ellie and Jason found a dead body in the hidden room in the basement. Around eight."

Right after he'd left. "Is she here?"

"She's back with the sheriff. She told me to ask you to join them if you came in."

He checked his messages and saw she'd texted him to come to the sheriff's office. Rosa escorted him to Sheriff Burchell's office, and he rapped his knuckles on the door. The sheriff opened the door and motioned him inside. Jason and Ellie were with him.

Ellie was seated in a chair and turned to face him when he entered. Her face was white and set. "You heard?"

"Rosa told me." He crossed the room and put his hand on her shoulder. "I'm so glad you're okay."

She covered his hand with hers. "The body and the note made it more real."

"What note?"

The sheriff went around his desk and picked up a paper. "This is a copy."

Grayson took it and scanned it. A shudder rippled down his spine at the malice in it. "This sounds personal. I don't get it."

Jason rose from the chair next to Ellie's and went to stare out the window. "I think someone is trying to scare her."

"He's doing more than scaring people. He's killing them."

Ellie's hand dropped away, and she shivered. "Clearly these are terrorists we're dealing with. But why target me? If Mac was involved, it had nothing to do with me."

He couldn't imagine her hurting anyone. Sweet, gentle Ellie was quick with an encouraging smile and word. He glanced at the sheriff. "Do you have an ID on the vic in the basement?"

"Not yet. Guy's Asian."

Grayson kept a protective hand on Ellie's shoulder and glared at the sheriff. "What are you going to do to protect her? She can't move into Shauna's now—not with Alex there. We can't risk his life."

"Or Shauna's and Zach's," Ellie said.

Where could he take her? These guys were pros. They'd killed that guy in a neighborhood surrounded by houses.

"We need a safe house."

Jason whirled from the window. "I know! Mac's ship. It will be hard for someone to get to it undetected if we're guarding it. They'll have to approach it in a boat. We can get a few of the townspeople to volunteer to help watch. I'll stay, of course."

Ellie shook her head. "I don't want anyone else in danger."

The sheriff looked up. "That's a good idea. Crime scene techs are done with it. I can probably swing some around-the-clock surveillance for a few days too." His lips twisted. "We're short staffed and under the gun with our budget."

Ellie rubbed her head. "I still can't believe this."

He'd scared her, and Grayson hadn't intended to upset her. "I'm staying on the boat with you too. You'll be safe."

Her face was pale, and her lips trembled. "I'm not sure any place is safe." Her gaze went stony and determined. "I have to work, though. I don't think they'll try anything in the daylight. I won't go to the house until it's light, and I'll return to the ship before it gets dark."

Grayson could see a dozen things wrong with her idea. "I don't like it."

"I don't either, but my carpenters are moving on to new jobs soon. I need to be there for the next two days to steer things in the right direction."

"I'll have a car parked outside her house," the sheriff said.

Grayson moved away and dropped into the chair next to her. "If we find out what happened to Mac, I bet it leads us right to whoever is behind this."

He was going to have to call in some chips with headquarters. They knew more than they were saying. Even if it meant losing his job, he would have to dig out the truth.

Chapter 26

*Just because construction isn't typically thought of
as a woman's job doesn't mean we aren't equipped
for it. We can do anything we set our minds to.*
—HAMMER GIRL BLOG

S hauna curled up on the sofa beside Zach. The two rott-weilers, Artemis and Apollo, snored at her feet, and Weasley lay belly up on her lap. She scratched the cat's belly and nestled under Zach's arm. He'd just taken allergy medicine, so the cat's presence should be all right for a while. "I should have called Grayson today."

He dropped a kiss on top of her head. "You don't want to smother him, honey. He still seems pretty shaken up by all of this. I think church was pretty overwhelming, too, with everyone coming up to him. And he's neck-deep in protecting Ellie."

"You think I'm expecting too much, don't you?"

"Maybe just too much too fast. He's got to figure out how to assimilate his adoptive family with his biological one."

"I have to admit I had a twinge of jealousy that he has another sister." She hated how petty she felt admitting it.

"It's understandable."

She sensed a coiled intensity in Zach, a distraction in his tone. Pulling away a bit, she looked up to study his beloved face with its strong jawline and steady gaze. "Something bugging you? Is it because I've been too focused on my brother? You're not feeling neglected, are you?"

He barked out a laugh and shook his head. "I wouldn't expect anything else, and I'm a little obsessed myself. I got a call from Grayson's sister Isabelle. She gave me the name of someone at CPS for me to talk to. I've tracked down the paramedic you found the day of the earthquake."

"You're kidding!" She felt like leaping from the sofa and dancing a jig, but she planted a joyful kiss on her husband instead. "You're amazing. Who is she?"

"You said she was blonde, right?"

"Yes." Her memories of the woman were clear because she'd been the face of hope in a scary situation.

He reached into his pocket and drew out a folded piece of paper. Unfolding it, he handed it to her. "What do you think?"

She stared at the grainy picture of a group of ten people dressed in paramedic uniforms. Two were women. She pointed to the blonde. "I recognize the smile. This is her! What's her name?"

"Olivia Norman."

She pulled out of his embrace and jumped to her feet. "Can we go talk to her?"

He shook his head. "Not easily. She lives in Rock Harbor,

Michigan. I doubt you want to wait to talk to her until we can get a flight out there."

She perched back on the sofa cushion beside him. "Do you have her phone number? Maybe we could call her."

He nodded. "And I know a little about her. She's fifty and moved away right after the earthquake. She got a job as a paramedic in Arizona and married two years later. They moved some and ended up in Rock Harbor, Michigan. She has a daughter and two sons. I called the sheriff in Rock Harbor, and he raved about her and her daughter."

"She was so helpful after the earthquake. I don't know what we would have done without her. Could we call her right now?"

He glanced at the grandfather clock. "It's almost eleven there. That's pretty late."

"Maybe not. Can we just try? Maybe she's a night owl."

"We're likely to tick her off. She probably won't answer anyway. Most people don't answer unknown phone numbers these days."

She knew everything he said was true, but she longed to find Brenna now that she'd found Grayson. Her phone was on the coffee table so she grabbed it. "I'll call."

"Put it on speakerphone if she answers." He pushed the paper with the phone number under her nose.

Her heart was trying to pound out of her chest as she punched in the number. The phone rang three times, and she resigned herself to leaving a message until the line clicked.

"Do you have any idea how late it is?" The woman's voice held outrage. "I never answer sales calls, but this is just too much. I'm going to report you."

Shauna quickly flipped over to speakerphone. "I'm so sorry for calling late, but this isn't a sales call. Are you Olivia Norman?"

"That was my maiden name." Her voice went wary.

"My maiden name was Shauna Duval. I wasn't sure if you'd remember me. You helped me and my family after the earthquake."

"I don't know what you're talking about."

"In Lavender Tides, Washington. You were a paramedic here, right?"

"Th-This is much too late for you to be calling. D-Don't call me again."

The click in Shauna's ear told her the woman had hung up. She stared at the screen, then turned off her phone. "That's so weird, Zach. Did you notice how she acted like she didn't know what I was talking about, then hung up when I mentioned Lavender Tides? And she sounded scared. You're sure it's the same woman, that the name is right?"

"It's her. I found a current picture on the Rock Harbor EMS website. She's older now, of course, but it's clearly the same woman."

She picked up the woman's picture and studied it. "I'm sure this is her. A hundred percent sure. But why wouldn't she at least talk to me about it? For all she knew I might have just been calling to thank her for taking such good care of us then."

"It's odd for sure. Let's try again tomorrow. Maybe she was just grouchy because it was so late. We could have awakened her or one of the kids."

"How old are her kids?"

"Grown, so yeah, that's probably not the reason." He consulted a file on his phone. "Her daughter is twenty-four, and she has two older stepsons."

"Brenna would be about twenty-four. She must have had a baby of her own." Shauna's gaze locked with Zach's, and she saw an awareness flare to life at the same time she began to wonder herself. "There's no record of Brenna at all."

"Let me see if I can find a picture of her daughter." He grabbed his computer and typed in a search string. "Here's her old high school website." He scrolled through several pages.

Shauna watched over his shoulder, and even before she saw the name, Bailey Fleming, she knew which girl was Olivia's daughter because she could have been Shauna herself at age eighteen.

She struggled to catch her breath. "We've found her, Zach." Tears burned her eyes. "We found her."

Lavender Lady was beautiful in the moonlight. Her tall masts reached for the stars, and the soft creaking of the ship shifting in the waves added to the Old World feeling as Ellie climbed the ladder to the deck behind Jason. Gray was on her heels, his keen gaze exploring every shadow.

The last ferry of the day chugged by, its lights bouncing off the waves. The sea wind brought the scent of kelp to her nose and left the taste of salt on her lips as she stepped onto the deck and put her kitten down to explore the new quarters. Ellie's gaze immediately went to where she'd seen Mac's blood. The stain lingered, and she shuddered.

She still trembled inside from the horrific events of the last twenty-four hours. Two dead. She had a sense of something momentous on the horizon, like a mythical sea monster about to devour them all.

Gray moved close to her. "Are there any lights on this thing?"

She caught a hint of his cologne, and it comforted her to know he was near. "There's a generator."

"I know where it is." Jason vanished into the shadows.

Gray's warm hand came down on her shoulder. "You doing okay?"

She tipped her head up to stare at him. "I don't know. What's really going on, Gray?" The halyards banged against the masts to punctuate her question.

"I think it's something big, Ellie. And I've got to stop whatever it is no matter what my bosses say."

Her gaze went to the masts. "This is a beautiful ship, Mac's pride and joy. I've been thinking about how she tried to cancel the tall ship flotilla that is coming this weekend. I thought Terrance might give us a peek into her state of mind, but what if the flotilla plays a role in all this?"

"What kind of role?"

She rubbed her head. "I don't know. She told the committee it would be dangerous. That has to mean something."

Ellie faced the shore where lights from town twinkled on the hillsides. Teenagers hung out on the pier, and she caught low hoots of laughter as they shared cigarettes and jokes. It was a carefree scene, and she wished she could capture that same sense that all was right with the world. She saw a few shadows and recognized Jermaine's slight form beside Stuart Ransom's bulk. Good people here in town determined to protect her.

Instead, she knew in her bones something was very wrong.

Gray's shoulder brushed hers as he leaned against the railing with her. "Do you know anything about the tall ship flotilla? Who books the appearances, that kind of thing?"

"Mac spoke with a guy in San Francisco when she came up

with the idea." She searched her memory. "Gun Moon. I only remember it because she joked about him being a cowboy with a name like that. He's from Korea and owns one of the tall ships, though he lives in California most of the time."

"I'll see what I can find out about him and the tall ship he's bringing in. When are they arriving?"

"Sometime on Thursday. The Parade of Sail wraps up the festival on Sunday. Twenty tall ships from three countries will be here."

The ship lights flickered and came on, and Gray straightened. "Let there be light." He looked around. "Nice ship."

"It was a pile of floating debris when Mac bought it, but it was cheap enough for her to afford. She's worked her tail off restoring it. She was built around 1920. Let's go belowdeck and take a look at where we can sleep. Mac had everything ready for a crew. She was in the process of interviewing."

Ellie led him to the stair entry, and they exited belowdeck in the grand salon. The odor of fresh varnish stung her nose. Newly recovered bench seats ran around the perimeter of the room, and a refinished wooden table and chairs sat atop the red Oriental rug.

"Nice," Gray said.

"I think the captain's and first mate's rooms are there." She pointed out two doors at the stern of the ship. "They both have heads in them. There are two smaller suites at the bow."

Gray poked his head into both rooms. "You take the captain's suite, and Jason can have the first mate's room. I'm going to stay up top and guard the ship tonight."

Jason ducked as he entered the salon. "Wake me at one and I'll spell you. We can each do four hours of watch."

Gray evaluated him for a long moment before nodding. "Thanks. You know how to handle a firearm?"

Jason headed for the ladder to the deck. "I'm an avid hunter. I'll take a quick run home and get my rifle while you look out for Ellie. I'll be back in half an hour."

Gray gestured to the captain's suite. "Get some rest, Hammer Girl."

Hammer Girl. It was a reminder that she was strong and resilient. Together they would get to the bottom of what was going on. She prayed they figured it out in time.

Chapter 27

*I can't tell you how many things I've learned to do by
reading and watching videos. Anyone can learn how
to wield a hammer or drive a screw into a wall.*

—HAMMER GIRL BLOG

The boat creaked and swayed in the gentle waves of the
bay. Leaning against a big mast, Grayson stretched out his
aching leg as he sat under the stars and pulled out his phone. He
needed answers.

Lance Phoenix, an FBI agent, was his best bet. Grayson had
worked with him on several investigations over the years. He
trusted Lance.

Lance answered on the first ring. "Bradshaw, what have you
gotten yourself into?"

"What are you talking about? I'm in the dark here. I was
ordered to stand down and leave this to the suits, but I can't. It's

spinning out of control here at warp speed." He told Lance what had been happening the past few days. "I'm aboard the tall ship where Mackenzie died, and I'm not sure how much longer I can keep her sister, Ellie, safe."

"She means something to you. I can hear it in your voice."

Grayson ignored that comment. His feelings had no bearing in the case. "What do you know?"

"You know my butt is on the line if I tell you."

"But you're going to do it anyway. Just like I'd do for you."

Lance chuckled. "Here's the scoop. Mackenzie Blackmore contacted the FBI two months ago and told them she thought a terrorist cell was going to set off an EMP bomb. Two agents were dispatched to talk to her, and she told them she was in a position to infiltrate the group. The FBI was reluctant to agree to it, but if they were going to stop the attack, they had to know the plan and the mastermind."

Grayson clenched his fists. "They let her do it?"

"And they're paying for it now. She texted them and told them she had the full scoop. Before they could meet, she was killed."

"They found her body?"

"Well, no, but they're sure she's dead."

Grayson winced. He sure didn't want to tell Ellie about this part of the conversation. "What about the cocaine theft from the Coast Guard hangar?"

"That was my part in it. I helped arrange for her to steal it and give it to her contact, Nasser, as a way to prove her loyalty. Unknown to him, Dylan Trafford was set up to be her cover story."

"Nasser." Grayson spat out the name. "Do you know how she found out about the plan to set off the bomb?"

"She fell for Nasser, if you can believe it. He told her about stealing the cocaine, and at first she went along with it. At the time I think she believed he was a drug lord. She had no idea he was planning this attack. Once she found out, she knew she had to get help."

Grayson had no doubt Nasser could charm the ladies with his dark good looks. At least Mac had enough sense to try to take him down before he killed thousands of people. "Why here, though? The area doesn't have a large population."

"That's the worst part. It's a trial run for a much bigger attack in San Francisco." Lance's voice was grim. "Unfortunately, with Mac gone we have no way of knowing how they're planning to deploy the bomb."

"You think it's here in the area already?"

"Almost certainly."

Grayson stared out at the lights along the shore. While the population wasn't enormous, there were good people here. He had to stop this. "Why was I told to stand down?"

"The FBI feared your poking around would make Nasser's cell move the attack up sooner, before they could track down the bomb. They're not having much luck, though. Maybe you will."

"Which is why you're telling me."

"You got it, Bradshaw. I know you, and you can be a help. Plus, this is personal to you."

"So all we know is Nasser's ISIS cell is playing a part."

"And the North Koreans. It appears to be a joint effort."

He blew out a harsh breath. "That's bad." A confirmation of his worst fears.

"Worse than bad."

"So we need to find the mastermind, the guy who is directing Nasser. And figure out what they are planning?"

"That about sums it up. Tall order for a tall guy."

"Do we have any idea when this is all coming down?"

"This coming weekend."

Grayson couldn't respond. Five days. The weekend would be here in the blink of an eye. "Thanks, Lance. I'll keep you posted."

"Do that. Good luck, Bradshaw."

The pain in Grayson's leg intensified as he ended the call. The task seemed impossible. But there had to be a way.

Mac sat on the floor in a corner of the room and stared at the door. This had been all her fault, really. All she'd had to do was tell Ellie about how stupid she'd been. Instead, she'd allowed herself to be pulled deeper and deeper into this until there was no way out.

She'd been an idiot.

These last few days staring death in the face had been a wake-up call. Deep down, she'd always been jealous of Ellie. Ellie was prettier, smarter, kinder, more talented—more *everything*—than Mac. If she had been able to bring down Tarek and his cell, her face would have been all over the news. The accompanying accolades would have been sweet. And maybe even Jason would quit looking at her with such contempt. Instead, she had walked right into a trap with no way out.

The sound of footsteps coming down the stairs brought her to her feet, and Mac stood facing the door with her hands clenched together in front of her. The key jangled in the dead bolt, and the door opened. Tarek stepped through, then closed it behind him. She backed away, though her traitorous heart wanted her to throw her arms around his neck.

He wore slim-fitting black trousers and a blue Oxford shirt. His dark hair gleamed as if he'd just gotten out of the shower. His gaze swept over her. "Looks like you're recovering."

"Why do you care? You're going to kill me anyway."

"I'm not going to kill you. Wang might, and I admit it's not what I'd choose. I find I have more feelings for you than I thought, though that fact won't change anything."

It was ridiculous how much his dark eyes moved her. She shook her head. "I wish you weren't involved in this. I love my country."

"You don't love anyone but yourself."

She'd met him in Seoul, of all places. An instant attraction had developed between them until she realized he was a bona fide terrorist. That had opened her eyes, but it hadn't driven out the feelings she still carried for him.

She reached toward him. "Let me go, Tarek. He's not your boss. You don't have to do what he wants."

"This is a joint effort, Mackenzie. It's the culmination of everything I've worked years to accomplish. America will finally pay."

She recognized the glint of fanaticism in his eyes. "What about my sister?"

"He's ordered for her to be killed." His white teeth gleamed in a mirthless smile. "I'm sure you miss her." He took one step closer to her. "You sealed your fate a long time ago, Mac." His eyes went hard, and he spun on his heel and stomped to the door, then slammed it shut behind him. The lock clanged into place, and his footsteps retreated up the stairs.

She put her face in her hands and let out a groan. She had to figure out how to get out of here and warn the FBI.

Mac paced the tiny cell with renewed strength and determination. There would be no more mistakes made that allowed her to escape. A new dead bolt and padlock had been added to the outside of her door, and the metal bed frame had been removed. The dirty mattress rested directly on the floor, and all other loose items had been taken away.

No tools, no weapons. But she still had her brain. There had to be a way out of here. She had to get out before Ellie was killed and the bomb was set off. But how?

She whirled toward the door when she heard a key scrape in the lock. The door opened, and Hyun stepped inside the room. Her dark eyes flickered stonily to Mac, then back to the floor as she set the tray with soup and water on the floor.

Mac sprang forward as the woman started to leave. "Wait! Please stay and talk to me a moment."

Hyun turned back toward her. "There is nothing for us to say."

"What could it hurt? I've been shut up here for days, and I'm going crazy in the silence."

The Korean woman eyed her a moment. "Wang was unhappy with me when you escaped. I don't care if you suffer from loneliness now."

Mac winced. "I'm sorry. You'd locked the door, and I managed to unlock it. It wasn't your fault."

The steely expression in those eyes softened. "That didn't matter. It was my fault."

Mac wet her lips and tried a tremulous smile. "I have money, plenty of money. I don't know what he's paying you, but—"

The woman's eyes flashed, and she held up her hand. "Death would be preferable to betraying the man I love." She tipped her head and studied Mac's face. "What did you do that he locked you in here? Were you a former girlfriend who disrespected him?"

"Wh-What? No, of course not. I didn't do anything to him. He plans to kill me. My blood will be on your hands."

"Better your blood than my own."

"Where are you from?"

Her shoulders stiffened. "From Hamhung." The woman turned and hurried toward the door.

Mac leaped after her, but the door slammed and the lock snicked before she could reach it. She slammed her palms against the door and groaned. She'd blown it.

Chapter 28

*You can never afford to let your trades work
without supervision. That's a good way to
have to redo plumbing or electrical.*
—HAMMER GIRL BLOG

G rayson's eyes ached from staring at the computer screen for
so long. All morning he'd been trying to find evidence
of the cocaine hitting the streets, and he'd finally found a large
uptick in overdose cases in Yakima. It might be the missing
cocaine, but if it was, he didn't like what he was seeing.

He had no idea how to tell Ellie what he'd learned last night
from Lance. He'd let Jason escort her to the Saltwater Point
house this morning and had gone to his place to work. If there
was a way to link the cocaine to terrorists in North Korea, he
wasn't seeing it.

His doorbell rang, and he glanced out the window as he got

up. Shauna and Zach were on the porch. His leg throbbed and accentuated his limp as he went to open the door. "Good morning." He glanced at his watch. "I guess it's almost lunchtime."

"We came to take you to lunch," Shauna said. "Ellie is meeting us at the Yellow Submarine in an hour. You hungry?" She stepped through the doorway with Zach on her heels.

"Starved." Grayson patted his stomach.

"There's something we want to talk to you about before we go. Got a minute?"

"Of course. Have a seat."

They followed him into the living room and settled on the sofa. He dropped into the chair across from them. Shauna's eyes sparkled, and she kept breaking out into a smile.

"Looks like something exciting, whatever it is."

"We found Brenna!"

"Already?" He wasn't used to one new sister yet, let alone a second one. "How'd you find her?"

She sent her husband an adoring look. "Zach found the paramedic who helped us after the earthquake."

Zach shrugged. "It was a joint effort, actually. Isabelle found a CPS agent who was able to supply the crucial information I needed."

Warmth surged in his chest. "She's a great researcher."

Shauna leaned forward. "Grayson, the paramedic *took* Brenna. That's why no one knew anything about her. There was no official record. She left the area right after the earthquake so no one would know."

"How do you know all this?"

She glanced at Zach who took out his iPad and handed it to Grayson. "Fourth row, third picture from the left."

Grayson scanned down the page, then gasped. "The girl looks just like you."

"She does. That's her senior year in high school."

His investigator brain was already running through charges against the woman. Kidnapping, taking a minor across state lines. The woman was in a heap of trouble.

He handed the iPad back to Zach. "Where's Brenna now? She's, what, about twenty-four?"

Shauna nodded. "Zach isn't sure where she is. That's where you come in. You think you can track her down with your investigative connections?"

"Probably. We know her name and location, plus where she graduated. Should be pretty straightforward. I'll see what I can find out."

He called a friend he'd worked with at the FBI on a joint task force and asked her to track down Brenna, a.k.a. Bailey Fleming, then ended the call. "I should know something within the hour."

Grayson wasn't sure what role Shauna expected him to play in this. He was happy to assist her with a location, but the thought of showing up on this young woman's doorstep to break her world apart didn't appeal to him. Would he rather not have known about Shauna? He liked his new sister a lot and felt a sense of connection to her that he couldn't explain. But there was no denying his life had been turned upside down, and he wasn't sure he wanted to do the same to Brenna/Bailey.

"You seem lost in thought," Zach said. "Anything wrong?"

"Just thinking about this Bailey and how she's going to take the news. You realize she won't know she's adopted. Well, not adopted. *Kidnapped* is a better word. I'm sure Olivia never formally adopted her. How could she?"

Shauna pushed her thick, black hair out of her face. "What about a birth certificate for school?"

"She probably got a forged one or something. I'm sure she found a way around it." Grayson's phone rang, and he glanced at it. "There's our answer already. I didn't think it would take long."

He answered the phone and jotted down everything his friend said. Bailey was living in Rock Harbor, Michigan, and worked as a nurse at an assisted living facility.

"Thanks so much, my friend." He ended the call and exhaled, then told Shauna and Zach what he'd found out. "I have her address and phone number. I'm not sure how you want to handle it, though. Having someone show up on your doorstep is a bit of a shock, you know. Or maybe you don't realize just how topsy-turvy news like this can be."

Zach shot a quick look at Shauna. "What do you suggest?" He put his arm around her as if to calm her.

"Maybe write her an email first. Give her all the information so she can digest it a bit, then let her call you," Gray said.

Shauna shrugged off her husband's embrace and leaned forward. "What if she calls her mother and doesn't believe us?"

"Then you go see her. She'll take one look at you and know it's true. Better yet, enclose a picture of you in the email."

"Of both of us," Shauna said.

"I won't bolster your story much. We don't look alike."

"That reminds me." Shauna drew a paper out of her purse. "Not that we weren't already sure, but the official DNA is back. We're siblings."

It wasn't anything unexpected, but it brought back Grayson's sense of being lost in a forest. "So I guess you're going to have to put up with me forever."

She smiled. "It's all I ever wanted." She handed him the document. "You can tell her how we found you and you didn't believe it at first either. We can show her the DNA report."

He had to admit her plan held merit. "Okay. I have her email. We can do it now if you want."

She shook her head. "Let's go have lunch. I want to think about what to say."

And he was happy to put off destroying the young woman's life. He'd thought his situation was bad, but hers was worse. The woman who'd raised her had actually kidnapped her. That was going to be earthshaking.

Wang slammed his fist against the wall in Nasser's office. "I don't understand why you can't find the tiles! I need that picture to get the codes. And Grayson Bradshaw is still alive. The mah-jongg tiles have to be somewhere in Ellie's possession."

This last bit of incompetence was intolerable. Nasser had bragged he could manage anything, see anywhere, and do what was needed. His confidence in the man had been severely shaken. He should have done this himself.

Nasser, relaxed and unperturbed, leaned back in his leather chair at the expansive desk surrounded by books. His dark eyes held more than a trace of contempt. "We've searched her house and Mac's apartment multiple times and can't find them."

He drilled Nasser with a quelling look. "You and your men are incompetent. Do I have to find men worthy of their hire?"

The picture contained a crucial pass code for detonation, and the clock was running out. He stared out the window at the neighborhood kids painting graffiti on the abandoned building across the street, then turned to look again at Nasser. "Sunday is go time. I must have that picture by then or I'll have to scrap the whole plan. And failure will not be tolerated."

Nasser reached for his cigar, then lit it and took a puff.

Wang waved away the stench of the cigar. Nasser offered him one, but he grimaced and shook his head. He planted his palms on Nasser's desk and leaned forward. "Find that picture. Tonight. Or you'll be the next one found dead in a basement."

"Of course." Nasser looked sufficiently quelled. "What about Mackenzie?"

"What about her? You have her safely locked up."

"Yes, of course. She is growing antsy, though."

"I don't care how she feels." He stared at Nasser, then grinned. "You care about her, don't you?" He hooted with laughter. "I never would have guessed you'd fall for a woman like her."

Nasser stiffened. "If I'd cared about her, would I have delivered her to you this way? Would I have let you embroil her in your plot?"

"Maybe. I think you wanted her, but she turned her back on you. She's attractive, I'll give you that. But don't let her get inside your head."

"Like Hyun got inside yours?"

Wang clenched his fists. "She's been a great asset to our work." He spun on his heel and slammed the door behind him. Stupid, stupid man. Nothing was going to stop this plan from coming to fruition. If Nasser couldn't handle it, Wang would do it himself.

❧

Ellie spent Tuesday removing old wallpaper and patching plaster in the House at Saltwater Point. She had hundreds of plaster washers and drywall screws ready, but the plaster was surprisingly sound except for one spot in a wall in the master bedroom and another in the ceiling of the living room. The whine of power saws and drills filled the house as workers began restructuring the place into a big, open space that would appeal to the majority of buyers.

Clint was arguing politics, as usual, with another worker. She would have to talk to him about working more and arguing less.

The more she worked in the house, the more determined she was to make it her own.

Jason poked his head into the living area where she rooted through her tools for a hole saw. "You're making some good progress."

"Yeah, I was about to drill some holes for plumbing in the new kitchen."

He grinned. "Don't trust the plumber, eh?"

"Not after the one who put the run of cabinets with the sink on the wrong wall in our last house. That set us back several days. I don't want a repeat. 'Verify all work' is my motto now."

There were circles under his eyes, and he had a bandage on his left hand, which wasn't unusual. Jason was a good carpenter but sometimes absentminded. He often had his country music cranked so loud it was no wonder he lost track of what he was doing.

"Did you get any sleep last night?"

He shrugged. "More than Grayson did. How'd you sleep?"

"In fits and starts." She inserted the end of the hole saw

into the drill. "I have to believe I'll find out the truth of what happened to Mac. And we have to stop whatever is about to happen."

"You don't even know what that is."

She heard the note of cynicism in his voice. She tightened the nut. "I know, Jason, but I have to try."

"Have you talked to your dad?"

"I tried to call him, but he's still in Africa on safari." She rose. "I'd better get cleaned up. I'm meeting Grayson for dinner."

She didn't wait for his reaction but headed to the garage. The only working bathroom in the place was in the apartment over the garage. Her hands shook as she washed the plaster dust from her arms and face, then headed for her truck. As she stepped outside in the sunshine, a truck slowed, then stopped in front of the house. Isaac Cohen.

The passenger window ran down, and he leaned over to peer up at her. "How's it coming in there?"

"Pretty well. Always slow at this stage, but we're getting the structure right."

"I heard the sheriff found a body. Any word on her identification yet?"

Her pulse galloped. "I haven't heard that. Are you sure?"

He shrugged. "I heard it at the coffee shop a few days ago. You'd think they'd know by now. It's not like she was wearing something nondescript. I mean, she had on an ugly green sweater according to scuttlebutt. He didn't ask you to ID her?"

She realized what he was talking about. "That ended up being a dead deer, not a person at all."

"Oh, well, sorry for saying anything then." He exhaled. "I was hoping for closure for you, for all of us."

"Thanks, Isaac. I know you all care about her too. I'll let you know as soon as I hear something."

"Thanks." His window went up and he pulled away.

For just a minute she'd hoped that they might at least know what had happened to Mac. The waiting was so hard.

Chapter 29

Wood is a wonderful material. It's almost
magical in the number of things you can do
with it when you have the proper tools.
—Hammer Girl Blog

The town in twilight was almost mystical with lights glowing from the cafés and small businesses that were still open. The old-fashioned streetlights added a fairy-tale touch to the scene. But Grayson knew the town wasn't as idyllic as it seemed. As he walked to Harvey's Pier to meet Ellie for dinner, he found himself staring sharply at every person he passed. Were they hiding their true identity behind a smile?

Laughing patrons spilled out of Harvey's Pier, and he eyed all the diners as he walked in the door. He spotted Ellie sitting at a small corner booth by herself. She stared into her plate like it was a foreign object, and he knew she was lost in thought.

He let his gaze linger on the way the overhead light glimmered on her burnished hair. She took off her glasses and put them beside her plate before picking up her fork and eating a bite of salad. She sure was pretty.

He veered around another group exiting the place and stepped into the restaurant. A country tune he didn't recognize blared from the jukebox and mingled with the laughter from the patrons. There didn't seem to be anyone watching her. He threaded through the tables to where Ellie sat.

"You got here a little early." He dropped into the chair opposite her.

She reached for her glasses and stuck them on her nose. "I didn't get a chance to ask you this morning if you talked to the FBI agent who might be able to tell you what was going on."

Great. Telling her wouldn't be easy. Maybe he should hold back some of it. He signaled to the server and ordered iced tea and a hamburger with fries. "Yeah, I got him last night."

Her gaze sharpened. "What'd he say?"

"They believe a major terrorist attack is coming this weekend, something joint between North Korea and ISIS."

Her glass stopped on its way to her lips, and she set it back on the table. "And what about Mac?"

How did he tell her that her sister had decided to be a confidential informant for the FBI? "This isn't easy to hear, honey."

"Tell me."

So he did. Her eyes got bigger when she heard the FBI had helped Mac steal the cocaine so she could infiltrate the terrorist cell. "They killed her, didn't they?"

"They think so, but her body still hasn't been recovered."

Tears filled her eyes. "What's next?"

"I'm trying to find some clue that will lead us to who is behind this attack and stop it in time. The bad thing is we don't even know *where* it's hitting. Here? Seattle? Yakima? No one really knows."

"Did you find out anything about the tall ship organizer, Gun Moon?"

"I looked him up. He escaped North Korea ten years ago and has lived here ever since. He became a citizen last year. Nothing points to anything wonky with him."

She drummed her fingers on the table. "When I was tossing and turning last night, I realized that if Mac was going to hide some kind of evidence, it might be on the ship. She spent so much time there."

"That's a great idea. We can start searching tonight."

He fell silent as the server brought their food, then he bit into his burger. The spicy jalapeños on his burger hit his tongue in a perfect combo with avocado and cheese. This place was good, but he couldn't wait to get to the ship and do a thorough search.

The clock was ticking down to Sunday.

Ellie's glasses steamed so badly she had trouble seeing. She paused and wiped them on her sweaty T-shirt. "It's hot down here without a breeze. Mac said the generator couldn't handle air-conditioning. It's going to be hot sleeping down here tonight."

Gray looked up from his knees in front of the storage space under a bench seat lining the wall of the salon. "I'll be on deck standing guard anyway. You could take a mattress to the deck and sleep up there if it gets too hot."

"Okay." She averted her gaze from the magnificent sight of him in gym shorts and a tank top. "Find anything?"

He dropped the bench seat back into place. "Not yet. A few specks of sand."

"There's a storage area in a bench in the smallest room in the bow. I'll check there." Ducking her head as the ceiling dropped, she squeezed into the tiny room that held only a single cot on one wall and a bench on the other. She lifted the lid and found a file folder. "Found something," she called as she carried it under a dim light and opened the cover.

Gray's bare feet slapped on the wooden boards as he rushed to join her. "What is it?"

"Looks like it's a manifest of all the tall ships in the upcoming event."

"Let's take it to the salon where the lighting is better." He held the door open for her.

She squeezed past him, and they pulled out chairs at the wooden table under the light. She slid the folder over to him. "Let's look at what countries are represented."

Gray slid his chair over close enough that his arm brushed hers. "I'm glad you found this. I wanted to request it, but I knew I'd be found out immediately. I don't like having my hands tied."

She ran her finger down the list of ships and countries, then paused at one. "Wait a minute. The *Elyssa Marie* is listed as an American ship on the brochure the committee gave me. This says it's Korean."

He frowned and studied the details. "I'll find out for sure."

"How can you do that when you're locked out? Your FBI friend?"

"Yep." He pulled out his phone and placed a call.

She walked around while he spoke to Lance. Gray put his phone away. "He looked it up while I was on the phone with him. It's Korean."

"Why is it wrong on the brochure?"

"Could be a typo or something else."

"I can find out." Kristy Gillings was the committee chairperson, so she called her. "Hey, Kristy, sorry to bother you in the evening like this."

"You're never a bother. What's up?"

"I was looking at the list of ships and countries represented in the flotilla this weekend. Is it accurate? I was wondering where you got the ships' countries of origin."

"Isaac got the list from Gun Moon, the guy in California who put this together for us. I typed it up myself. Is there a problem?"

Ellie forced a lilt to her voice. "I was just wondering what we were going to see. There are several countries represented: America, England, China, even Korea."

"I don't think we have any from Korea, though they have several they sometimes display. It should be a packed festival. Mac was brilliant to come up with this. There's no word about her, is there? I'm sure I would have heard."

"No word. Thanks, Kristy. See you this weekend."

Ellie ended the call. "She contradicted me about Korea, so their information is wrong. It came from Gun Moon."

"Even though he looks clean, I'll ask Lance to take a closer look at him." Gray sent off a text to his friend.

What did it all mean? "Mac mentioned the danger of bringing the ships here. Is there a way to stop it? Does the FBI know she tried to stop the ships from coming?"

"I'll make sure Lance knows." He sent another text, and his

phone dinged almost immediately. "Lance says I'll have more info by morning. Maybe we're getting somewhere."

He draped his arm around her, and she leaned into his strength. "Let's go up top to cool off."

His warm breath whispered across her neck and cheek. How did he make her feel so accepted for who she was?

Chapter 30

*Lack of confidence is a killer when it comes to
design. The fear inside makes us wonder if we
can really combine lavender and pale green.*
—Hammer Girl Blog

It was a beautiful evening for a seafood boil aboard ship, but Ellie was too on edge to enjoy it. The thought of an impending terrorist attack made her want to crawl out of her skin. She glanced at Gray, who sat on the deck chatting with Jason, and she forced her attention back on preparing the food. He drew her in ways she couldn't even name.

It was silly, though. He wasn't going to look at her any special way. Not when he could have any woman on the planet.

She got the outside gas burner going and went to fill the big pot from the water hose Mac had connected to the potable water source. When it was half full, she started to lug the pot back to the flame, but Gray leaped up.

"That's too heavy for you. Let me carry it." He hefted it away from her and carried it back to the burner.

With any other man she might have been offended at the insinuation that she couldn't do something, but he made her feel cherished. *Cherish* was a word she hadn't thought much about, but she liked the sound of it.

"Is it seated on the burner okay?" he asked.

She checked the level and nodded. "Neanderthals are good to have around on occasion."

"I like being here for you. For anything."

She couldn't bring herself to look into his eyes. He surely didn't mean it the way her heart took it. She swallowed and turned up the heat, then sprinkled in Chesapeake Bay seasoning, a few cloves of garlic, and some sliced lemon. "It shouldn't take long for dinner to be ready. Maybe forty-five minutes. If you're hungry, there's a veggie platter and dip in the galley fridge."

"I wouldn't say no to it. I'll get it." He ducked down the ladder.

Out of his presence she was able to catch her breath. Being around him was like riding a roller coaster of emotions that left her exhausted. The water started boiling, and she dropped in fingerling potatoes, carrots, sausage, and corn. The seafood would go in once the vegetables were almost done. Individual butter warmers waited along with fresh bread on the folding tables they'd set up. He wouldn't leave hungry.

Her gaze strayed to the ladder as Gray emerged with the veggie tray in one hand and the kitten in the other. Good grief, he was handsome. Such a big guy but so gentle and kind. Most of the big men she'd met liked to throw their size around, but he seemed to understand how intimidating he could be and made allowances. She hadn't even known him a full two weeks, and she was already smitten.

Danger, danger.

He set the tray on the table in front of Jason. "Eat up before my sister gets here with Zach and Alex or you may be out of luck." The kitten snuggled against him. "Mia was meowing at the ladder, and I couldn't bring myself to ignore her. I think she was afraid to try to climb it."

"You're a pushover just like Ellie." Jason snagged a couple of carrots.

The lights on a small boat bobbed in the water offshore, and Ellie tensed until she recognized Shauna.

Shauna waved. "You guys up there?"

"We're waiting on you," Ellie called.

Shauna, pink-cheeked and smiling, climbed the ship's ladder with Zach behind her. "I asked my mother-in-law to keep Alex for a while. He's not fond of seafood, and I wanted a chance for us to compose a letter to Brenna. I've got my part done."

Zach carried a plate of brownies, and he put them on the table by the veggies, then grabbed a couple of cucumbers as he lowered himself into a chair beside Jason and Grayson.

Shauna joined them and set down the computer she carried. "See what you think about the first part of the email I composed."

Ellie went to join them for a few minutes while the vegetables cooked. "This has to be exciting, Shauna. I'm so happy for you!"

"I'm thrilled. Let me read it to you since there are so many of us." She cleared her throat. "'My name is Shauna Bannister. My maiden name was Duval, and I have reason to believe you are my baby sister, Brenna, who disappeared twenty-five years ago after being born during an earthquake in Lavender Tides, Washington. I know this has to be a shock since you likely have never heard any of this. Your mother was the paramedic who assisted our mother in your birth, and she helped save your life. However, I believe she took you out of the collapsed grocery store and made you her own. There was never any record of you after the earthquake, and she has refused to talk to me. I think you can see from my attached picture that the two of us look very much alike.'"

Shauna stopped and looked up. "Do you think she will even read this? I'm not sure I would after the baby-sister thing." She sighed and rubbed her eyes. "Maybe this is the wrong thing to do."

Zach squeezed her hand. "I don't know any other way to handle it, Fly Girl. There's no easy way to do it."

"Let's pray for her to be receptive," Gray said. "Let's wait a bit to send it, then if there's no answer from her, I can fly there after things are over here. Maybe I can even talk to her mom and ask for her to tell the truth."

Ellie took his statement for what it was—a wake-up call for her to guard her heart. He wasn't going to be here long.

The ship swayed and clanged with the tide. Grayson's belly was pleasantly full from the crab boil, but all his senses were on high alert as he watched out over the waves for any boats headed their way. He couldn't remember when he'd last enjoyed himself so much. Shauna and Zach were good people, the kind who immediately put you at ease and made you feel ten feet tall.

And Ellie. His gaze cut to where she slept on a bunk mattress under the stars. She lay on her side, her right cheek turned sweetly up for the kiss of a moonbeam. A fanciful, almost poetic thought. He used to read poetry in high school but had given it up for dry subjects like math and social studies.

Her lips pursed as though she were kissing someone in her sleep, and he wished he was the lucky one. Long lashes cast shadows on her cheeks, and even her ears were cute. He liked everything about her.

She'd blush if she awoke and saw him staring. He rose from his seat against the mast and went to the railing. Though it was nearly two, he wasn't tired enough to awaken Jason who was sleeping on the deck in the bow. The shapes of townspeople watching the ship moved along the beach, and he spotted a bonfire.

A whisper of sound lifted on the salt-laden breeze, and he cocked his head. Just the wind or the creak of the ship? A sixth sense told him it was more than that. The noise seemed stealthy yet purposeful. He stood as quietly as he could and tried to get a fix on where it was originating from. He caught a whiff of gasoline. From the generator or something more sinister?

He went on full alert and hurried on bare feet to rouse Jason, who awakened in two seconds. Grayson held his finger to his lips and motioned for the other man to follow him. He gestured for Jason to move to the starboard side while he went to the port side. Access by ropes was available on both sides, and he didn't want to be surprised. He shot off a quick text to the sheriff asking for backup, then sank to his knees at the railing.

He wanted to get Ellie belowdeck, but he needed to surprise their unexpected visitor. Or visitors. Gun in hand, he crouched at the rail by the ladder and listened. Someone was climbing up. They had to have put in from one of the offshore islands or their sentries on shore would have seen them and alerted him.

He'd rigged floodlights to illuminate the ship's hull, so he reached over and plugged them in. Someone cursed, and Grayson popped up his head and looked over the side. Two men, one holding a can of what had to be gasoline, swung on the rope ladder like ugly spiders.

He pointed his gun at them. "Hands up!"

In that instant gunfire broke out on the starboard side, and he turned to see Jason grappling with a figure dressed in black. An ambush. Jason thumped the guy over the head with the butt of his rifle, and the man tumbled back into the water.

A bullet zinged by Grayson's head from one of the men on the port side, and he returned fire. He heard Ellie moving on her mattress.

"Stay down!" He shot off a volley of bullets at the figures, and one shouted and fell into the water. The one with the gas can still clung to the rope.

The guy looked up at him, his face covered in a black ski mask. He dropped the gas can into the water and pulled a gun from his belt. Grayson shot his wrist, and the gun went flying into the bay. He wanted to catch one of these guys alive. They might be persuaded to talk.

He gestured with the gun. "Climb up here. Slowly."

The guy looked at the gun, then let go of the rope and fell into the water. Grayson slung his leg over the railing and began to clamber down the rope. He needed to haul one of the assailants in, but by the time he reached their inflatable, there was no sign of them.

He returned to the deck to make sure everyone was okay. Ellie rushed to him as soon as he stepped aboard, and he embraced her. "I'm not hurt." He looked over her head at Jason, who was clambering over the rail too. "I couldn't catch one either. You okay?"

"Yeah, just disgusted," Jason said.

Sirens blared from the shore, and two sheriff's cars careened to a halt at the pier. "There's an inflatable at the bottom of the rope. You mind going after the sheriff?" he asked Jason.

"Nope." Jason's mouth was grim as he went past them and climbed over the railing.

Grayson didn't want to tell Ellie they'd come to burn up the boat—and them.

Chapter 31

Always be prepared for the client not to like
something. They might tell you one thing but really
want another. Some people are hard to please.
—HAMMER GIRL BLOG

Ellie sat on a camp chair and stared blankly around the living room. The House at Saltwater Point was taking shape. The open floor plan now let light in from front to back, and the grand spaces allowed the full beauty of the tall ceilings to shine.

In the bathroom she marked one more wall for removal. She'd come up with a floor plan that used a small linen closet in the hallway to enlarge the master enough to squeeze in a double sink vanity, which would help make the room more functional.

Footsteps echoed in the hall outside the master bedroom, and she turned, expecting to see one of the crew, but the sheriff stood outside the door.

"I tried knocking, then came on in when no one answered. I saw your car here so I figured you were working and didn't hear me at the door." His eyebrows gathered in a pained expression.

She backed away at the pity in his eyes. "You found Mac?"

"Well, we don't know for sure yet, Ellie. A woman's body was recovered from the bay this morning. Th-The fish have done a number on it, so we haven't been able to identify it yet. Identification will have to wait for DNA results."

"Clothing maybe?"

"As I said, the fish." His mouth twisted. "There was no clothing recovered."

She grasped for any way of identification. "Hair?"

"Brown. Long enough that it appears to be a woman, though the coroner hasn't taken a look yet. We just don't know, but I wanted you to have a heads-up."

Ellie fisted her hands. "You think it's her, don't you?"

"Well, we don't have anyone else missing at the moment, though with the ocean currents, the victim could be from anywhere, even Canada. But yes, I do think it's possible."

Ellie clutched at her stomach and swallowed. "Could I see the body?"

"I don't think that's a good idea. If it's Mackenzie, you don't want your last memory of her to be that painful. We'll have DNA back in a few days."

"I might . . . recognize something."

"Believe me, if there was anything recognizable, I would ask you to take a look. Some of the limbs are missing, Ellie. Much of the flesh. I hate to be so graphic, but putting yourself through that wouldn't be of any use."

She gulped and nodded. "Okay. Any other news?"

"We got an ID on the vic from your basement. It's a man by the name of Gun Moon."

Ellie took a step back and put her hand to her throat where her pulse throbbed. "Gun Moon? He was the man Mac contacted to arrange for the tall ship flotilla."

"Well, someone didn't like him much. He was garroted."

Was he one of the terrorists, or just someone who got in their way? Gray needed to know about this. "What about last night? Anyone see the attackers come ashore?"

The sheriff shook his head. "At least Grayson and Jason were prepared to protect you. I'm tempted to take you into protective custody. Your luck is going to run out any day."

"You can't do that! We have to figure this out before Sunday."

"And that's the only reason I haven't done it." He fingered a long black sideburn. "Just be careful."

She nodded. "You haven't heard from my dad, have you? I've tried calling him, but he's on safari."

"He hasn't been in contact with you?"

She shook her head. "He's not what you'd call an involved parent. He has his own life."

"You might try him again." Everett's mouth twisted, and he frowned. "Well, I'd better get out of here. A deputy is stationed outside as usual. Let me know if you need anything."

She sat on the floor staring out the big rear windows at Rainshadow Bay. Maybe the sheriff was right. Though she'd left a message for her dad, he might be waiting for her to call with more information.

He answered on the third ring. "Have they found your sister?"

He sounded entirely too calm, and she clenched her left hand into a fist in her lap. "Not yet. How are you holding up?"

"I'm still in Africa. We hit a hotel with phone service and internet today, and I just got your message."

Likely story. He probably got her message days ago. She hadn't even known he was going until a couple of days before he left. His abandonment of her and Mac had happened long ago, but the reminder of how it continued closed her throat and brought tears to her eyes.

"You should be here, Dad. Mac is in trouble and maybe dead. How can that compare with a trip?"

"You're being your usual melodramatic self, Ellie. I don't think this conversation is going anywhere. Let me know if you hear anything about Mackenzie."

The phone went dead, and Ellie stared at it disbelievingly. He'd just hung up, which told her what she'd already known. He didn't love her or Mac. Not one bit.

The day boasted only a few clouds in the deep azure of the sky. "I was told this neighborhood in Port Angeles might yield some clues to the missing cocaine, but I've got my doubts."

Ellie didn't reply. Ever since Gray had picked her up at the house before lunch, she'd been quiet. She'd told him about her call with her dad, but there was nothing he could do to fix it, though he wished he could. She'd begged to come with him today, but the outing didn't seem to have lifted her spirits.

"Wait here." He parked along the street and got out to the stench of garbage burning and the smell of cabbage. Looking around he spotted an old school. He approached a group of teenagers laughing and smoking cigarettes near a basketball court and waited for one of them to notice him. They all looked to be juniors and seniors in high school. Or maybe dropouts, for all he knew. Two of them had pants so big they barely hugged their hips, and he caught the skunky scent of marijuana on them.

One of the tallest boys nudged the guy next to him. "Cop," he muttered.

Grayson held up his hand. "I'm not a cop. I'm trying to find a missing woman." He pulled up a picture of Mackenzie on his phone. "You see her around at all?"

The boys looked at one another, then to the ground. Several shook their heads without looking at Grayson.

The tall black-haired boy hesitated, then shook his head too. "Nope. What'd she do?"

He didn't buy their denials, and he couldn't tell them she was dead or they'd really clam up. "Someone attacked her and hauled her off, leaving a lot of blood behind. We're afraid she'll die without medical treatment." He passed the picture to the other five. "Take a good look."

"We're no snitches." The redhead hauled his pants up a few inches as he sneered.

"Look, I'm not going to turn you in for the pot you're smoking or anything else. No one will know you gave me any information. I've got a feeling you know something about this woman. Do you want to be responsible for her death?"

The black-haired boy who appeared to be the leader frowned and stared at the picture. "She might have been hanging around this dude in a black car."

"A Taurus?"

He shrugged. "A Ford, yeah. I didn't pay attention to the model."

"When was this and what did you see?"

"About three weeks ago, wasn't it?" he asked the redhead.

Redhead scowled but nodded. "Watch what you say, Dex." Dex shot him a deadly look, and Redhead put his hands up. "What? Dex is a nickname, not your real name. That's not telling him anything."

"Shut up," Dex growled.

Grayson held out the picture again. "Like I said, I don't care who you are or what you're doing. I just need to find this woman before it's too late. What did the man look like?"

"Dude was driving, and she was in the passenger seat. She jumped out while the car was still moving. It was something else, man! She rolled on the pavement like she was a stuntman or something, then got up and dusted herself off."

"Did she get away?"

"She argued with him for a minute, then took off running and got into the grocery store." Dex pointed out a run-down store on the corner. "A little while later some dude came to get her. She was crying, and he was patting her back and stuff. They walked out and went around the corner. That's all I know."

Had to be Trafford. Or did it? "What did the guy look like?"

Dex looked down and kicked a stone with his ratty shoe. "It was Nasser."

"Tarek Nasser?"

"Yeah." Dex glanced around and lowered his voice. "A terrorist you don't ever want to meet. He's heavy into cocaine trafficking."

Finally, a decent lead. "Where can I find him?"

Redhead shook his head. "You'd better listen up, man! You don't want to mess with him. If he has her, she's dead anyway."

"You ever been with him yourself?"

Dex shuddered. "No, and I don't want to. He hangs around the liquor store down the street once in a while, but it would be a fluke for you to find him. It's usually one of his lackeys who hits the store for supplies."

"A terrorist, like, for real? One who bombs buses and things like that?" Grayson asked.

"His group deals in drugs to raise money for terror camps. He's downright scary."

Dex grabbed Grayson's arm. "You won't say you even heard me say his name, right? I don't want to be worrying about him taking me down one dark night."

"I won't mention I even talked to you boys."

They were still muttering among themselves when he walked away. While Grayson was here, he might as well check out the liquor store. He might just get lucky, or he might be able to follow one of Nasser's men to their lair.

He slid back under the steering wheel. "Those kids saw Mac with Nasser and told me where he often hangs out."

She brightened. "That's great news!"

"It's in this same neighborhood. I'm going to check it out."

"Let me go in. A woman is less threatening."

She had a point. "If the store's empty, we might give it a try."

And if it brought her smile back, all the better.

Chapter 32

Never, and I mean never, tackle more than one
room at a time. Do the one job first or you'll end up
living in a disaster zone for months or even years.
—Hammer Girl Blog

G ray parked in front of a run-down brick building with
one *E* out in the neon beer sign hanging in the window.
"It just opened, and it doesn't look like there are any customers.
You sure you want to go in by yourself?"

She opened her door. "I want to do it."

"I'll keep watch out here and come get you if anything looks
dangerous."

The store looked empty when she approached the plate-glass
window. Glancing inside, she saw a skinny male clerk behind
the counter. When she opened the door and stepped inside, the
place smelled yeasty, like spilled beer, and it was none too clean.

The clerk glanced her way. His black eyes examined her face. "Can I help you, miss?"

"Um, I'm looking for a missing woman I thought you might have seen." She pulled out her phone and showed him Mac's photo. "Recognize her?"

The clerk stared at it. "I think I saw her a few weeks ago. She didn't buy anything, though. She just strolled through the aisles and kept looking at the door every time someone came in. I thought maybe she was supposed to meet a boyfriend here or something, but he never showed. She left after about an hour."

Ellie dropped her phone into her purse. "Did you speak to her at all?"

"I asked her if she needed any help about three times, but she always said no."

The guy was readily answering questions, so Ellie decided to take a chance. "You know Tarek Nasser?"

The clerk rubbed his kinky hair and backed away, glancing at the door. "Everyone in this part of town knows him." He dropped his voice. "Or knows of him."

"Did the woman ask about him?"

The clerk shook his head. "She just hung out watching the door."

"Did she speak to anyone else?"

The young man shook his head again. "That's all I know. I only remembered her because she was a looker."

Ellie knew it was a long shot. "Thanks anyway."

"If she has anything to do with Nasser, though, she'd better be careful. We had two kids in my neighborhood killed in drive-by shootings last month. They were part of Nasser's gang."

"Do you know anyone else who is with him? Or any idea where he is holed up?"

The man's eyes nearly rolled back in his head, and he stepped back. "Don't ask and don't tell when it comes to Nasser. I've heard he flays the skin from his enemies. It might just be a rumor, but I don't want to find out."

"Thanks for your help." Ellie started for the door when the guy called her back.

The clerk looked down at the floor. "Look, don't say where you heard it, but you might check out the cabin at the end of Gandy Lane. It's not here in Port Angeles, but up in the mountains. Not many know it's back there. Don't even try to drive there. You'll have to walk, and be careful."

"You must want this guy caught to risk telling me where to look."

The man nodded. "My younger cousin got mixed up with him and he's dead now, thanks to Nasser. I'd like to see him shut down."

"Does he have many men working for him?"

"Probably ten or so."

Enough to mount a formidable defense with the right weapons, and Ellie suspected the guy had the best weapons out there. "Thanks again."

She exited into a fine drizzle that had already dampened the sidewalk and road. She slung herself into Gray's SUV. "He remembered Mac, but she didn't talk to anyone. She kept looking out through the window like she was watching for someone."

"Probably Nasser."

She told him about the Gandy Lane cabin. "Maybe the FBI could check it out."

"I'll call Lance."

She listened with half an ear as he told Lance what they'd learned. It felt important, and she prayed they managed to stop the attack before it began. Surely the FBI was making progress. She had to believe that.

He ended the call and glanced over at her. "How about we get out of this neighborhood and get some lunch?"

She forced herself to smile and nod, though she wanted to rush out to Gandy Lane and see what was happening there. "Sounds good."

Grayson had found a surprisingly good hole-in-the-wall Mexican restaurant with picnic tables looking out on the fall foliage. The temperature hovered near seventy, so it was pleasant enough to sit outside at a secluded table and eat their lunch. Ellie had fallen into silence again, and she kept looking out at the glorious landscape of gold and orange as if it held the secret to all her questions.

The spicy aroma of cumin and peppers mingled with the scent of pine and loamy soil. It was a feel-good kind of moment, but he couldn't seem to get to that emotion with her staring anywhere but at him. There was a curious tension coiled around her, and he was on tenterhooks waiting for the hammer to fall.

He scarfed down his enchiladas. "I think I'll see if the sheriff has any idea about that body he found."

"Oh, would you? I've been trying to be patient."

"He probably doesn't know anything yet, but I'll ask." He texted the sheriff and got a reply in seconds. "The blood type is wrong for Mac. It's not her."

Tears sprang to her eyes. "Oh, Gray, that's wonderful."

But it didn't mean Mac wasn't dead.

Chapter 33

When choosing a color for a room, consider
the measurements of the space. More wall
space makes the color seem deeper.
—HAMMER GIRL BLOG

F riday night came too soon for Grayson. A dinner party was
not his type of event, but having Ellie on his arm made up
for his discomfort with the tux. When had he last worn a tux?
Probably to his sister's wedding.

So much was riding on this evening. Ellie looked stunning
under the glow of the chandelier. Her light-brown hair was up
in some kind of fancy do that left little twists of hair touching
her cheeks. He didn't think he'd ever seen her in makeup, and
tonight she wore only a light touch, but skin like hers didn't
need much. The dress hugged her curves in all the right places,
and though he knew she felt it revealed too much, she had her

shoulders squared and her head up. No one would know how uncomfortable she was.

Guests milled around the expansive room that held a massive marble fireplace soaring all the way to the fifteen-foot ceiling. The ultra-contemporary home had to be fifteen thousand square feet, and this room was easily fifty feet long. The party spilled out through an open sliding wall that connected with an enormous flagstone patio. Bar-top tables had been brought in, and servers offered flutes of champagne and hors d'oeuvres on black trays. Everyone was dressed to the nines. He'd thought about opting for a sports coat, but he would have been out of place, and they wanted to mingle and try to discover something helpful. He wanted to blend in with the sea of black suits.

He scanned the crowd. "Do you know what Terrance Robb looks like? I've never met him."

"Oh, yes, I know both of them. I babysat for them."

"So we want to know what Mac told him about the flotilla."

She nodded. "He might have done some digging into whatever she told him. Even if he discounted it, there might be a lead we can use."

"Hmm. Lots to dig out at a party where it's going to be tough to get them alone." He stopped and took her hand. Her fingers closed around his, and he liked the feel of her trusting hand in his. "I think that's Rear Admiral Hutchinson, Candace's father."

Grayson had met the man a few times over the years, and he recognized the leonine head of white hair topping an aquiline nose and chiseled chin. Hutchinson stood talking to a blonde woman who hugged his arm affectionately. "Is that his daughter?"

"Sure is." Ellie started that way, but Grayson caught her arm. "We probably ought to talk to Candace alone. We don't want to get thrown out before we have a chance to learn something. Let's mingle and look for her husband."

She nodded, and he tucked her hand into the crook of his elbow. A server passed, and he snagged a couple of tiny pastries for them. His was gone in one gulp, which left him eyeing hers longingly.

"You can have it." She lifted it to his lips, and he opened his mouth.

Her fingers grazed his lips, and he kissed them lightly before she could snatch her hand away. "Tasty."

Her cheeks went pink at his forward remark, and she looked away.

"Sorry," he said. "I didn't mean to embarrass you."

"I'm not embarrassed." Her choked voice told a different story.

Why did he like to make her blush so much? And heaven help him, he liked being with her in more ways than he could count. He was in serious trouble. Her business was firmly established here, and his work was in Seattle, hours away.

She inclined her head. "Don't look now, but there's Terrance. He's by himself too."

Grayson gave a surreptitious glance to the corner. Robb was about six feet tall with blond hair and a rangy build. He had a slight pudge from sitting at a desk all day. "Let's go talk to him."

She nodded, and he tucked her hand into the crook of his elbow. "You start the conversation since you know him," Grayson whispered.

They reached the man, and Ellie extended her hand. "Mr.

Robb, so good to see you again. My partner and I just bought your house in Lavender Tides, and you're going to be so pleased with what we're doing to it. It will have a wonderful open floor plan when we're done, and we're putting in top-of-the-line finishes."

Robb took her hand. "Ellie, I haven't seen you in ages. You're all grown up. And I'm glad you're pleased with the house. You'll have to let me know when it's done. I'm sure Candace will want to take a peek at it." His smile widened to show perfect white teeth. "Though maybe that's not safe. She'll likely want to buy it back for a vacation getaway."

"She might," Ellie agreed. "Your wife has good taste. Mr. Robb, have you heard about my sister, Mackenzie? She was attacked and has been missing. There was a lot of blood at the scene, and the FBI thinks she was killed. We haven't found her body."

His smile vanished. "I hadn't heard about it, but I'm so sorry. Any idea what happened?"

Ellie shook her head. "We're still trying to figure that out. We've been researching her last few weeks, and we heard she wanted to cancel the tall ships flotilla. When the committee refused, she said she was going to talk to you because letting them come here was dangerous. Can you tell me what she said to you?"

"She did come to see me. She believed someone named Gun Moon planned to set off an EMP bomb. It was pretty far-fetched, of course."

And Gun Moon was dead. "Did you investigate it?"

"Just a cursory look. She was very distraught about it. I'm not sure where the notion came from."

"Mr. Robb, someone killed Gun Moon and left his body in your secret basement room."

The man blanched. "Murdered?"

"Garroted. An efficient execution method often used by ISIS."

"If the CIA can be of any help, be sure to let me know." He looked over her shoulder. "My father-in-law is beckoning me. Good to talk to you."

Once he was out of earshot, Grayson steered Ellie deeper into the corner. "He didn't really investigate it. If he had, maybe Mac would still be with you."

"Now what?" Ellie skirted the patio in the shadows with a glass of iced tea in hand.

The party had started to thin out a bit, and they still hadn't had an opportunity to talk to Candace. People stood under gleaming lights on the patio, and some had wandered down to the edge of the water.

"Let's give it a little more time to see if we can catch Candace by herself," Gray said.

"What do we hope Candace can tell us?"

"Maybe she overheard Mac talking to her husband. He's trained to spill nothing. She might offer some kind of insight. It's worth a shot."

She'd found it hard to keep from staring at him all evening. The tux spanned those broad shoulders without a wrinkle, and the contrast of black and white was an amazing look on him. Tonight was a Cinderella night for sure, but she knew she'd transition back into a scullery maid much too soon.

A group of women began to disband, and she spotted Candace's blonde head walking down to the beach. "There she is. Let's go."

Gray clasped her hand. "Steady. This yard is soft, and one of your heels could snap right off."

Whatever reason he wanted to give for holding her hand was fine by her. She clung to his strong fingers as they hurried to catch up with the other woman in her flowing pink gown. She looked like a true princess with her shining blonde hair piled high on her elegant head. Ellie could never dream of appearing so beautiful and put together.

The moon glimmered on the waves rolling to shore, and the lights on passing boats added a romantic touch to the scene. She caught the scent of the blazing lanterns. A foghorn echoed across the water and blended with the *putt-putt* of the engines. The distant murmur of people from the party talking and laughing grew louder, and Ellie knew she had to stop Candace before other partygoers distracted them.

Ellie's ankle turned under her and she nearly fell, but Gray caught her, and they both stumbled out of the lights from the yard lamps and into the shadows from the trees lining the property.

Gray caught her against his chest as she reached down to rub her ankle. "Are you okay?"

"I think so." She tried to put weight on her foot and winced. "Yikes, I think I sprained it."

"Let me see." He knelt and probed the tender flesh with gentle fingers. "It's already starting to swell. You need to prop it up and put ice on it."

Ellie glanced out to where she'd last seen Candace and saw that Terrance had joined her. They stood only a few feet away, but the shadows hid her and Gray from view. She opened her mouth to call to them when she heard Terrance say her name.

"Did you see Ellie Blackmore?"

"I thought I saw her here. I haven't had a chance to talk to her. Why, what's wrong?"

Gray swooped Ellie into his arms and stepped farther back into the shadows. His breathing slowed, and Ellie matched his light inhales and exhales.

"She came with a Coast Guard investigator. Try to stay out of her way. I think she's only here to ask questions. You'd think her sister would serve as a warning to let things be, but that doesn't seem to be the case."

Ellie's blood roared in her ears. Was he saying he had something to do with Mac's death?

Gray pressed his lips to her ear when she started to struggle to be put down. "Quiet." His breath barely puffed against her skin.

She relaxed against his chest. They needed to get the information any way they could. Now wasn't the time for confrontation.

Candace's voice got softer. "Do you think she knows you were told to make sure the flotilla came here?"

"I don't see how she could. There was nothing fishy about it."

"You need to get her out of here," Candace said. "I don't want to talk to her."

"The party's nearly over. You cut the cake, and it's almost gone. Half the guests have left. Maybe they did too. I haven't seen them for a while." He took his wife's arm.

"What about Mackenzie?"

"I haven't been able to find her. Her disappearance wasn't my doing. You thought I had her hauled off?"

Candace shrugged her slim shoulders. "It made sense after

she waylaid us with all those demands about stopping the flotilla. Why were you told to get it here anyway? It seems like a small thing."

"It doesn't matter. Let's just get through tonight and put it behind us."

"So who do you think took her?"

"She stole some cocaine. That's all I know. She's not our problem."

Hot tears flooded Ellie's eyes. Mac wasn't a problem—she was a living, breathing person. To hear these two discuss her possible death so callously took her breath away.

Someone called Candace's name, and she turned and waved. "Be right there." She turned back toward her husband for a moment. "Make this go away, Terrance. This *cannot* derail us after all these years."

"It won't, my dear." He retreated toward the house, then disappeared into the last of the guests milling in the great room.

"Let's get out of here," Grayson whispered in her ear. "There's a lot to talk about and to investigate."

"You can put me down. I can walk."

"You don't weigh anything, and I don't want us to be seen. We'll skirt the side of the house and have a valet fetch my SUV. Hang tight."

His long legs ate up the yard, and she clung to his neck with both hands. While she'd dreamed of being in his arms, this wasn't quite the way she imagined.

Terrance had been asked to make sure the flotilla came here. What did that mean?

Chapter 34

Put investment pieces front and center in a room.
You want visitors to notice the room's best assets.
—HAMMER GIRL BLOG

Two ice packs swaddled Ellie's swollen ankle, and she sat nestled on the sofa in a bright-red throw Grayson had found in the hotel room closet. Cooler air had blown in with a storm tonight, and it was pleasant with the window open. The FBI had stationed several agents in the hallway, but he was still on high alert.

The Robbs' callous conversation had convinced him dangerous forces were swirling closer to them. Who would have asked him to make sure the flotilla didn't get canceled? The FBI? Maybe they thought if it got canceled, the terrorists would escape them and set off the bomb in a more highly populated area. This might have been their best shot at catching a big cell.

She yawned. "I'm pretty tired. I'd better get to bed. The agents are still out there?"

"Yeah, I checked when I locked the door. I'll be here, though."

"Why, Mr. Bradshaw, are you trying to get rumors started by staying here alone with me all night?" The teasing light in her eyes faded, and she shook her head. "On second thought, I doubt that would happen. People would take one look at you and know I'm not your type."

He grinned and leaned over to capture a curl grazing her cheek. "What's my type?"

"You know, tall, willowy blondes with some kind of fashion sense. A gorgeous woman who looks good on your arm." Her voice shook and went husky.

That rankled. "I think you need to get to know me better. I like someone real and fresh with glowing skin that doesn't need makeup. Someone who knows her way around a hammer and crowbar." With every word, he moved closer until he could run his fingers down the side of her face. "Someone with skin as soft as silk and amber eyes that show her soul."

Her lips parted, and her eyes were luminous. "I-I think you're teasing me."

"I might be, but that doesn't mean it's not true." He tipped her chin up, then brushed her lips with his. Her lips were incredibly soft, and she stirred all his senses.

He dropped his hand. "And you're way too tempting. I'd better help you to bed before I lose my morals." He scooped her up in his arms and carried her out of the living area into the bedroom and laid her on the bed and tucked the covers around her.

He kissed her on the forehead, his lips lingering for a moment, backed away and shut the door behind him, then headed for the sofa where he pulled out his phone and called Lance.

"Bradshaw, you have a death wish? It's after midnight."

"And you don't even sound sleepy."

Lance gave a low chuckle. "Caught me. I'm up binge-watching war movies." The man studied war games like some people studied poker moves.

"I had an interesting conversation with Terrance Robb tonight. He claims he was told to make sure the tall ships flotilla went off as planned this weekend. Who would have ordered that?"

"Strange. You have a theory?"

"I wondered if it was the FBI. Could he be working with them? Maybe they didn't want to scare off the cell and thought it was better to try to catch them here in a lower-population area."

"I haven't heard any rumors like that." There was a distant *ding* on the other end of the phone. "Oh, hey, that query on Robb came back already. He's not working with the FBI, but we've suspected him of selling information to the North Koreans."

"So if we didn't tell him to make sure the flotilla exhibition took place, it might have been the North Koreans. Maybe he's part of the plot."

"He's on a watch list. I'm going to report this."

"Thanks, Lance." He ended the call.

The door to the bedroom opened, and a tousled-haired beauty peered out. "Who were you talking to?"

"Lance." He told her what he'd found out. "Think about who might be good friends with Terrance. You'd know that better than I do."

"I will. Good night." She closed the door again.

Just in the nick of time. He'd been about to cross the room and take her in his arms again.

Ellie's ankle was much better by morning, but she still limped a bit as she held on to Gray's arm while walking to a table at the Rainshadow Brewhouse. The aroma of espresso and pastries made her mouth water. She hadn't eaten much at the party last night, and her stomach was protesting.

"I'll get us coffee and bagels," Gray said.

She watched him head for the long line at the counter. He stood a full head above most of the other people waiting, and several women turned toward him and smiled. Since last night she'd felt shy and uncomfortable. She wished she could believe the sweet words he'd said to her.

The door opened, and she caught sight of a familiar uniform. Sheriff Burchell scanned the crowd, then nodded when he saw her. He must have come inside looking for her because he headed straight for their table.

He pulled out a chair and joined her.

Her pulse surged. "Have you found anything?"

"Sorry, no, but Gray left me a message saying he had some things to talk over. I was about to call him back when I saw you guys in here."

Grayson balanced the coffee and bagels on a tray as he joined them at the table. "I saw you come in, Sheriff, so I got you a black coffee. That okay?"

"Great." Everett took the cup and set it down. "What's going on?"

Gray put down the tray and lowered himself onto a chair, then launched into what they'd found out last night. The sheriff's expression stayed impassive, though he nodded several times.

He took a sip of coffee and huffed out a breath. "So why am I just now hearing that terrorists may be targeting my town? The FBI should have told me about this weeks ago."

Ellie paused as she reached for her breakfast. "You didn't know?"

"Nope. I only knew about the missing cocaine. Now you're telling me we might be dealing with an EMP bomb. *Tomorrow?*"

"You've lived here your whole life. How well do you know Terrance Robb?"

The sheriff took a sip of his coffee. "Pretty well, actually. Candace is my cousin. Might as well tell you that right up front. She's a hard woman to please—likes the best of everything. Terrance has been a saint dealing with her. He's a good guy. I wouldn't want you to suspect him."

"Do you know who his good friends are?"

"He's got lots of friends. I couldn't even begin to count all the committees he's been on through the years. Anyone needs a little help with something and Terrance has always been right there. I always thought he had political aspirations, but he's never run for office." He chuckled. "Maybe he thought the power would go to Candace's head."

Everett snagged a spare bagel. "Have you seen the tall ships? They're still out in the straits, but man, they're beautiful. White sails billowing in the sun and hulls gleaming."

A kernel of a thought rolled around in Ellie's head. "I haven't gone that way. We'll take a look."

The sheriff, his cheeks bulging with bagel, took his coffee and rose. "Later," he mumbled past the food in his mouth.

As soon as he was out of earshot, Ellie leaned closer to Gray. "What if we took a skiff out and asked to look around the ships? You think they'd let us? I could pretend to be Mac. They'd all know her name. Maybe it would work."

"They're not going to let you into any cabin with a bomb in it."

"We could split up. I could keep them distracted while you looked around."

"Ellie, those boats carry quite a few sailors. I'd be caught the minute I went belowdeck."

He was right, and she knew it. "So we're back to working with the FBI."

Gray's gaze held hers. "I'd like you to leave the area until Monday when this is over."

"You know I can't do that, Gray. The people I care about are all here. And why haven't the authorities ordered an evacuation? Why hasn't anyone told the sheriff what's going on?"

"The threat is too nebulous. We don't know any specifics, not even where this is supposed to happen."

"Mac was convinced the ships were a threat. That has to mean something."

Without realizing it, she'd reached for his hand, and his fingers curled around hers. "I don't want to lose you, Hammer Girl. Not when I've just found you."

"I-I don't want to lose you either." She couldn't look away from the intensity of his gaze. His blue eyes held more warmth than she'd ever imagined to find.

"Tell you what—let's get a tandem kayak and paddle out to

the tall ships. Maybe we'll hear something. I'd like to take a look at *Elyssa Marie.*"

She gulped the last of her coffee. "That's a great idea. What time do we have to be back to meet the FBI?"

He grimaced. "Four. I've ordered some drone pictures of the cabin on Gandy Lane. That should tell us a lot about what we're up against."

Chapter 35

A beach theme makes everyone relax. There's
nothing better than reconnecting with the water.
—HAMMER GIRL BLOG

Ellie inhaled the scent of the sea—kelp, salt, and sand. The sun glimmered on the waves. A ferry blew its horn on its journey to Whidbey Island, and she returned waves to several of the passengers leaning on the railing.

Their oars dipping into the placid water calmed the nervous energy zipping up and down her spine. She let her oar rest atop the kayak and exhaled. She stared at the way Gray's hair curled at the nape of his neck. His muscles flexed as he paddled, and she had to restrain herself from leaning forward and laying her palm on his back. Even from behind, he was so doggone handsome.

He pointed his oar at a small, uninhabited island. "I'm thirsty. Can you hand me a water?"

"Sure." She lifted the lid of the cooler and grabbed them both a bottle of water.

A dolphin leapt from the water to their right, and it startled her enough that she overreacted. Gray tried to correct the kayak's bounce at her sudden movement, but his jerk amplified the kayak's movement, and when she reacted as well to keep the kayak from tipping, her hand flew across the side of her glasses, and they flew off her face into the water.

"Easy, Hammer Girl. We're all right." With a few deft strokes, he had the kayak settled and turned sideways in his seat. "You lost your glasses."

Her hands flew to her face. "You're right. I'll never find them."

"Uh-huh." His hand *almost* hid his smirk.

There was too much pleasure in his noncommittal grunt, and she stared at him suspiciously. "It sounds like you're glad I lost my glasses."

His grin was wide. "You don't even need them. I've seen you take them off when you're concentrating and need to see really well. Why do you do that?"

Her cheeks heated, and she took a sip of her water. "Let's eat our snack now and catch our breath. That scared me." She handed him a baggie of cookies and took one for herself. If a man could be beautiful, he was, though he'd frown at such a term. But beauty meant perfection, and everything about his physique was unmatched by any other man she'd met in her life.

"You said you've never dated much, but do you have a girl-friend now?" She put her hand to her mouth. "Sorry, did I just say that out loud?"

He swallowed the last bite of his cookie. "You sure did. And I'll answer it if you tell me why you wear glasses when you don't need them."

"I shouldn't have asked." She balled up her plastic bag and reached for his.

He caught her hand in his and turned it over so it was palm up. He took the baggie away and tossed it into the cooler. His thumb made circles against her palm, and he made no move to release her.

"I told you I've traveled around too much to date very often, but there's a little more to it than that. I was a bit of a freak in Japan. My size and all."

"I can imagine you towering over all your friends. That had to be a bit intimidating."

His touch on her hand was making it hard to keep her breathing in an even pattern, and her pulse was jumping all over the place.

His gaze never looked away as he brought her palm to his lips in the gentlest and most tender way possible. "Then I went to college, but I knew I wanted to be in law enforcement so I was pretty focused on that, though I dated a bit. Nothing serious, though. I've been moving around a lot, and I've never really met anyone who tugged at my heartstrings."

He kissed her palm again, then moved up to her wrist. "Until now, that is."

He lifted his head and reached for her at the same time she moved toward him. His lips covered hers with a gentle yet masterful touch, and she was lost.

❧

Grayson had kissed other women before, but kissing Ellie was like coming home to a place filled with stability. He cupped her cheek in his palm and kissed her again. Her arms were around his neck, and he never wanted to let her go.

But he needed to.

Pulling back, he rested his cheek against hers. The sun was high overhead and heated his skin. Or was it Ellie? Her amber eyes were huge and pensive, and her skin looked even more golden in the bright light.

"I wish I had a jacket. You're cold."

"I'm fine."

In spite of her assurances about being warm enough, he could feel shudders rippling up her spine.

"I'm a little like the sea creatures here." Her fingers curled around his hand. "You wanted to know about my glasses, and I'll admit I wear them as a shield."

His fingers tightened protectively around hers. "A shield from what?"

"From being seen too closely. From being known too well. The people I loved most in the world have always condemned me, and I never felt very worthy." She made a face. "Do I sound like a crybaby? Even talking about it makes me feel raw and exposed. Believe me, that's a sensation I've avoided most of my life."

He dropped her hand, then gripped her shoulders. "You have no idea how amazing you are, do you? Loving, kind, and beautiful, any parents would be thrilled to have you for a daughter. And I'm honored to call you a friend. You make me want to be better, to give more and love more."

Her eyes filled with tears, but at least she held his gaze. "I don't deserve those kinds of accolades. I'm no one special."

He grinned. "I told you that you didn't know yourself well. I've never met anyone like you, and I want to woo you if you give me the chance." Her skin was incredibly soft.

Woo was an old-fashioned word, but it was how he felt. She deserved the best he could offer.

"I–I'd like that."

He dropped another kiss on her head. "I'd better check my email again for those drone pictures."

She lifted her head and nodded. "It's probably going to take another hour to paddle out to the *Elyssa Marie*."

Grayson dug his phone out of the baggie in the cooler, then called up his email. There were the pictures, but they weren't what he'd hoped to see.

He looked up. "The pictures are here, but the place looks empty. Nasser might have flown the coop."

If Nasser was gone, they had no real leads to follow. He prayed they'd find something at the ships.

Chapter 36

*The most beautiful home means nothing if it
has no soul or character. Some things can be
added, but you can't mimic the real thing.*
—HAMMER GIRL BLOG

The beautiful estate looked empty, but Wang's reconnais-
sance had told him the Robbs were here for the weekend.
They were the only ones in residence too. Her parents had left
this morning on a trip to Europe, so no one would interrupt the
little tête-à-tête. He'd pretended to be an installer for a new,
free security upgrade to their current system, and Terrance had
given him a code to get in. All he had to do was wait until they
were in there alone, then let himself in through the back. He'd
parked around the block and had walked here so no one saw
him. Easy peasy.

He could have instructed Nasser to take care of this loose end, but it hadn't seemed prudent. He no longer trusted Nasser.

Wang crept through the darkened rooms toward the family room where the two of them were watching a movie. From here it sounded like a cop show with guns blaring and people yelling, a perfect cover-up for any noise they might make. Though there were no nearby neighbors, so he should be able to do what was necessary without incident.

He stopped in the doorway and peered into the room. Dimly lit by one lamp and the television, the room held overstuffed leather furniture, recliners, and several expensive tables. It was a cozy room, the perfect representation of the perfect place to curl up with popcorn and watch TV.

Their backs to the door, the Robbs sat at opposite ends of the leather sectional. Candace held a Kindle and wasn't looking at the TV at all. Terrance seemed engrossed in the action taking place. Neither seemed aware that everything was about to change.

He pulled out his gun and stepped into the room, moving quietly until he stood between Terrance's view and the TV. "Hello, old friends."

Terrance sprang to his feet and reached for the gun lying on the coffee table beside him, but Wang got there first. "Uh-uh, that's not okay. Sit down." He motioned with the gun, and Terrance sank back onto the sofa.

His mouth tight, Terrance glanced around as if looking for a weapon. "What are you doing with that gun?"

Candace edged to the front of the seat cushion and sent a thousand-watt smile his way. "Well, hello there, it's good to see you."

"I'm sure it's not." He waved the gun in his hand. "At least not with this pointing your direction. The safety is off, by the way. It won't take much for me to blow your brains out. I don't trust you, Terrance. It's coming to an end tonight." Wang swiped his arm at the lamp by his side and swept it off the table to the wood floor where it shattered.

Both Robbs jumped, and Candace finally lost her superior attitude. She huddled in on herself, and tears began to leak from her eyes.

Terrance clenched his hands together in his lap, and his face went red. "We can end our partnership. Just tell me what you want me to do."

Wang had to hold back a grin. Terrance would clearly love to tackle him and bash his head in. Luckily, he had no weapon that could stand against this gun. "What did you tell Ellie and Bradshaw?"

"Nothing. She asked if Mac had come to me and asked me to pull strings to get the flotilla canceled. I told her that she had, but that I'd investigated and found nothing."

"Did she accept it?"

"I think so."

"You're the loose end, Terrance. They'll find the money in your overseas accounts, and it will all come crashing down. You'll tell everything you know, and I can't have that."

Terrance reached toward him. "Look, we can work this out."

Moments later Terrance and Candace were both dead. He grabbed the candle lighter on the fireplace mantel and lit the curtains on fire, then some paper he found. Smoke billowed as he walked away.

He'd thought clearing out the deadwood would feel better

than it did, but the only sensation he had was emptiness as he walked away.

Grayson's jaw dropped the moment he saw the flotilla of tall ships. Their sails billowed grandly, and their masts reached for the clouds. He could have sworn heavenly music played as he stilled his oar and watched as they sailed past.

"I've never seen a more beautiful sight," Ellie whispered. She was in the stern of the kayak, and she'd stopped paddling too. Her large eyes glowed with fervor. "Now I know why Mac wanted them here. It's like stepping back to another time, one populated with the myth and magic of the sea. I can almost hear pirates and the clash of swords."

Grayson grinned and began to row again. "And I thought I heard music. Got any idea which one is *Elyssa Marie*?"

"I saw a picture. She's a clipper like *Lavender Lady*. Most of the ships in the flotilla are barques and schooners." She reached for binoculars and focused them. Moments later she pointed. "There!"

The ship was the one closest to them. It had three masts and a square rig. Fully manned, the crew scurried around the deck, and he saw no way of sneaking aboard.

Ellie rose and waved to the crew. Most of them waved back, though the ready smiles ceased as Grayson brought the kayak closer to the boarding rope.

A man in a blue uniform leaned over the railing. His beard and mustache were more white than brown, and he wasn't smiling. "We can't allow you to board, miss."

"I'm Mackenzie Blackmore. I'm here to welcome you."

The man's mustache twitched, but Grayson wouldn't call it a smile. "Captain Arnett, Ms. Blackmore. I know your name, of course, but I still can't permit you to board. If you'd like to tour the ship tomorrow, I'll be happy to escort you personally." His gaze flickered over Grayson.

"I have a clipper too, did you know? *Lavender Lady* is beautiful." Ellie gave a vague wave. "She's moored over there."

"There aren't many of us in the flotilla. Are you going to join us tomorrow?"

Ellie's smile faltered. "I plan to."

"I will look forward to it." The captain tugged the brim of his hat. "If you'll excuse me, I have quite a lot to attend to. I hope to see you tomorrow." He moved away from the side and out of sight.

Ellie slumped. "Well, that was a bust."

"Let's just hang out here a bit. Maybe act like you've got a problem so they're not suspicious."

"Oh dear, my contact popped out." Ellie spoke loudly as she began to feel around the bottom of the kayak.

The murmur of voices was too soft and distant to make out any words, and Grayson wished he had a listening device. They weren't going to get anywhere with this. He shook his head at Ellie, and she climbed back onto her seat and picked up her oar.

The captain's voice bellowed out, "Move it! Wang will be here in two hours. It had better be shipshape."

Wang. Could it be the same man they'd been looking for? It had to be, didn't it?

"Did you hear that?" Ellie climbed back onto her seat and picked up her oar. "Could we just have the FBI move in after we think he's aboard?"

"I'd better at least let Lance know."

He paddled them a distance out from the boat, then pulled out his phone and called Lance. His friend promised to pass along the information.

Ellie's nose and cheeks held a bit of pink from wind and sun. "What'd he say?"

"He's going to let those in charge of the investigation know."

Her golden-brown eyes examined him. "But you don't think they will? You look down."

The kayak's bottom bumped sand at the boat launch by Harvey's Pier, and he jumped out and pulled it ashore. Holding out his hand, he helped Ellie out. Her face was set and strained.

"I'm tired of bumping into dead ends." He tossed his oar into the bottom of the kayak. "I want Nasser. He gave me this limp, and he killed my best friend. I'm beginning to fear he'll never be brought to justice. He'll just go on killing and destroying people's lives."

Ellie reached for him, and he pulled her close enough that he could feel the thump of her heart.

"I'm sorry," she said. "I didn't know. No wonder you've been so driven. What happened?"

He rested his chin on her hair and inhaled her sweet aroma. "We were hot on his tail and thought we had him cornered on a remote farm near Chicago. It was an ambush, though, and I heard him laughing as his men rushed him out. The guy's a devil."

He felt her head move as she nodded. Nasser couldn't get away with this. Grayson couldn't live with it.

Chapter 37

The second most important room in the home is the bathroom. Clear glass doors can make the space seem bigger because you can see all the way through.
—HAMMER GIRL BLOG

Ellie leaned her head back, then stretched her cold feet closer to the heat blasting from under the dash in Gray's SUV. She was nearly dry after rowing across the bay and getting warm in here, plus the huge sweatshirt Gray had dug out for her helped.

She thrust her hands into the pockets. "I'd hoped the agents would have some idea where to look for Nasser and his men."

"The man is like a phantom. Every time I get close, he vanishes with no trace. I hope the FBI is finding out more than we are."

She stared at the passing cars. "Could we go by Mac's office? I want to look through her desk one more time and maybe talk to some students. I got to thinking that I didn't check to see if anything was taped to the underside of her desk. It's probably silly, but I have to feel like I'm doing something."

"You have a key to get into the university?"

"Yes. I'll call Penny and let her know too, just in case someone calls to tell her someone is in Mac's office."

He slowed as they entered the town limits and shot her a glance. "I'll do lookout."

"The university is right in the middle of everything. I think we're safe. What I'd really like is for you to run and grab us some coffee while I take a quick look in the office. I'm still frozen." Her phone rang, and she glanced at the screen. One of her employees was calling. She was tempted to just ignore the call since she was in no mood to discuss the house, but it might be important.

"Hey, Clint, what's up?"

"Sorry to bug you, but I can't find Jason. He was supposed to help me lift that beam into place in the living room, but he's not answering his phone."

"Don't worry about it. We'll see what we can do on Monday."

"It's going to put us behind schedule."

"I know, but there's nothing we can do about it now. I could try to help lift the beam, but I'm not sure I could carry my end. I guess I can give it a try, though. I need to run by anyway and get my computer."

"I can do it. I'd rather you weren't anywhere near the house now that the terrorists know you've been staying there." Grayson took the phone from her. "Hey, Clint, if all you need is a strong back for a few minutes, I can help you. How long will it take?" He nodded. "Uh-huh. I'll be right there."

He ended the call and handed the phone back to her. "It won't take long. You head into the office, and I'll run over to the house, then grab coffee. I'll be back soon." He leaned over to brush her lips with his. "Be careful."

She patted his cheek with her palm. "I'll be fine. Extra-hot latte."

"I got this."

She slid her phone into the pocket of the sweatshirt, then smiled and opened her car door to slide out. "I'm going to lock the door behind me. Text me when you're here, and I'll unlock it."

"Will do." He let her out in front of the doors, then pulled out of the lot.

On a Saturday afternoon the only students around were ones using the library or heading to the gym. She had to use her key to get into the office building. Her footsteps echoed loudly on the marble floors, and the clatter set her teeth on edge and made shivers run down her back. She hurried to Mac's office, unlocked it, then stepped in and flipped on the lights. She texted Penny to tell her what she was doing. She slipped off her shoes and padded toward Mac's desk. Setting her shoes on the floor, she pulled out the chair and crawled under the desk to look around. It was dark under there, so she turned on her phone's flashlight and shone it around.

Nothing was taped to the metal underside, and she exhaled. "Doggone it. I was sure there'd be something."

Talking to herself made her feel a little less vulnerable and alone. She crawled out from under the desk and looked around. Mac's desk was clear and held only a calendar.

She had to be missing something, but what? The sheriff had

taken Mac's computer so she couldn't even look through files. A long expanse of lateral filing cabinets occupied one wall. Had anyone looked at Mac's student notes?

She called Penny. "Did anyone take over Mac's classes? Are her class notes still here?"

"Yes, the classes were reassigned. I think her notes are probably still there. She usually transcribed everything in the computer so there shouldn't be anything in the physical files that isn't in the computer."

"Thanks, Penny." She ended the call, then glanced at the time on her phone. Where was Gray? She called him but got his voice mail, so she left a message telling him she was ready to be picked up and that she'd just head over to the Brewhouse to wait. But when she didn't get him after trying again, worry began to gnaw at her. Why wasn't he answering his phone?

Maybe the sheriff would run her out to the House at Saltwater Point.

Perspiration dripped from Grayson's forehead and landed on the floor below him. His cell phone rang a few minutes ago, but he hadn't been able to get to it. It had taken longer than he'd expected to heft this beam up here. He perched on the top of the ladder with the beam on his shoulder and struggled to get it into place. He finally got it positioned, and Clint managed to nail it securely, raining drywall dust onto Grayson's head in the process.

He coughed at the dry dust in his throat, then retreated down the ladder. "You weren't kidding—that thing was heavy."

Clint scampered down his ladder too. He wiped the sweat from his face and left streaks of white along his cheeks. "We usually have more men on it, but at least it's done. Thanks for your help."

"Glad to do it. I'd better get out of here and pick up Ellie."

"I'm sure she's fine. How about some cold water or a Pepsi for the road? I've got a bunch on ice."

His mouth was as dry as a desert wind, and his tongue felt coated with gunk. "I wouldn't turn down some water."

"This way," Clint said. "It's in the kitchen."

Rolls of drywall tape, drywall tools, buckets of mud, and stacks of wallboard covered the floor. Only pipes poking through the floor and the wall identified the room as the kitchen. Clint opened the red metal cooler and pulled out a dripping bottle of water that he tossed at Grayson.

Grayson uncapped the water and drank half of it. The delicious wetness was heaven.

Clint popped the top on a Pepsi and chugged it too, then wiped his mouth with the back of his hand. "So you have something going on with Ellie?"

His tone was casual, but Grayson checked his expression anyway. Was the guy interested in her too? "I like her a lot."

"She's a nice person. When I came to town two years ago looking for a job, I didn't really have any skills. I'd taken care of my sick mom for some years, and when she died, I didn't know what I could be good at. I'd done some work around the house since we couldn't afford to hire it out. I ran into Ellie at the coffee shop and didn't even have money for anything bigger than a small drink. She bought my coffee and breakfast, then listened to my tale of woe. An hour later I had a job working on her houses."

While it didn't surprise Grayson to hear Ellie's kindness detailed, it still warmed him. "That's a pretty cool story."

"It is. And I have to say it causes me grief to have to hurt her."

Before the words could register, he had grabbed a heavy pipe wrench and brought it crashing down on Grayson's head. He went down hard and the lights went out.

"I'm probably being silly," Ellie told the sheriff as he parked his vehicle behind Gray's SUV in the drive at the Saltwater Point house. "I'm sure they're probably still up on the ladder."

"No lights on," the sheriff observed.

She stared at the house as she unfastened her seat belt. "Clint's truck isn't here."

The unease she'd worked hard to push aside came rushing back as she glanced inside Grayson's SUV to see the keys dangling from the ignition. She went up the porch to the entry and tried the door. The knob turned under her fingers, and she pushed open the unlocked door and flipped on the light. "Gray?"

Her voice echoed in the empty room. The heavy wooden beam overhead proved Clint's request had been valid, which should have reassured her. Where was Gray? He wouldn't have left his SUV behind when he knew she was waiting for him to pick her up. And he wasn't answering his phone.

Her footsteps echoed as she walked toward the kitchen where she found more confirmation that something was wrong. A bloodstain spread out on the dusty plywood, and Gray's phone, screen shattered, was in the corner. Water had spilled from an uncapped bottle.

Horror kept her rooted in place, and she licked dry lips. "They're both missing."

The sheriff was looking more and more troubled. "I'm going to call for help from the state and FBI." Everett took out his phone and moved to the door.

While he stepped outside to make the calls, Ellie wandered through the house and tried to think of anything Clint might have said that would indicate where he'd taken Gray. Nothing came to mind. Clint was always on time, a hard worker, and well liked by her and Jason as well as the other employees. Had someone harmed both of them, then stolen Clint's truck?

Everett ducked back inside. "I have to go. Terrance and Candace Robb just died in a fire at her father's estate. Come on and I'll drop you at home."

She backed away and shook her head. "That can't be an accident. You go on ahead. I'll take Gray's SUV."

Distracted, he nodded and rushed for the door. A sense of hopelessness made her want to sink to the floor and bury her face in her hands. If the Robbs hadn't been able to escape whatever web was closing in on them, what hope did she have? She couldn't give in to weakness, though. There had to be some clue to find Gray.

A light tap came at the front door, and she looked up to see Isaac smiling through the glass. Maybe he could get her aboard that ship. It was the only place she knew to look for Gray.

She unlocked the door and opened it. "What are you doing out here?"

He lifted a brow. "I saw the sheriff's car pull out with its lights flashing and wondered if you needed help. Everything okay?"

"Gray is missing." She pointed out the bloodstains. "I think he might be on board one of the tall ships, the *Elyssa Marie*. Do you think you could get me aboard? We saw the tall ships today."

His smile vanished. "This looks serious, Ellie. What's the sheriff say?"

"The Robbs died in a house fire so he was on his way there. The FBI should be here soon, but I can't stand around waiting. I have to find Gray. Can you get me aboard that ship now?"

A frown crouched between his eyes. "Maybe. Let me see what I can do."

He pulled out his phone and placed a call, then turned his back to her and walked a few feet away while he spoke with someone. His smile came easy as he ended the call and turned around to face her. "Success! Let's get going. You have a weapon?"

She shook her head. "No weapon." Her bear spray was her only defense.

"Let's go." He took her arm and hurried her out the door to the drive. "We need to hurry."

She wanted to ask him why the huge rush, but if she showed any reluctance he might call it off, so she just nodded and kept up with his rapid steps. Once she got to the car, she'd text the sheriff and let him know where she was.

Isaac's car beeped when he unlocked it, and he slid behind the wheel while she went around to the passenger side. She buckled up, then pulled her phone out of her pocket.

She'd barely started to type the message to Everett when Isaac grabbed the phone out of her hand. Before she could respond, he lowered his window and tossed it out onto the road.

He pulled a revolver from his pocket and laid it on his left thigh. "I don't think you'll need that any longer."

The look in his dark eyes quelled the argument building on her lips. "Isaac?"

Could he have something to do with this? He'd told her that he'd insisted Mac go through with bringing the tall ships here, but he didn't seem a likely person to be behind a terrorist attack. She thought he was Jewish, so surely he wouldn't have teamed up with ISIS. What could possibly be his motive?

He smiled. "Don't worry. I've made arrangements for lover boy to join you too. He's way too tenacious to leave wandering around looking for you. You wanted to know what was coming down, and you'll both get a front-row seat."

Chapter 38

*Light does more than illuminate a room. It adds
ambience and elegance as well as a certain style.*
—Hammer Girl Blog

When Grayson awoke, he was trussed up and in a place with
no light. He shook his head to clear it, then became aware
of the sloshing of water. He was tied up in a box of some kind.
Clint's words just before he knocked him out reverberated in his
head. *Have to hurt her.*

He thrashed against his bonds, but the ropes lashing his wrists
together didn't budge. It was too dark to see, and the quarters
were too tight for him to sit up, but he squirmed around trying to
feel for anything he could use to cut through the rope. The box
appeared to be empty except for him.

A motor rumbled from somewhere, and he had a sense of
bobbing. Was he on a boat?

He had to get free. He rolled onto his back and tried to leverage his legs against the trunk, but the space was too narrow to get a good angle. He couldn't even bang his feet against the metal in hopes someone would hear.

The boat lurched to the left, and Grayson's head bounced up to hit the ceiling. After what seemed an eternity, the boat stopped, and he heard male voices in the distance. Footsteps came his way, and a key grated in the lock. The lid rose, and a bright flashlight shone in his eyes. Hard hands grabbed hold of his arms and hoisted him out of the trunk. Two of Nasser's thugs.

"What'd you take *him* for?" The younger man shoved Grayson ahead of him to a dock, and they both leaped onto it.

Clint's voice spoke out of the darkness. "Nasser wants him. He's got plans for him."

A chill ran up Grayson's spine at Clint's grim tone. Nasser's plans were sure to involve torture and death.

At least his feet weren't bound. If he found the opportunity, he'd race for the water and try to escape them. He turned his head slightly to look to his right and caught his breath when he saw a tall ship. It was too dark to identify. How far were they from people? He saw no lights in the distance except on the ship.

The men marched him along the dock to a skiff, then threw him into the bottom of it. He hit his bad knee and bit back a yelp of pain. Agony rose up his thigh. Gripping his knee, he sat up as the boat ferried toward the ship. Was Ellie on that ship too?

The skiff bumped the ship, and Clint yanked him to his feet. "Climb."

If he had his hands free, Clint wouldn't be able to shove

him around so easily. He kept his head down as though he were resigned, but his mind raced with escape plans. He needed to get his hands free, and he needed a weapon.

Grayson rubbed his knee. "I'm not sure I can." While his knee throbbed, it wasn't as bad as he made out.

The younger man prodded him with a gun. "I'd just as soon shoot you and feed you to the sharks. Don't tempt me."

"Back off," Clint snapped. "I told you—he's Nasser's."

Grayson gritted his teeth and put his right foot on the ladder. Using more of his biceps and less of his leg muscles, he hauled himself up the ladder until he lay gasping on the deck.

A man waiting at the top hauled him to his feet and marched him into the hold. Grayson's knee gave out as he started down the ladder, and he tumbled the rest of the way to the floor where he lay stunned. Pain hit his shoulder, and his knee increased its complaint to a scream.

His captor leaped after him and pulled him to his feet again, then guided him past some ominous-looking contraption to the bow of the boat. They had to thread their way through crates and barrels to a tiny cabin. The sailor shoved him inside and shut the door behind him.

The bomb was probably on this ship, and he had to stop it.

Ellie hadn't wanted to see the tall ship quite this way. She stood on the deck of the *Elyssa Marie* with the stars gleaming down. It should have been a beautiful sight to see the ship lights reflecting off the water in the strait, but this was anything but a pleasure sail. The ship was moving farther away from shore, and she had to fight with the terror telling her to fling herself overboard and swim for land.

Sailors, both men and women, scurried to their duties. Most of them appeared to be Asian, and none of them talked to her when she spoke. Maybe they didn't even speak English. The answers were on this ship, and she couldn't escape her duty to do what she could to stop the mass chaos and loss of life from radiation poisoning.

Isaac's grip on her arm was hard, and she let him shove her toward the ladder to the hold. He'd refused to answer any questions on the ride here, and she'd finally given up and turned to watch the dark woods as his vehicle zipped past them. At one point she'd tested the door, but the lock didn't budge. And it had been too dark when they passed another vehicle to motion for help.

They reached the ladder, and she wrenched her arm free. "Where are you taking me?"

"Why, to your sister, of course. Isn't that what you wanted?" He inclined his head. "What are you waiting for? She's down there."

Dead? She was afraid to ask so she started down into the darkness.

When she reached the floor, she paused to let her vision adjust to the dimly lit space. She was in a huge area with no cabins. Various machinery parts she couldn't identify occupied the space, and it wasn't nearly as finished or as beautiful as *Lavender Lady*.

An older Asian man grabbed her arms and propelled her toward the stern. He opened a door and shoved her inside. She fell onto a hard, wooden bench.

"Ellie?"

She looked up at the familiar voice and saw her sister, pale and disheveled, sitting on the bench. "Mac? Mac, you're alive!" In seconds they were in each other's arms. She didn't mind her sister's greasy hair and rank body odor. She was alive. That was all that mattered.

Mac pulled back to stare in her face. "How'd you get here? You shouldn't have come."

Ellie told her about Isaac's offer to show her the ship. "I wanted to try to stop the bomb. I-I can't tell you how happy I am to see you. We all thought you were dead."

"Well, it was supposed to look like that. I was really stupid, Ellie. I thought he loved me."

"Isaac?"

Mac shook her head. "Tarek Nasser. We were making it look like I was dead so I could go with him. We'd taken blood over several weeks' time and planned to spill it on board. With my disappearance, I would be presumed dead."

How incredibly cruel to preplan something like that. Didn't she think of how Ellie would feel? "That's what happened." Ellie's gaze landed on a crusted-over cut on Mac's forehead. "But then you were really attacked?"

Her sister nodded. "I came to in a cellar. Tarek found out I'd gone to the FBI. I never intended to turn him in—I just wanted him to cancel his plans."

"What's he going to do?"

"He and Isaac are setting off an EMP bomb. It will launch from here into the atmosphere to take out electronics in the area and scatter radiation all along the Pacific Northwest. ISIS then plans to mount an attack in San Francisco."

Exactly what Lance had told them. "We have to stop it."

"I tried to convince Tarek, but he's firmly aligned with Isaac. Everyone calls Isaac 'Wang,' which means 'king' or 'ruler.'"

"I thought Isaac was Jewish. Why is he involved in this?"

"He's the liaison with the North Koreans. When he was getting his doctorate, he sneaked into North Korea on a dare, was recruited by them, and has been on their payroll ever since."

It still made no sense to Ellie. "Why would he betray his country?"

"He's heavily into politics, and he's disillusioned with America. He feels an EMP war would shake things up, take us back to basics, and make the citizens remember who we were when we first became a nation."

"But people would die." Why did anyone become this radical? Ellie couldn't wrap her head around it. "We have to get free and stop this. Gray doesn't know where I am."

"Gray?"

"He's the Coast Guard investigator here looking into the theft of the cocaine."

Mac's face reddened. "I was so stupid, Ellie. Looking back, I realize just how stupid. I hate that you got dragged into this. Did Isaac get the message in the mah-jongg tiles?"

It all clicked. "He's been targeting me because of the message? There was a picture in the box that Gray said was some kind of hidden message. I think the FBI is still working on figuring it out."

"It's the codes he needs to set off the bomb."

"Does that mean Wang can't detonate it without that message?"

Mac shook her head. "I'm sure he had the codes delivered another way by now."

Ellie moved close enough to bump shoulders with her sister. "I'm just overjoyed you're alive. Listen, I have an idea. Can you ask a sailor to let you go to the bathroom? I'll distract him, and you can get up top. You're a strong swimmer. Get to shore and call the FBI."

"I-I don't know if I can make it, Ellie. I'm still so weak and dizzy."

Ellie stared at her sister's face, still bruised. Even her hair held traces of blood. They must not have allowed her a shower since she'd been attacked. Though Ellie wasn't a strong swimmer, she had to try. "Okay, I'll get help."

Mac adjusted her posture and raised her voice. She shot off a rapid-fire question in Korean. A few minutes later a sailor stepped into the room and grabbed Ellie by the arm. He pulled her into the bigger room, then shoved her toward the head.

Chapter 39

We could take advice from shipbuilders. They know
how to pack a lot of functionality into a small space.
—HAMMER GIRL BLOG

G rayson, his hands bound behind him, sat on a wooden
bench in a tiny cabin in the hold of the ship. His knee
throbbed, and something wet obscured his vision and trickled
down his face. The coppery taste of the moisture on his lips told
him that moisture was blood. No matter how much he strained,
he was unable to budge the ropes. He figured Nasser would be
there any minute.

The door to the cabin opened, and Jason tumbled inside and
hit the floor. His hands were bound behind his back, and blood
trickled from his nose and mouth. He struggled to his feet and
staggered over to the bench.

"How'd you get here?" Grayson asked.

"I spotted Ellie in a car with Isaac. She had her shoulder pressed against the door like she was trying to get away from him. I followed them at a distance and saw him tie her up and row her out here. I had an inflatable raft in my truck so I left a message for the sheriff, then paddled out to the ship. I tried to climb up on the aft side, but someone spotted me. Where's Ellie?"

Ellie was in danger, and Isaac was behind this. "I haven't seen her, but if she's here, we need to find her."

"What's going on?" Jason's brown eyes were bewildered. "Why would Isaac bring her here? I don't understand."

"We knew there was a mastermind behind a terrorist plot to set off an EMP bomb. Mac's involved somehow, but we don't have all the details of that. Isaac must be Wang, the mastermind."

Jason slumped against the seat. "Wow, I had no idea all this was going on. So Isaac orchestrated the attacks on Ellie?"

"Apparently, though we still don't know why." And why bring Ellie out here?

The door opened, and Nasser stepped in. His dark eyes held a triumphant glint, and his grin revealed the most obnoxious gloating. "Bradshaw, we meet face-to-face at last."

"What have you done with Ellie?" The muscles in his arms tensed as he wrestled with the rope.

"She's safe and sound. For now. I can't tell you how much pleasure it will give me to see you both go down with this ship. I'll finally be rid of you. It's been a long time coming."

"Let her go. She's done nothing to you."

"She and her sister nearly derailed my plans." He tipped his head and studied Grayson. "Romantic attachments can be so messy. I think I've learned my lesson this time. You won't have a chance to learn from your mistakes."

A shout came from outside somewhere, and Nasser turned to the door. "I'd better see what's going on. I'll be back." He stepped into the hold and pulled the door shut behind him.

Now was the time.

Grayson twisted his wrists together, but the ropes didn't budge. Most sailors knew how to tie knots good and tight. "We've got to get free. Let me see if I can untie you."

He moved until his back was to Jason's and tried to loosen the knot with the limited movement he had in his fingers. The rope was too stiff and tight to make any headway.

"I can't get it. See if you can do anything with mine."

Jason fumbled with the knot for several minutes. "I'm not getting anywhere. We need a knife or something sharp." His head came up. "I don't think they took my box cutter. It's a flat piece of metal with a slit in it, so they probably missed it. See if you can get it out of my back pocket. It might work."

Jason turned his back to Grayson, and Grayson fumbled with his numb fingers to try to reach the box cutter. The rough hemp scraped his wrists as he worked to get it. "Got it."

He maneuvered the slit so the rope could slide into it and reach the blade. The rope was a little wide, but after some twisting, he felt the hemp move.

"I'm free!" Jason tossed the rope to the floor and took the box cutter to Grayson's bonds.

In moments Grayson's hands were free too. He twisted them around to get the blood flowing to his fingers again, then moved quietly to the door. He couldn't see much through the window, so he opened the door a crack. They seemed to be in the bow of the boat, and crates and barrels filled the space outside the cabin. He motioned for Jason to be quiet, and they moved through the obstacles. Voices came their way, and they ducked down behind some barrels.

There were few cabins here, and Ellie was in none of them. The only space to be searched was the hold at the stern. The men moved through the shadows, and when they were gone, Grayson checked several rooms along the hold. Most held bunks, but a movement in one of them made him stop. Mackenzie sat on a bunk. Ellie would be so relieved to discover she was alive.

Jason made a small sound behind him, and his eyes widened when he saw his ex. Grayson held his finger to his lips.

Boots stepped onto the ladder at his side, and he ducked back into the shadows with Jason. Isaac moved nimbly down the steps, then turned and went back to the room they'd vacated. They would only have moments to get out of here.

How long had Ellie been in the head? The sailor would be pounding on the door any minute.

A heavy fist beat on the door, and the sailor shouted in Korean. She had no idea what he was saying, but she knew he was about to come barging in.

"I'm ready!"

He shoved open the door and glared at her before saying something else in Korean and jabbing his thumb toward the room. She nodded as though she understood and shuffled after him. There had to be a chance to make a break for the ladder and freedom.

Another sailor hailed him, and he pointed for her to go back to the room as he stepped over to talk to the other man. This was her chance. The ladder to the deck was only five feet away. Moving as silently as she could, she moved toward it. The two men seemed deep in conversation, and she prayed she'd escape without them noticing.

She'd put one foot on a step when her captor started to turn. He'd see her any moment and give a shout. Before she could decide what to do, Mac kicked at the door and called out in Korean behind her.

Both sailors turned away from Ellie to stare at the door, and Ellie scurried up the ladder as fast as she could. She poked her head out under the stars and looked around. Several sailors stood talking at the bow, and she caught a few words of Korean. And Clint was with them. Her hands curled into fists, and she wished she could pummel him. Had he killed Gray? She couldn't bear to think of what was happening to the man she loved.

Yes, *loved*. She could admit it now that she feared she'd lost him.

She didn't have the luxury of striking Clint. To the port side, farthest from the shore, the railing was unprotected by any sailors. She darted for the side and slung one leg over the railing.

Clint turned and spotted her, shouting after her. He rushed toward her, but she jumped over the side before he could reach her, then dove under the water. The grip of cold water squeezed the breath from her lungs. She had to get help before hypothermia took her down.

She swam for the bow, which would be the opposite direction they would expect since it faced out into the strait. A splash came when she surfaced close to the hull, and she kept her head down. Just as she thought, the sailor was swimming toward the stern.

She dove under the water again, then set off into the strait toward a tall ship moored in the distance. All her fears about sharks swimming under her tightened her chest, but she pushed away her terror and set off again. If she could get aboard one of the ships, the captain could call the Coast Guard. She had to get help for Mac. A large wave swamped her, and she went under, then came up with saltwater burning in her nose and throat.

Her strokes seemed ineffective and helpless. She paused to tread water and catch her breath. The cold water stole her strength, and she wished she could stop the fight, sink under the water, and sleep, but she couldn't fail. Mac was depending on her. And the entire region was at risk.

She started for the ship again, and a cramp seized her left leg. Biting back a cry, she paused again and massaged it.

"Help me, Lord." She floated on her back a moment and looked up at the stars. She had to get to the other ship.

Had to.

Panic drove her on, past her own endurance, and she glanced behind once to see no one was in pursuit. Two splashes nearer to the shore were likely from sailors dispatched to find her. She gritted her teeth and moved to the ship's side by the ladder. Pausing, she treaded water and shouted, "Help!"

She grasped the rope ladder with numb fingers and began to climb as several sailors looked over the side of the boat. "I need help," she gasped.

It was all she could do to climb up to the deck. When she practically fell over the railing, a deckhand dropped a blanket around her shoulders. "Call the Coast Guard." Her teeth chattering, she told him what was happening, and he raced to radio the Coast Guard for help.

She prayed they arrived in time. Those madmen were likely to simply set off the bomb early.

In moments Isaac would see he was gone. Grayson darted forward into the hold, then held his hand to his lips and slipped into the room to pull Mac to her feet.

"I'm a friend of your sister's," he whispered. "I'm with the Coast Guard. We have to get you out of here."

He led her out the door and propelled her toward the starboard side of the hold. There was a small space between stacks of crates, and he wedged in there with Mackenzie and Jason. Running footsteps came back their way, and they all froze, ducking down even farther.

Isaac shouted, and his footsteps pounded back up the steps.

The search would be on. "I have to stop the bomb," he whispered in her ear. "Jason, you get her out of here."

Her lips flattened, and she started to shake her head. "You might need us."

"You need to get out of here." From his training he knew there were small nuclear weapons, but to set one off as an EMP, it would have to be able to be launched into the atmosphere. He walked around the hold looking at the contraption he'd seen when he first came down.

It looked like a small, narrow cannon, but if this was it, the nuclear rocket wasn't loaded yet. Where could it be? He eyed the crates and found one with the lid partially pried off. He wrenched it off the rest of the way and looked inside. Then gulped at the sight of what was clearly a bomb.

Mackenzie's shoulder pressed against his. "That's it, isn't it?"

"Yeah, it has to be." There was a control panel where the codes would be input. Was it armed even now? He looked closer and saw the clock wasn't ticking down. "I don't think it's armed yet."

A bullet whizzed by his head, and Jason fell hard against a crate, then landed on the floor. He didn't move. "Get down!" Grayson jerked Mackenzie down with him, then peered over the top of the crate to see Isaac advancing toward them with a gun. Two armed men were behind him. Grayson curled his hands into fists and wished he had his firearm. He spared a glance at Jason, but the man wasn't moving. Blood poured from a wound on his arm and another on his head.

Grayson motioned to Mackenzie to crawl through the tunnels created by the stacks of crates. "Make a little noise," he whispered. When she started to the starboard side, he moved port side and peered past the edge of a crate to see Isaac and his henchmen moving toward the other two.

Lord, help me. Grayson barreled out of the cramped space and leaped on top of Isaac's back before the man could swing his gun around. He wrestled Isaac around toward the other two men so he was facing them, then grabbed at Isaac's gun. It wavered close to Grayson's head, and Isaac's mouth was stretched in a snarl as he struggled to pull the trigger.

"Shoot him," Isaac yelled.

The other two men tried to circle around him with their guns, but Grayson kept Isaac in front of him. He managed to squeeze Isaac's wrist in a tight grip, then shook his arm until the gun went skittering across the floor. Grayson kept Isaac's arms pinned behind his back and used him as a shield.

He spun him around closer to the other men. "Throw down

your weapons or I'll break his neck." Isaac struggled to free himself, but Grayson easily kept him under control. "Tell them to throw down their weapons."

"Shoot him!" Isaac shouted again.

Footsteps thundered above them, and a man called out, "Coast Guard, drop your weapons."

Isaac fought with renewed strength, but Grayson kept him locked down. The men looked at each other, then tossed their guns to the floor.

Grayson thought it was all over until he heard a war cry behind him and turned to see Nasser barreling down the ladder toward him with a saber in his hand.

Chapter 40

Master the hammer and you master renovation.
—HAMMER GIRL BLOG

Heavy rain began to fall and thunder rumbled over the waves, but from the Coast Guard boat, Ellie watched men grappling on the deck. Had someone saved her sister? She shivered as the cold rain penetrated her clothing. She heard a cry that sounded like her sister and sprang to her feet. Before any of the personnel could stop her, she scrambled from the boat to the ship, their yells for her to stop ringing behind her.

A wooden locker stood open next to the ladder that led to the hold, and she spotted a hammer and snatched it up. It would have to do. She advanced down the ladder with the hammer ready. The scene below seized her gut. A swarthy man was cutting at the air with a very sharp-looking saber. His cruel laughter rang out, and Gray backed up as the man advanced.

Nasser?

Without thinking she threw the hammer like a hatchet. It flew end over end in a perfect arc to strike Nasser on the back of the head. He fell face-forward without a sound.

Ellie's heart kicked in her chest. Her mountain of a man was still standing head and shoulders above lesser mortals. Their gazes met, and he raced toward her. "I always knew you could wield a hammer like no one else." His big arms pulled her into a fierce embrace. "Thank God, Ellie. Mackenzie told me you'd gone for help, but I was so afraid you'd been captured."

She lifted her head. "Mac's okay? Everyone's fine?"

He hesitated. "She's fine, but Jason was shot. He's over there. Mac is with him."

She pulled away. "I'd better see."

She found Mac kneeling beside Jason, and her face was streaked with tears when she looked up. "Ellie, he's not waking up." She was holding a blood-soaked T-shirt to the side of his head.

The hard wood bit into her bare knees as she knelt on Jason's other side. She touched his cheek. "Jason, wake up." He didn't stir. She shook his shoulder. "Jason, wake up." She pressed her fingers against his neck and felt his pulse, weak and thready.

His eyes didn't flutter, and he made no sound. Did he have brain damage? "Is a doctor coming?"

Mac wiped her cheeks. "I think so. He can't die, Ellie. I was so mean to him. I discovered pretty early on that I didn't really love him. I just wanted someone of my own, I think. But I didn't have to be so cruel."

Ellie touched her hand. "I think he knew you didn't mean it."

Mac removed the T-shirt to look at the wound. "D–Does that mean you think he's going to die? He's not bleeding as much."

Ellie didn't answer because she didn't like Jason's labored breathing or his pasty color. She wasn't a doctor, but he looked bad.

Jason groaned, and she touched his cold cheek. "Jason?"

He muttered something she couldn't understand, then his eyelids fluttered and opened. He blinked and stared, then blinked again. "Is it night?"

"Yes, it is." She glanced around. The hold was lit with several lights. "Want to sit up?"

He nodded, and she helped him up and into a chair. He ran his hand over his face. "Man, it's dark here. Where are we? I can't see a thing."

Her gut clenched, and she moved to kneel in front of him. "Can you see me, Jason? I'm right here."

He shook his head. "It's as black as a cave, Ellie." His eyes were bloodshot and unfocused.

She touched his face. "Do you see anything, Jason? Any light at all?"

"I told you—it's like a cave in here! Why do you keep asking about it? Can't you see how dark it is?" He whipped his head around. "There's just nothing here."

She tried to tell herself it was just trauma from his head injury, but what if he was permanently blind? She couldn't bear to think about it.

She moved aside when the paramedics arrived and prayed. Jason had always been her rock. He never should have been here in the first place. She couldn't bear for him to be blinded while trying to help her.

She heard voices behind her and turned to see Coasties taking Nasser up to the top deck on a stretcher.

She rose and hurried up the ladder and found that Clint and

Isaac were in custody too. Isaac glared at her, but she held his gaze defiantly, and he looked away. A beautiful Asian woman in cuffs stood close to him.

Rain began coming down in sheets. It soaked her hair and dripped down her face as it made its way to her skin. She hadn't fully warmed up from her swim across the strait, and shivers radiated up her spine. She moved a few feet closer to Gray and waited for him to see her. She didn't want to interrupt if he was telling the Coasties what he'd done with the bomb. What she really wanted to do was throw her arms around his neck, but that might embarrass him, and she'd die a thousand deaths if he pulled away from her.

He glanced over the head of the closest Coastie, and his blue eyes warmed. "You should have seen her throw that hammer."

One of the Coasties turned to look at her. "She swam the strait to the ship and called us here. That one's a keeper, Grayson."

"I never doubted it for a minute." He opened his arms, and she ran into them.

After the horrendous events of Saturday, no one wanted to be alone. Ellie and Gray crashed at Shauna and Zach's house. Ellie got the spare room, and Gray slept on the sofa. Mac and Jason were both in the hospital. Zach fixed his Mickey Mouse pancakes for breakfast, and the sweet aroma mixed with the bacon cooking in the oven. The sound of cartoons played softly in the living room where Alex sat playing with his Legos, the dogs curled on either side of him. The cat was in hiding.

"I could eat a horse." Ellie poured herself a mug of coffee and joined Gray at the table where he sat nursing his dark brew.

There were circles under his eyes, and his hair was still wet from his shower. His limp was obvious this morning too. He'd probably need to see his physical therapist again. She felt just as ragged as he looked, though she'd barely moved all night long.

He eyed her over the rim of his cup. "You ready to face the onslaught of media and questions from the FBI today?"

"I think so. As ready as I'll ever be. I want to go see Mac and Jason today too."

Shauna, her black hair up in a messy bun, turned toward the living room. "Alex, breakfast."

"Okay, Mom."

"I'll go with you," Gray said. "That is, if you'd like me to."

"That would be great."

How soon before he left Lavender Tides? The thought of him leaving was like looking down into a dark abyss. He'd said some sweet things when they were kayaking, but in the cold light of day, she wasn't sure if he'd meant all he said. Seattle was over two hours away, which wasn't that far, but life had a way of turning frantic.

Still dressed in his pajamas, Alex ran into the room and scooted up to the breakfast bar where Zach had placed his pancakes.

The doorbell rang. "I'll get it." Shauna wiped her hands on the large red apron she wore, then hurried out of the kitchen.

Ellie recognized the sheriff's deep voice and wrinkled her nose at Gray. "The interrogation is about to start."

"We might find out more background information too." Gray's gaze flickered to Alex. "We might want to go outside to the deck to talk to him."

Zach turned off the stove and went to put his hand on Alex's shoulder. "Hey, buddy, how about you and I take the dogs outside? It's a nice day, and we can eat on the deck."

"Cool!" Alex grabbed his plate and followed Zach out the back door with the two rottweilers on their heels.

The sheriff's heavy tread came their way, and his expression was somber as he joined them in the kitchen.

"Coffee, Sheriff?" Shauna asked. "We have pancakes and bacon too."

"I'll take the coffee, but I've already had breakfast, thanks." Everett pulled out a chair and sat at the head of the table. "You both look a little worse for the wear. How're you feeling, Gray?"

"I'll live. Did any of them do any singing in the jail last night?"

"Clint talked a lot. He says Isaac shot the Robbs, then set the house on fire." He took a sip of the coffee Shauna handed him, then set it on the table. "Terrance had been on Isaac's resource list for several years, and he didn't want a loose end around waiting to spill the beans on him. He mostly didn't trust Candace. Her constant purchases were what fueled Terrance's never-ending need for money, and Isaac thought she was a loose cannon."

Ellie shuddered. So much death. "What about the body in my basement at the Saltwater Point house?"

"Gun Moon was one of Isaac's moles, and he was getting cold feet. He went to the house to warn Ellie that she was in danger, and Isaac sent his henchman to kill him there."

Ellie hugged herself. "What a terrible, ruthless man. What about the bomb?"

"Stopped from being armed, pretty much in the nick of time." He stared at Gray. "Thanks to both of you."

"It was Gray," she said at the same time he said, "It was Ellie." Her cheeks burned at the tenderness in Gray's eyes when she looked his way.

Gray's gaze never left her. "If she hadn't gotten the Coast Guard to us in time, I don't know that I would have won the standoff with Isaac's men. What about Nasser?"

"He's not saying much, as we expected. But at least you got him."

Gray grinned at her. "Hammer Girl took him out. I'm going to enjoy calling William's parents to let them know he's finally going to pay for their son's death."

"What's next?" Ellie asked.

"The FBI are on their way, so I'm sure you'll have to go over what happened several times. Isaac, Hyun, and Nasser are all in custody with their men. I'd guess you'll have to testify whenever the trial comes up." The sheriff swallowed down the last of his coffee and rose. "I'll let you have a little peace before the craziness starts."

He tipped his hat and headed for the door. Gray leaned over and took Ellie's hand. "Let's go see Mac and Jason before the suits get here. I think we both need a breather."

Just what she was hoping to hear. "I need to take a quick shower."

"I'll walk down to the water. Whistle when you're ready."

His blue eyes held a promise that made her heart stutter in her chest.

Chapter 41

The budget is always important. You must count
the cost before you begin any renovation.
—HAMMER GIRL BLOG

Grayson tossed rocks into the rolling waves in Rainshadow Bay. The salty tang of the sea on his lips blew the last of his sleepiness away. He watched a ferry chug toward Whidbey Island. When this was all over, he wanted to spend some time getting to know this place.

He had a lot of thinking to do. He'd barely slept last night, and though he'd tried to blame it on the pain in his leg, he knew better. The real pain was the thought of leaving here, of missing Ellie. Seattle wasn't that far, but far enough that it could be difficult with his crazy work schedule. He'd done what he set out to do, and Nasser was facing justice. Maybe it was time for him to reexamine his goals and figure out where he went from here.

Pebbles tumbled down the hillside, and he turned to see Zach coming to join him. The dogs scampered ahead of him and ran to nose the remnants of a tide pool.

"You doing okay?"

"Yeah, just trying to figure out life. A month ago I had no idea how differently I'd feel about everything." Grayson rubbed the head of one of the dogs as it thrust its nose into his hand.

"Need a sounding board? I know what it's like to have your whole life turned upside down."

He probably did. Grayson had heard a little about how things had been after Shauna's first husband died. "I thought I had my career and life all mapped out. Everything is turned on its head."

"This is about how you feel about Ellie, isn't it?" Zach tossed the Frisbee in his hand, and the dogs ran off to chase it. "While I'm not an expert on the topic of love and marriage, I can tell you that finding the right woman is worth turning your life in a totally new direction. You don't want to leave her, do you?"

Grayson shook his head. "And I don't want to leave Shauna now that I've found her. Or this place that suddenly feels more like home than anywhere I've ever lived. But yes, it's mostly Ellie. She's special, and I think we might have a future together. I don't want to give up seeing her every day."

"What are your options?"

"I could put in for a transfer to one of the Coast Guard stations here. Maybe Port Angeles."

"You've done your homework."

"Seattle is more of a boon to my career, which is why I took it in the first place, but it's too far away to drive every day. Port Angeles is close enough, but since it's small, I'd be able to get some experience in a lot of different things. The variety might be interesting, but am I trashing my career by asking for a transfer?"

"I'll pray about it with you. God will give you direction on what you're supposed to do."

"Thanks, I'd appreciate it." Several seagulls landed nearby and approached with beady eyes looking for food. "How'd you know Shauna was the right woman for you? I don't have much experience with long-term relationships."

"I couldn't imagine life without her in it. It was as simple as that."

"I'm pretty much already there. Here I am thinking about asking for a move that could either be the biggest mistake of my career or the best."

He couldn't leave her. He loved watching her smile slowly blossom across her face. He loved the way she pushed her glasses up on her nose and looked at him so earnestly. He loved the golden lights in her hair and the way it curled in the humidity of the ocean air. She believed in those she loved with all her heart, even when they had hurt her. He hoped to see those amber eyes look at him with that same unshakable loyalty someday.

A smile lifted Zach's lips. "You already know what you want to do."

"Yeah, I guess I do."

Zach tossed the Frisbee to the dogs again. "Has Ellie talked to Mac yet?"

"She tried calling the hospital this morning, but the nurse said she was sleeping. Jason too. We're going to head that way soon. There's still the loose ends of the cocaine theft to tie up."

A bandage around his head, Jason's eyes were open to the ceiling, and he lay motionless and lethargic on the bed. He didn't turn his head when Ellie entered with Gray on her heels, even though the *whoosh* of the door was loud in the quiet room.

Ellie's shoes squeaked on the tile floor as she approached the bed. "It's me, Jason. How are you feeling?" He still didn't turn his head to face her. "Jason?"

"Did you come here to stare at the blind man, Ellie?"

She winced. He'd never spoken to her with such a sharp, sardonic tone. "We came to see how you are. I thought maybe you'd like to know exactly what was going on."

"I'm used to being kept in the dark. Especially by women in your family. I heard her, you know." He gave a harsh bark of laughter. "I've always heard about people who are unconscious hearing things going on around them. I heard her say she figured out pretty quickly she didn't love me."

Ellie stepped closer and laid her hand on his arm, but he shook off her touch. "Jason, it wasn't you. Mac is . . . broken somehow. She had this thirst for some kind of crazy adventure. I don't think she even knows herself why she did all this."

She laid out everything for him—the cocaine theft, the way Mac had gotten involved in the terrorist plot, everything. Jason listened, his face devoid of expression.

"We're going to go see her now, and I'm sure we'll find out more," Ellie said.

He finally turned his head her way. "She's not going to jail, is she?" He laughed again, a humorless sound. "Just like always, she landed on her feet. She's like your cat, Ellie. Nine lives and all that." He flung his arm across his eyes. "Just leave me alone. Go back to your sister and mother her like you always do."

Stung, Ellie drew back. "I don't mother her."

"You've always mothered her. You're so afraid of letting some-one down that you never made her stand on her own two feet. This is your fault."

Gray stepped forward. "That's enough. None of this is Ellie's fault. She got pulled in like everyone else. I've had enough of people blaming her to avoid taking their licks like an adult. Whatever Mac did or didn't do rests squarely on her shoulders."

"I suppose my blindness is my own fault too."

"It's no one's fault. You think you're the only person who's ever had to deal with an unpleasant circumstance? Your life isn't over even if you never see again, and you're whining when you don't even know if that's what'll happen. It's not the tragedy that can ruin you—it's your own attitude toward it. You can let adversity make or break you, Jason. It's up to you."

The words hammered into Ellie's head. Even if Jason never took them to heart, she understood in an instant what Gray meant. And how she'd been guilty of it herself. She'd let the tragedy of Alicia's death and the things her parents had said to her sink in too deeply, had let it define her.

Nothing could define her unless she let it. She had God in her life to heal those broken places, but she hadn't let him do it. She'd held her pain to her heart like a lovey she couldn't give up.

No more. She could let it go now. Gray had taught her so much in the short time she'd known him. This time when she put her hand on Jason's arm, he didn't shrug it off. "What's the doctor say, Jason?"

"That time will tell. The blindness was caused by the blow to my head when I fell and not the gunshot, which was just a flesh wound on my arm. My brain is swollen, and the visual cortex might be involved. We'll know more in a few days or a few weeks." He turned his face toward her. "What am I going to do if I stay blind, Ellie? I can't work. I can't drive."

"You can pray, Jason. I will too. God will take care of you no matter what happens."

He swallowed and closed his eyes. "Leave me alone, please. I'm tired and my head hurts."

She squeezed his arm and pulled her hand away. Gray steered her toward the door, and they stepped into the hall. She wasn't sure she was ready to talk to Mac yet, but she had to. Gray needed answers.

And so did she.

Chapter 42

*Disaster can strike any home project. A stray
ladder, a lid not completely secured on a paint
can. Always be prepared for the unexpected.*
—Hammer Girl Blog

Ellie and Grayson walked through the hospital halls dodging squeaking carts and bustling nurses. The beige walls smelled freshly painted, and an undertone of antiseptic lingered. Grayson glanced at Ellie's set face. This was going to be hard for her, especially after hearing Jason was still blind.

Grayson put his arm around her shoulder as they rode the elevator to the fifth floor. "You doing okay?"

"I'm still trying to wrap my head around all this, you know?"

The elevator dinged, and they stepped onto Mac's floor. Rosa sat on a chair outside a room two doors down from the nurses' station. It had to be Mac's room.

Rosa rose as they approached. "I thought you'd be along anytime. She's awake and has been asking about you."

"When will she be released?" Grayson asked.

"Probably tomorrow. Her lawyer has already been here. Go on in." Rosa opened the door for them.

The room was a private one with sunlight streaming in a big window. The walls were a pale green, and the soundtrack to the movie Mac was watching was on low.

Dressed in a blue-and-white-striped hospital gown, Mac sat in an orange vinyl chair with her bare feet on the tile floor. She'd lost at least ten pounds, and her legs looked frail. Her hair had been washed but not dried and it frizzed around her head.

Ellie's sneakers squeaked on the floor, and Mac looked up. Her eyes widened, and she didn't smile as she rose to grip the rail on the bed.

"Mac, how are you doing? You've lost weight."

"I'm okay. Did Isaac hurt you?" Her blue-eyed gaze raked Ellie from head to toe.

"Not really. Gray is a little worse for wear with his bum knee, but we'll all survive."

"How's Jason?"

Ellie winced and looked down at her hands. "He's blind, Mac. At least at the moment. We're hoping once his head trauma heals, his sight will come back."

"Oh no. He has to see again!" She looked over at Grayson. "I know you're with the Coast Guard, but I didn't catch your name."

"Grayson Bradshaw."

"He's Shauna's long-lost brother," Ellie said. "Not that it matters right now, but it's a wonderful turn of events."

"And now you're here to question me."

Ellie pressed her hands together. "I mostly wanted to make sure you're okay, but yes, Gray will have questions."

Arms folded across his chest, Gray stood where he was. "I do need some answers."

Mac squared her shoulders and set her cup back on the tray. "It all started when I went to South Korea. I met Tarek there, and to tell you the truth, I fell hard for him. Then little by little I found out he was a terrorist. I was so disillusioned and I broke it off. I tried to put it behind me and move on. Then I ran into him again at a restaurant in town when I first started dating Dylan."

She shook her head. "I still can't believe I let myself fall for it." She sent a pleading glance toward Ellie. "Then a day or two later Tarek found me walking along the shore of Rainshadow Bay late one night. He told me he'd never gotten over me and that he wanted us to be together, that he was willing to give up his vendetta against my country. He said he was being pressured, though, and he had to deliver enough cocaine to buy his freedom so we could leave all of that behind."

Ellie sighed. "Oh, Mac."

"I know, I know. Oldest trick in the book. He said he knew Dylan would show me where the cocaine was if I asked him, and that he'd arrange for some men to help me. Once it was delivered, we could be together."

"So you did it," Gray said.

She nodded. "But not for that reason. By that time I saw him clearly. I called the FBI and told them what I'd discovered. They arranged for me to get the cocaine to prove myself to Tarek and to be able to be on the inside of the plans."

"Why didn't you tell me?" Ellie's voice was small and forlorn.

"Ego. If I delivered the cocaine, I'd be the hero." She gave a heavy sigh. "Then I was at Monte's house learning about ham radio." Her voice rose. "We stumbled on a broadcast in Korean, and I recognized Tarek's voice. I realized the cocaine was about to fund something really terrible and horrendous."

"An EMP bomb," Gray said.

Mac nodded and clicked off the television, then reached for her water and took a sip. "I'm so thirsty all the time. They didn't give me much food or water." Her raspy voice showed the damage to her throat. She sat down and clenched her hands together in her lap.

Mac stared at Ellie. "I've always been jealous of you, Ellie. I loved you and hated you all at the same time. You're always so calm and in control. You always do the right thing. Just once I wanted to do the wrong thing and have fun doing it." She pushed her curly brown hair out of her face. "It sounds so crazy to even say that. So stupid. I *was* stupid to get involved with Tarek."

Ellie went to stare out the window at the parking lot below. She leaned her head against the glass for a long moment.

"Ellie? Don't you have anything to say to me?"

Ellie turned to reveal a pale, strained face. "I don't know what to say, Mac. Why would you be jealous of me? You had the best job, an exciting life, the most friends. I could never compete with you. I never even tried. And I killed our sister. I live with that mistake every day."

"It was an accident. And you were a kid. Sheesh! You need to let that go, Ellie." Mac waved her hand in a dismissive gesture. "You have always had something so valuable—a genuinely good heart. You always see the best in people. I hated that, but I can't even tell you why. Jason always saw through me, you know."

Ellie gave a slight shake of her head. "I'm nothing special, Mac."

Mac's eyes went frosty. "Stop it! I can see the way you're internally making excuses for me. But I don't want your pity. I'm being as honest as I know how." Her voice quavered, and she fell silent.

Ellie took a step toward her. "I forgive you, Mac."

Tears flooded Mackenzie's eyes. "I didn't even ask for that."

"You don't have to ask."

Gray cleared his throat. "Where's the cocaine now, Mackenzie?"

"I don't know. I gave the cocaine to Nasser like I was supposed to."

At least jail wasn't in her future. That would be a comfort to Ellie, and he'd figure out the rest of it.

Ellie lifted her chin and closed her eyes, relishing the touch of the sun's warmth on her skin. The ocean raged against the rocks below, but she felt safe with Grayson's strong arm around her waist. They'd come straight here to Saltwater Point so she could let the scent of the sea wash away the taint of the hospital.

She examined how she felt and realized she truly had let go of her disappointment, pain, and shame. Only God could have helped her release it, and she already felt lighter. It had been hard to carry that all these years.

She rested her head on Grayson's broad chest and listened to his heart thump under her ear. He guided her to a giant boulder looking out at the expanse of gray, stormy sea as thunder rumbled. The salty breeze carried the scent of ozone to her nose too.

He sat on the rock and pulled her onto his lap. "We won't be able to stay long. The storm will be here in a few minutes."

The thunder rumbled a warning again, and she rested her back against him. It felt as though nothing could hurt her if she was near him. Gray was a rock every bit as dependable and stalwart as the boulder. The thought he would be leaving soon was more heartbreaking than what she'd already gone through.

She pushed away the despair that was creeping into her heart. He was here with her in this moment. It had to be enough to see her through the lonely days and nights without him. When had he become as important to her as breathing? The love blossoming inside her had surprised her when she wasn't looking.

She forced a bright note into her voice. "So, you'll be leaving soon."

His arms tightened around her, then one arm came under her knees, and he turned her on his lap so she was sideways and looking up into his face. "Maybe not."

A tiny ray of hope began to push away the gloom she felt. "What do you mean? Don't you have to get back to work?"

He pressed his lips to her cheek and spoke against her skin in a gentle voice. "I've put in for a transfer. I won't hear for a few weeks, but there are several possible stations here. I think I've got a good shot at being reassigned." His right hand cupped her cheek. "Here's the thing, Ellie. I don't want to leave you. I hope that doesn't scare you. I know we haven't known each other that long, but I think we might have a shot at a future together. I'm not willing to throw that away. Not even for my dream job."

She searched his face, examining his tender expression and tentative smile. "Y-You aren't leaving?"

He shook his head. "Not for long, at least. I promised Shauna

I'd go talk to Brenna, and I'll need to report back to work until my reassignment is approved, but I won't be gone long. Will you wait for me? Don't go running off and dating some pinhead while I'm gone, okay?"

It was too good to be true, and she reached up and pinched her arm. "Ow, that hurt. I don't think I'm dreaming."

His grin widened. "You're not dreaming, but I might be because I think you're saying you feel the same way."

She planted her palms on his cheeks and nodded. "Kiss me, Gray. I don't think I'll believe it until you do."

She closed her eyes as his lips, gentle and exploratory, came down on hers. Lightning crackled overhead and thunder crashed as she reveled in the passion rising between them. His arms tightened around her, and she wrapped her arms around his neck. They should get to the SUV, but she didn't want to leave the haven of his arms.

He lifted his head, and she tightened her grip on his neck. "I don't want this moment to end. It might not be real."

As the rain came, he lifted her in his arms and carried her toward the SUV. "This is the beginning, Hammer Girl. Only the beginning."

A Note from the Author

Dear Reader,

It's been so wonderful to hear from so many of you about The View From Rainshadow Bay! I hope you enjoy this next visit to Lavender Tides.

I'm a major home renovation junkie. My husband and I love working on houses! We love tiling, laying hardwood floors, design, everything. I'm addicted to *Fixer Upper* and meeting Chip and Joanna Gaines would be a dream come true. About the only thing we watch on TV is HGTV. Like I said—major junkies! So Ellie's profession has a whole lot of my passion in it.

I'd love to see pictures of things you've been doing in your own homes so shoot them off to me and let me drool over them. I love to hear from you!

Hugs to you!

Colleen

colleen@colleencoble.com

Discussion Questions

1. Have you ever suffered from a trauma you had trouble getting past? How did you do it?

2. Sin can be a slipperly slope of one poor decision leading to the next. What was Mac's first mistake?

3. Ellie used her glasses as a way to protect herself. Have you ever used something to hold others at a distance?

4. Grayson's foundation was shaken when he discovered he was adopted. What would be the hardest thing to get past in that situation?

5. Ellie always believed the best in those she loved. Why do you think it was important to her?

6. If you were going to receive upsetting news like Grayson when he found out he was adopted, would you prefer it to be in person or to have a letter that prepared you first?

7. Terrorism is hard to wrap your head around. What do you think drives it?

8. It's often harder to forgive ourselves than to forgive other people. Why do you think that is true?

Acknowledgments

I'm so blessed to belong to the terrific HarperCollins Christian Publishing dream team! I've been with my great fiction team for fifteen years, and they are like family to me. I learn something new with every book, which makes writing so much fun for me!

Our fiction publisher and editor, Amanda Bostic, is as dear to me as a daughter. She really gets suspense and has been my friend from the moment I met her all those years ago. Fabulous cover guru Kristen Ingebretson works hard to create the perfect cover—and does. And, of course, I can't forget the other friends in my amazing fiction family: Becky Monds, Kristen Golden, Allison Carter, Jodi Hughes, Paul Fisher, Matt Bray, Kimberly Carlton, Laura Wheeler, Jocelyn Bailey, and Kayleigh Hines. You are all such a big part of my life. I wish I could name all the great folks at HCCP who work on selling my books through different venues. I'm truly blessed!

Julee Schwarzburg is a dream editor to work with. She totally gets romantic suspense, and our partnership is pure joy. She brought some terrific ideas to the table with this book—as always!

My agent, Karen Solem, has helped shape my career in many ways, and that includes kicking an idea to the curb when necessary. We are about to celebrate fifteen years together! And my critique partner of twenty years, Denise Hunter, is the best sounding board ever. Thanks, friends!

I'm so grateful for my husband, Dave, who carts me around from city to city, washes towels, and chases down dinner without complaint. My kids—Dave and Kara (and now Donna and Mark)—love and support me in every way possible, and my little granddaughter, Alexa, makes every day a joy. She's talking like a grown-up now, and having her spend the night is more fun than I can tell you. Our little grandson, Elijah, is fourteen months old now, and we are expecting a new sibling in May. Exciting times!

Most important, I give my thanks to God, who has opened such amazing doors for me and makes the journey a golden one.

RETURN FOR MORE ADVENTURES IN
LAVENDER TIDES!

(novella)

(available January 2019)

Available in print, e-book,
and downloadable audio

THE
ROCK HARBOR
series

Colleen Coble returns
to Rock Harbor

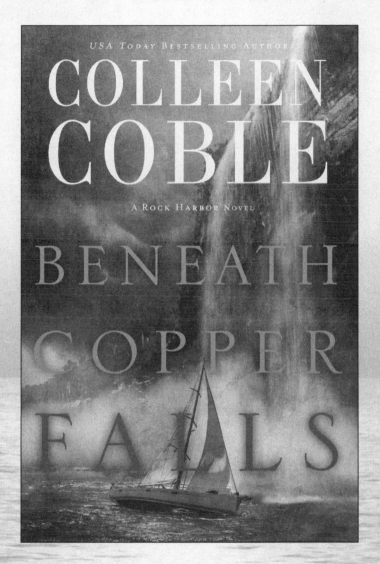

Available in print,
e-book, and audio

COMING FALL 2018!

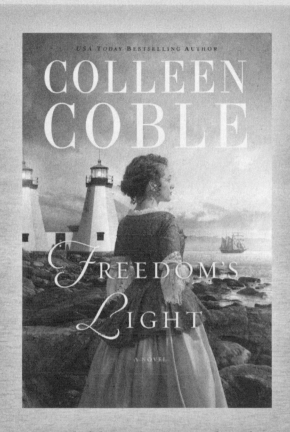

USA TODAY BESTSELLING AUTHOR

COLLEEN COBLE

FREEDOM'S LIGHT

A NOVEL

Available in print, e-book, and downloadable audio

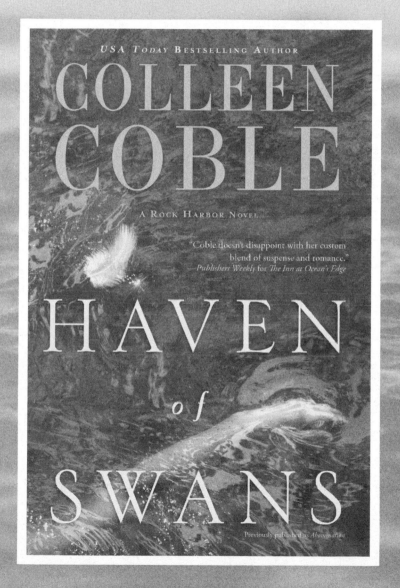

THE
SUNSET COVE
series

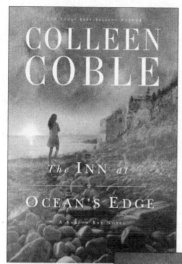

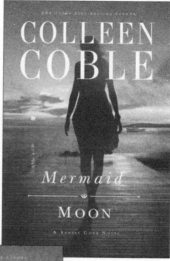

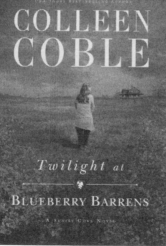

AVAILABLE IN PRINT,
E-BOOK, AND AUDIO

AVAILABLE IN PRINT,
E-BOOK, AND AUDIO

AVAILABLE IN PRINT,
E-BOOK, AND AUDIO

THOMAS NELSON
Since 1798

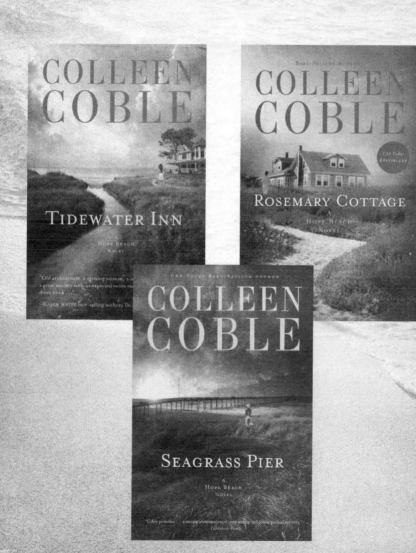

About the Author

C olleen Coble is a *USA Today* bestselling author and RITA finalist best known for her romantic suspense novels, including *Tidewater Inn, Rosemary Cottage,* and the Mercy Falls, Lonestar, Rock Harbor, and Sunset Cove series.

Visit her website at www.colleencoble.com.
Twitter: @colleencoble
Facebook: colleencoblebooks